NOT A THROUGH STREET

NOT A THROUGH STREET

ERNEST LARSEN

Random House
New York

Copyright © 1981 by Ernest Larsen

All rights reserved under International and Pan-American Copyright Conventions. Published in the United States by Random House, Inc., New York, and simultaneously in Canada by Random House of Canada Limited, Toronto.

Library of Congress Cataloging in Publication Data

Larsen, Ernest, 1946-
Not a through street.
I. Title.
PS3562.A733N6   813'.54   81-2775
ISBN 0-394-51941-8   AACR2

Manufactured in the United States of America

2 4 6 8 9 7 5 3

First Edition

for Sherry
　—from the first word to the last

Only the bad in history is irrevocable: the unrealized possibilities, missed opportunities, murder with and without legal procedures, and that which those in power inflict upon humanity. The other is always in danger.
— MAX HORKHEIMER

Acknowledgments

All finished work, even a labor of love, is the accumulated result of collective efforts. Among the many friends who nudged or pushed me in the right direction, I wish to thank in particular Hannah Green, Joel Oppenheimer and Harriet Millner for their sustaining love and support.

I also wish to acknowledge gratefully the generosity of The MacDowell Colony, thanks to which I was able to get this book on the road.

NOT A THROUGH STREET

1

O<small>N</small> my last night but one as a taxi driver in Manhattan, the dispatcher gave me a cab that wanted desperately to die. At each agonized turn it begged me in the aggrieved tenor of hopelessly broken shocks to put it out of its misery. It took the corner at Fourteenth Street so hesitantly that the warning lights on the dash had time to glow red and then fade consecutively. On the straightaway up Eighth Avenue I could have had time to read and compare the prices on the menus in the windows of the Cubano-Chinese restaurants, but I didn't because it was raining and I was still persuading myself that fares were out there waiting for me in the downpour.

I kept glancing out the side window anyway, since the pitted wipers spread a smear the color of dirty dishwater across the windshield. That's what smog is, I thought lamely, dishwater in the sink of the city. I scribbled a note of the idea on the clipboard next to me while the cab inched along. I had lots of ideas then, ideas for stories that would do everything for me except lift me bodily out of the cab, and I put them all down on paper.

A gust of wind blew in. I started to roll up the window

and saw the man hailing the cab three cabs in front of me. I didn't stand a chance so I shifted my foot to the brake and watched as one cab slid past him, and two, and three, all empty but all blinded by the rain.

I thanked my peripheral vision. Once, during parents' week at one of the rundown Catholic grade schools my mother sent me to, the squat little nun, groping for some crumb of praise to offer her, ended up with, "Mrs. Hobart, your Emma has, I'm quite sure, the best peripheral vision in any of the higher grades." My mother is not an entire fool. She cuffed me later, saying, "Sure, she means you got eyes in the back of your head, you little witch."

Such flashes of memory and fragments of thought are the only kind you get when you drive a cab. The traffic, the lights, the need for speed and quick reflexes erase anything more substantial. But I felt guilty for thinking about peripheral vision when I pulled up to the man waiting in the rain. The reason I felt guilty was standing next to him, tapping a white cane with disembodied regularity at the edge of a puddle, his eyes not blinking as the rain ran down his forehead into them.

The man who had signaled opened the passenger door. It took a while because it stuck, but when he had it open he herded the blind man into the back seat, slammed the door, and leaned his wet face into my open window to thank me before walking away. His face was kind as well as wet. "We didn't think we'd ever get anybody to stop," he said. He smiled and the rain dripped from his nose onto my shoulder.

The blind man wanted to go to an uptown hotel I'd never heard of. That wasn't a good sign. The ones you don't hear about are the ones nobody takes a cab to.

"Where is that?" I said, too loud, as if deafness was his problem.

"I don't know," he said amiably.

It made sense that he didn't know but I needed a little

more to go on. We were already on our way uptown. "Any idea?"

"Don't worry," he said. "You'll see it." The idea that fleabags and welfare hotels fling themselves at you from blocks away would occur only to a blind man. "I just started living there. You're a cabdriver. You must have seen it. In the seventies. Welfare hotel—you know the one?"

"East or West?"

"Near East Seventy-sixth maybe." All the way up Eighth he'd mutter, "Can't miss it." And then he'd say, "Paradise Hotel," and spell it for me, just in case I wasn't used to long words.

At Columbus Circle I swung through the dark entrance to Central Park Drive. Maybe if the windshield wipers had been sharper I'd have noticed the pond covering half the street before I got to it. I think not. I was too rattled. For a cabdriver the most unnerving thing is not knowing exactly where you're going. The cab charged the pond. The drive curved east and then uptown. I was on the second curve, holding on to the wheel like a life raft, when the cab rolled to a stop without moans or squeals.

I put my hand on the ignition key and closed my eyes for a second. The rain drummed louder on the roof now that we were stalled in the wilderness of the park. The cab was tempting me to rush it.

"Are we stopped at a light?" the blind man asked.

I thought about lying. Then I said. "We're fine. I just stalled for a second. Too much rain. Just give it a rest and it should start right up."

"Where are we?" It was the first time he wasn't smiling.

"In the middle of Central Park."

Still no smile, but it can be hard to read the expression of a man without eyes in the rain, at night, in the park. Instead I turned the key. Nothing happened. I turned it back.

"Here's what we'll do," I said, "I'm going to stop another cab for you. This one's going nowhere."

He nodded. "Hotel Paradise."

He was taking it well, but Central Park was the last place I wanted to be hanging out at night even in the rain. Nevertheless I stood for five minutes watching cabs speed up as they approached me and waiting for a dozen arms to reach out of the darkness all at once and pull me into the bushes. It took five minutes for it to occur to me that no cabbie in his or her right mind would stop at night in the middle of the park. I opened the passenger door. "I'm not having a whole lot of luck. What we have to do is walk out of the park, and I'll find you a cab on Fifty-ninth Street."

I held my umbrella over his head and guided him by holding on to his upper arm. It was as spindly as a twelve-year-old boy's.

"I'm really glad I got such a friendly cabdriver," he said, meaning it. We walked slowly, and when we were halfway across the drive with cars swerving around us, horns blaring, rain and wind whipping our bodies, he stopped suddenly and said, "I've forgotten something."

I backed him closer to the cab so we wouldn't be run over for at least another sixty seconds. "Whatever it is I'll mail it to you."

"No, I have to pay you. Here, hold this." He handed me his cane and pulled an old wallet from his pocket. It was a children's plastic wallet with pictures of the Flintstones on it. Inside was nothing except a twenty-dollar bill. "Is this enough?" he asked.

I looked closer to make sure it wasn't play money. "I'll have to see if I can change it," I said, slid the umbrella under my arm, and reached automatically for the twenty. The wind swiped the umbrella and it flew over the cab down the drive, end over end. I grabbed the blind man's wrist, stuck the cane in his hand and curled his fingers around it. "Stay exactly where you are. The umbrella just ran away. I'll be right back."

Two cabs were stopped near the blind man by the time I got back. It hadn't occurred to me just to leave him alone. One cabbie had his arm around his shoulders. The Flintstones were gone. The second cabbie jumped out of his cab. Only he didn't look like a cabbie. "Aren't you Harold from the Paradise?" he asked the blind man.

"Yes," said the blind man, "that's where we were going."

"You can't walk there in the rain," he said. It sounded like an order.

"Who are you?" asked the blind man. "How do you know me?" He slapped the cane hard and fast against the pavement. It was an extension of his nerves.

"I know you, Harold, I know you fine. Remember that fight you were in last week with Otto?"

The cane stopped. "You the cop?"

"You got me." He turned to us, all business, a general dismissing his troops. "I'm not a cabbie. I'm a police officer cruising the Park undercover. I'll take Harold to the Paradise."

The other cabbie took his arm off Harold's shoulder. Maybe Harold wasn't quite as lovable now.

A moment later I was standing in the rain alone with the umbrella under my arm.

I needed to sit down a minute before walking—or running—out of the park to call my garage, so I went back to the cab. I was chilled through and shaking. I automatically put the key in the ignition. The cab started immediately. The meter lit up, reading $3.80. I stared at it while it ticked away and then punched the button much harder than necessary to turn it off. Naturally it didn't respond, and I had to hit it again. It would take me at least half what was left of the shift to make up that fare from my tips. I was accountable to the garage for the $3.80, the kind of account I paid without complaint, because I didn't want to give the dispatcher elbowroom to patronize me, a "girl" beat for another fare. My garage hired women, though they didn't like to and had always warned me away from the night shift—even though it's the only way a part-timer can make enough money to get by.

I never found out the address of the Paradise Hotel, so I know only by hearsay that it exists. But each tip I got for the rest of the night provided the occasion to decide over again the exact moment on that ride that I'd gone irreversibly wrong. Because I'd fallen, somewhere along the line, into the trap of letting it all wash over me.

Picking up the blind man was purely an accident. I could easily have been cruising down a hundred other blocks at that moment. But accidents are usually what you make of them. Either that—or the jagged second of surprise grabs you and pushes you in its direction. Picking him up was a cue. It set in motion from a dozen corners of Manhattan all the accidents and near-accidents that were in a matter of hours to crowd against one another that August of '74.

I call them accidents when they may not have been, when it was probably more a case of accidentally on purpose. "Accidentally on purpose," was my mother's favorite cliché. She attached it to every act of will that went astray. It covered a lot of ground for her, for a wily half-educated intelligence militantly opposed to the experimental. I couldn't blame her for that—she had her reasons. An accident, my father's death at the age of twenty-eight on a construction site of suburban tract houses, had broken her prospects for a secure future.

When drunk she'd use the phrase "accidentally on purpose" to characterize my father's death, almost as if she counted it an act of provocation against her. But this was just self-protection. "Accidentally on purpose." Invariably she changed her mind right away. "Bite my tongue. It's true he was always the careless type. Not careless—reckless. And he worked too hard. He swung his hammer so hard that when it missed its spot on the window frame he flew right out the window after it. It was only three stories, but the foolish man made the most of the three stories. Spat his brains all over his own hammer."

With that she'd make to toss down another swallow and stop, looking at me with a wave of sentiment bathing her eyes. "It was his foolishness made me love him, Emma, made you, made us marry when we were too young for it. So I warn you"—her voice, in another violent swing of mood, ran as cold as the ice sloshing in the glass her hand gripped—"don't do anything on impulse. It will just totally screw you permanently up."

I'd look at her hand holding the glass for dear life and determine not to heed her. In this as in all her warnings I disobeyed her. The upshot was we were usually in a process of disowning each other—I for her caution in making nothing out of her life beyond the grim reckoning of a carpenter's widow's pension, she for my recklessness in making nothing out of mine, "a girl bright enough to sit with the best of the brains in City College and too bright to sit there long enough to do herself any good." When her resentment—in some ways justified—at my refusal to be properly upwardly mobile had sat long enough on the burner, she'd begin to complain about the disgrace of having her only daughter a cabdriver. I'd spoken to her over a month earlier across the hum of the long-distance wire from Chicago. She'd started out fine, or rather haltingly, no longer knowing what was safe to talk about and so deferring actual talk. But in the end she couldn't hold it in, even in the midst of pretending to back away from controversy. Like all mothers of her generation, she dutifully called me on occasions. This was one.

"It's amazing, Emma."
"What is, Mom?"
"Time. Why at the age you are today, your father and I had been married, had you, had our first house; we'd

done so much. We were going on with our lives." She put a lot of emphasis on that "we."

"At the age I am today Dad was dead already a full year, Mom."

"Yes," she said, "but that was by accident."

She'd still been a young woman when it happened. Instead of using it, one way or the other, she let it use her. Ask her what she was, she'd say, "The widow of a carpenter." By accident. No wonder I treated every little accident that came my way as a summons. That's the way I tried to treat the soaking wet blind man in the back seat of the cab.

By the time I got home—three in the morning—the rain had stopped, and it was as hot and muggy as it's supposed to be in New York in August. I didn't turn on any lights. I didn't speak to the cat. I didn't look at anything. It takes two or three hours to recover from driving unless you go right to sleep. I didn't go to sleep. I lay there thinking about the blind man in the rain. Some accident had struck him blind just as an accident caught my old man's hammer in Brookhaven or Fairlawn or Riverview or Elkwood or whatever the name was of that prefab subdivision of humanity.

It was the aura of accident, of freedom, however illusory, that had attracted me to cab-driving after I dropped out of City College with less than a year to go. It was survival on a minimum investment of time and commitment, the only job I could think of that didn't mean somebody leaning on your shoulder so as to push your nose closer to the grindstone. "Shabby way to make a living," my mother said. Right, but I'd never told her that's why I liked it.

Except there were nights I didn't like it, when it scared me a little, not because it was dangerous—that fear was the condition of the job that kept me awake. I got scared when I couldn't sleep afterwards, particularly when I was alone. I got up and threw some water on my face from the kitchen tap. My face was caught in the little mirror above the sink, so I had to look at it. I was in the mood to be merciless. The wiry body escaped criticism. The face in the mirror looked exhausted, the brown hair disheveled, half-circles under the gray eyes that seemed a little big for the rest of the features. It was a face with too much emphasis in it. I always looked better in snapshots ("Look how pretty you are in this one," my mother said ten times or twenty, turning the album pages), the impatience wasn't visible then or the bad habit I had of tapping my forehead as if sounding for mineral deposits. I didn't have a face you'd trust right away unless you caught me smiling, and I didn't smile that much. Some people were made uncomfortable by all those clashing lines (forehead, cheekbones, nose, jaw). They seemed to imply the archaeological impress of a discordant universe. There was a saving grace though. You didn't easily get tired of it. It was dramatic, people said.

I wanted to make a judgment on that face. I wanted to make it answer for the long night, for its turn toward the bizarre and accidental. Pick up a blind man standing in the rain, and you get a fast glimpse of a smear of unconsidered social combinations (blind men fighting it out in welfare hotels, cops masquerading as cabbies). For the first night in a month I wasn't thinking about how hard it was to sleep alone. I'd found something else to keep me awake. I didn't have to think about Hoyt. . . .

2

When the phone rang what seemed like minutes later, my body waited for Hoyt to answer it because Hoyt always would when I worked so late. But Hoyt wouldn't any more. The bed didn't hold his weight. And the tremor in my fingertips and forearms and the knots in my back weren't there just because I'd been driving a cab till after three in the morning. They were still there because his weight wasn't, to mold, stretch, smooth and soften.

The ringing went on so long I opened my eyes. Direct sunlight cut into my vision. A little dizzied, I sat up, reaching automatically for the robe that should have been strewn across the sheet. I'd left the phone on the floor at the edge of my bed where it was crossed by a sharp-edged sunlit bar.

I leaned over the bed and upended the green receiver. Its cord writhed, making it look like a reptile being tortured in the sun. I poked it with my finger. "Listen," I said, "it's too early to be calling people." I thought I could hear breathing coming from it. "What do you want?"

"A guaranteed annual income, lunch at noon at B&H, and, let's see, a certain soft crevice at the base of your neck for my personal use shortly after noon." Hoyt's was the one voice that could victimize me.

"I'll see what I can do," I said and hung up.

I was abrupt enough for him to call me back. But the phone sat there quietly while I dressed. I was getting good at overprotecting myself, keeping the door shut. Instead of talking, I'd hang up and then wish he'd call back.

I dialed his number and let it ring. When we still lived together eating lunch out was a prelude to an afternoon in bed. To the point that the suggestion to go have Chinese food for lunch was an invitation to make love. But since the moment I'd asked him to move out and he'd stormed through the place throwing his things into his big black trunk, mixing long stares and cold silence, and I stood in the middle of the room watching him, trying to mitigate what I'd said, which was impossible because I'd said it and meant it but didn't somehow expect him to be so angered by it, since that moment over a month before, he'd never invited me to lunch.

He called every so often, and I called him a little less often, and we saw each other a few times, and there had been tears in his eyes and in mine, but only because we didn't chance talking about what was between us and so by mutual consent the anger was left to lie low, like a dog on leash.

It began out of talk—out of words, random ideas that maybe would never have been acted upon unless you think talk is just action bought cheap. We'd already been together nine months, long enough to learn to read each other's silences and omissions, long enough so that I knew what it meant when he spoke too soon or hesitated or held his body a certain way, or if not what it meant, at least that it meant something, and I'd have to find out what. It was my idea of being in love that what you knew gave shape to what you could know.

This was my idea, but it wasn't a program—it was just part of the way I saw things, and I was more naïve then. This was early in 1974, and it was raining, and I was trying to decide if I should go to work or not. It wasn't a day I usually worked, but a rainy Friday night can mean good money for a cabdriver. Hoyt was lying in bed reading and I was at a table writing and we'd had lunch out that day. Chinese.

Then I realized he wasn't reading even though the book was propped in front of him.

"No good?" I asked.

He looked up. "It's well enough written—for a thriller."

"But you'd stopped reading."

"I guess so," and he put the book down on the sheet and stretched. For a moment I could see the outline of his ribcage. He was well-made.

"You going to work?"

At another time he'd have said, "You're not going to work, are you?"

"I should. What's bothering you? You're down about something."

"No, I'm not. Go ahead writing."

"It doesn't matter. It's not working out any better than it ever does."

His face went blank, his lips flattened. "I see," he said, picked up the book and turned onto his belly.

"You can say something if you're thinking it," I said.

He turned back, leaning on one elbow. "I would say it if I could formulate it." He glanced out the window. "It's raining. It's 1974." He paused dramatically. "I'm thirty years old."

I had to smile. "I thought all you cared about was moo shu pork with four pancakes and going to bed afterwards because it's the best thing to do on a rainy day."

"Theoretically that's true. And practically it's true. But theoretically we neither of us believe in monogamy and yet here we are, nine months later, monogamous. What if we all of a sudden thought we should get married or something? It's 1974, Emma."

I liked it when he used my name, slapping it on the end of his sentences, like a conviction. "Go out and try somebody else if it will prove something. Wait till the rain stops, though."

He didn't laugh and neither did I and it went on like that, neither of us saying exactly what we intended, but still intending what we said.

I didn't go to work that night. And when we were both in bed again I made him stretch and I counted his ribs. I can't remember how many I counted. I can't remember why it started this way, but it started. Maybe after that we were never altogether free in each other's arms again. Desire became the desire to be what we were. Such a meager little misunderstanding at the root of it, like a dream you forget on waking that disturbs you for the whole day.

After that we were either fighting or we were in bed making up, with little middle ground. Hoyt became obsessed with "wasting time" and spent most of his talking about wasting it. He was right—there was a lot of waste; we were knee-deep in it.

One day he started pestering me to quit cab-driving and find something less marginal. "You should give yourself a deadline," he said. "Six months or a year, and if this writing trip is going nowhere, give yourself a break and quit hacking. You barely know the world exists any more."

"Look, you're the one that's feeling all the pressure. Why don't you—?"

"I'm already looking, Emma."

"Don't Emma me with that smug tone. You don't know yet what real wasted time feels like. I hope you connect with something you want. Then you'll get a line on what you're talking about now."

"I will," he said, "I will, and you're wrong."

I don't mind being wrong; the questionable part is

living with somebody who thinks you are. It was an emotional burden I couldn't handle. A few days later I told him he'd have to stop pressuring me. "You're panicking. I won't panic with you. You seem to think your life is going down the drain."

"And you seem to be the only person around who doesn't know the sixties are over and not coming back. But if you like, I'll stop hassling you. That's it."

So he did, and it got worse, and two days later I asked him to leave. In asking I was only telling him I meant what I said—that if he was upset then he'd have to find a way through it that didn't mean putting me through it first. All he heard was what I said. And he opened his big black trunk.

That came after he started talking about "broadening his sexual expression." That wasn't even a way he talked, so I didn't swallow it. But I didn't like it anyway. Monogamy was never an overriding issue with me but fidelity was, so I showed him the door before what I knew was coming knocked on it.

Hoyt thought me moody. That excited him. Then when we fought, we both found out he couldn't handle it. You're not rational, he said. Be reasonable. Think it out. Fidelity was never just about sex. His face was red as he stood above the trunk, but he was pretending to be calm. Of course I asked him didn't he want to talk some more about it, and of course he said he didn't see the sense.

I'd told him he was pushing his dissatisfactions with himself off on me. He had this habit when we started fighting of putting on all his clothes. I'd never called it to his attention. That's what he did the first time, the time that started it all, when it was raining and so quiet. He got out of bed as we got angrier and put on all his clothes.

"You going somewhere?" I asked him in the middle of it.

"I might be. I should go somewhere. At least that would give me the illusion of movement."

I asked him what that meant.

"Nothing," he said. He slipped a work shirt over his chest and started buttoning it.

Now I couldn't see the hairs that curled around his left nipple. He didn't have any around his right nipple. That physical anomaly had been a conversation piece at least two or three times. Now I couldn't see them. But I didn't want to. I was angry. My fingers were tight around the edge of the typewriter.

"Why don't you just write?" he said. "That's your way of shutting out reality—so go ahead and write. Shut it out."

I didn't have an answer for that.

So now, since I never got Hoyt on the phone, I crossed the Bowery on my way to Second Avenue on my way to B&H to meet him.

Where I live teeters on the edge of several New York City neighborhoods without sliding into any of them—Little Italy, Soho, Chinatown, the Lower East Side. When he moved his stuff in, Hoyt said, "Now I don't know which community to identify with."

This part of Second is a short walking tour of failed intentions—first the subway's aborted diggings, then the morose spillover of winos from the men's shelter, then the seedy, boarded-up remains of the Fillmore East, relic of the sixties. I steered my way through it without noticing, replaying moments from the last few fights, second-guessing myself. I should have said this. And then Hoyt would have said that. And then we'd have looked at each other and seen what we both meant, and the contradictions would have melted like tar in the street under the noon sun.

A few weeks after the split-up he called and for the first time didn't sound half-dead. A new job. I didn't listen too much to what he said. I was annoyed that he was so enthusiastic. After his long series of jobs on underground rags that sank under him, sometimes with his help—

he'd written two or three glittering, semislanderous articles and claimed that he'd provoked one bomb threat—he'd surfaced by signing aboard as a second-string investigator for a muckraking Washington columnist. At lunch, he looked as if the exercise was doing him some good. He brought his lox-and-cream-cheese-on-pump-with-tomato-and-onion sandwich up to his wide mouth. They were frying my potato pirogen. I jabbed my finger into the saucer of sour cream on the table. It was smooth and cold, like a reality check.

B&H is a dairy restaurant about as wide as Kate Smith, with a counter and stools the length of one side and five or six thumbnail tables along the other wall. Hoyt sat across from me at a table in the back, his chestnut hair cut shorter than when we'd lived together, his summer suit a little wilted. We'd exchanged comments about the suit. We were trying to be nice to each other.

Swallowing a bite, he started talking about his job again. We'd met with a light embrace, like friends, and now his tone was friendly. "The part that bothers me is that whatever info I scrape up is screened and combed and nitpicked at five different levels, submitted to the research department and the legal department and rewrite. And then it sees the light of print."

I licked the sour cream off my finger. "And you don't recognize it anymore."

He nodded, eating again, and I said, "Even then, newspapers influence almost nobody in this country."

Instead of answering he kept eating. He finished one half of the sandwich and reached for the other.

I said, "You don't have to agree with me to keep talking to me. I just don't think these regular newspapers mean much as far as changing anything goes. But you know that."

He put the sandwich back on the plate without biting into it. Then he put his thumbs on the edge of the table, leaning toward me a little. "Emma, I can't close off all my options. If I stay out of it—out of everything—waiting right through the seventies, I'll go bananas. You don't have to tell me what a low level I'm starting at."

There was a strain in his face that I wanted to ease. But I didn't let myself. I said, "I had a friend, an acquaintance, who suckered herself into seeing *The Graduate* five times. She thought the truest moment was when the guy by the pool said, 'Plastics.' Given the right context I know I could be that dopey and so could anyone, so could you, Hoyt. I don't think there is anything wrong with starting somewhere. It's just a question of . . ." I couldn't think of the right word. "Of direction."

"Uh-huh," he said, his tone different. "Well, at least my direction isn't uptown downtown eastside westside ten hours a night."

I thought of the blind man for an instant. "At least I'm not kidding myself," I said. The waiter slid a plate of seven golden-brown pirogen onto the little table. He sneered at Hoyt and said, "If you're with him, you are," and walked back around the counter. Hoyt watched him. "I'm not pretending I'm doing something relevant," I continued. "I know I'm disengaged. But what do you tell yourself—that you're being effective?"

"What if I do?" He flared up, then calmed down and said, "I'm not twenty-two any more, Emma. I'm almost thirty-one. I'm fed up calling a roach hole home."

"I don't blame you," I said.

I had, but I no longer wanted to. The truth was I was getting tired of an accidental life. I dipped the pirogen in the sour cream. Physical actions are so pure. "Is it interesting, at least?" I asked. It would have to be interesting. But I needed to get him on neutral ground, out of the sun, on to something that wouldn't hurt us both.

"Of course it's interesting. Scandal always is. Right now, don't tell anyone, I'm digging into that Berndt death."

Congressional aide suicides in bathtub. The newspapers flap about it until the tub overflows with irrelevant facts that no one can sort out, and the woman is still dead, the one fact that can't be rearranged. Well, loss can't really be rearranged either. It will retain its taste, long after lunch is over.

"*National Enquirer* stuff, Hoyt, catching Congressman Wincey in his silk stockings with his pants around his heels."

Hoyt smiled, shaking his head, and pulled a paper napkin out of the steel dispenser. He wiped it across his lips slowly.

"Your mouth wasn't dirty," I said.

"I know," he said and leaned over the table to kiss me.

It lasted only a second, but it brought everything to the surface with a fatality that surprised me. When I looked up, Hoyt's wide-set eyes were on me. When I spoke, my voice sounded low and tense. "Why try now, Hoyt? You haven't been able to all along. You never even suggest we meet, and then you call and invite me—very flip on the phone you were—here where it's so cramped we couldn't possibly really talk. Why? You packed your bag like a good boy. You were happy to leave. You went out and got yourself a nice challenging job. What does seeing me do for you? Is this becoming friends?" I sounded as if I was jeering, though again I didn't want or intend to. "Well, maybe I don't want to be your friend. I'm not the friendly type. You are. That's why you go out and make good. That's okay. I think that might be the best thing for you. I do. But don't put on your suit and call me and . . ." I stopped.

He didn't say anything. Now he looked tense. The hand that had reached for the sandwich was now on the other side of the table gripping mine. That was better than kissing me.

"Never mind," I said. "Tell me about that Berndt stuff.

What was she, a spy, an informer, did Wincey cut her loose, is that why?"

He bit his lip. We weren't eating, and it was lunchtime, and several people stood crowded near the door craning over the sitters for a free table. We were taking up space. "Eat, Emma. Go ahead. I didn't . . . I don't want to be friendly. That's not what I want at all." He paused. "I went and got this job out of desperation, you know that."

It cost him a physical effort to say it. I could see his chest, the whole upper part of his body, trying to meet the intelligence in his eyes. When they connected he had the will to be as direct as he could be. He wasn't absolutely good at it—at being direct—and it could deplete him fast if I didn't respond. It was a pattern, a way we gave each other things, and I couldn't withdraw from it yet.

"You got it because you're good at it. I'm not trying to turn all this into some goddamn moral quest, you know."

But I didn't know. I am too moral, in a certain way. Once you got hold of Hoyt—he had hold of me now, and I couldn't decide if he felt strange because it had been so long or because he was really foreign—once you got hold of him, he gave, and I didn't want him throwing it away on a job that would suck him dry, leave him with scraps and a little money and the constricted look of bitterness that comes from having wasted your time.

"You should realize that I'm not going to either," he said.

We held that, not saying anything more for a while. "Anyway," he said finally, "the whole Berndt thing smells a little worse than the usual sex-scandal crap. Payoffs look like a possibility. No way her salary could ever manage the car she drove or cover her swank apartment."

"You going to be the mucked rake that makes the American people so riled and self-righteous they throw the bastards out?"

"Maybe."

"So a cleaner set of bastards whose hands aren't so deep in other people's pockets can get a chance, right?"

"Maybe we can't expect any better than that at the moment. Expectations change. The scale—"

"At this historical moment you mean. What should I do? Go register Democrat? Is that on your scale?"

He waved his hand at me. I could remember when a wave like that, so light in its dismissal, could have crushed me. I ate my last two pirogen without speaking. He finished off his sandwich the same way. When only crumbs were left on our plates one of us would have to say something. He pushed his plate away. He opened his mouth at least twice before he spoke. His voice was tentative.

"When I called you I thought we'd eat here, be more relaxed eating together, maybe be able to sort out some of our mistakes. I guess I guessed wrong."

"You didn't. I even tried calling you back because I was too curt on the phone. It's a bad habit."

"Oh, I understood that. I called you from a booth uptown. I was trying to get the Berndt woman's mother to talk to me, which turned out to be a fiasco." He looked up suddenly. "Maybe you'd like to try. You'd be better at this than me."

"At what?"

"You could get her to talk. She must know something. Mothers always do. But she smelled me a mile away. She won't talk to reporters."

"Hoyt."

"Forget it. Forget I mentioned it."

"Did you call me before or after you screwed up your interview with her?"

"Wait a minute. That's not fair—"

"Why should I be fair?"

"Emma, I'll explain. I called you because I wanted to have lunch with you as we used to, and talk things over as we used to, assess things, and . . ."

"And what?"

"And maybe you'd like me to come home with you after."

"It's too sudden."

"Sudden? It's been weeks since we were together. Weeks."

"That's what I meant—sudden."

"This suit doesn't affect what's under it, Emma."

"I should hope not. Then you'd be in trouble. No, Hoyt, truth is I was—"

"Why not? We still—" He couldn't figure out what he wanted to say or else he stopped himself from saying it. We still what? What did we still have or want or what were we still? If he knew at that instant he couldn't say what it was—it was inexpressible. Still. "I was hoping..."

"So was I. So why can't we—we have the same feelings."

I didn't want to let the thread go either. "Maybe we can. I don't know. I just feel sad about it."

No doubt he had a right to be annoyed with me, but I wished he hadn't shown it just then. It was his expression, the skin lifting a little around his cheekbones so that his eyes narrowed and made his beautiful face a little ugly. I wished he hadn't because I was on my way to seeing him more objectively. But a look, even a brief one, can change a lot and I was in control no longer. I had to protect myself. So I did. I uttered a cliché, sounding like a toughened young woman who was used to keeping men at a safe distance. "Sorry, it's just not in the cards."

There are a hundred, or anyway a dozen responses to such a refusal that would brush it away or incorporate it even, make it sound funny enough that we could both laugh at it. Here we are, finished eating and saying silly things because we're nervous and lonely, but don't worry, we can relax. Hoyt didn't choose any of the hundred or the dozen. His voice changed again. "Not in the cards. Is that where we're at—lost in the shuffle?"

He leaned back in a gesture I knew meant he was

reaching into his pocket for money. "You give up awful easy," I said. It sounded, I guess, like a taunt to him. It's true I didn't want him to know he'd hurt me. But if he knew me at all, then he'd see that at once. Why was this all so complicated?

In a moment by unspoken agreement, we were out of our seats and edging up the narrow aisle, Hoyt in front so I could see the back of his neck just inches away, that vulnerable bit of bare flesh between his hairline and his collar. B&H had never seemed so small. My lips were inches from his neck. I could have leaned forward and kissed him. When we got to the cash register in front, I let Hoyt pay and brushed past him and the people waiting for seats. B&H was air-conditioned, but I couldn't wait to be out in the heat.

I glanced up Second Avenue at the marquee of the St. Marks Theater. It said BURN in big black letters and below that, $1.00 AT ALL TIMES. An outdated political slogan popped into my head—the kind of thing once you think of you can't get rid of: Burn, baby, burn.

Hoyt straggled out. "How 'bout an egg cream?" he said.

I shook my head no and then said yes. We walked over to Gem's Spa on the corner. The BURN sign got larger. Hoyt leaned close to me. I thought he might be trying to bridge the gap.

"Listen," he said, "this is going to sound paranoid, but tell me if you think that guy in the blue suit is following us."

I didn't see anybody in a suit. "Everybody but you is dressed normally, Hoyt."

He smiled, unconvincingly. "No, I mean it. A sort of stocky guy, brown hair."

As we turned into Gem's Spa I scanned the sidewalk. No suits. We shared a chocolate egg cream. It was so cold it hurt my teeth. Too many intense feelings in one day, baby. I held out the nearly empty glass to Hoyt so he could get the last gulp.

He took the glass in one hand and my wrist in the other. Burn, baby, burn. "I'm sorry," he said. "I've done all this wrong. I've said the wrong things. I'll make it up to you. I swear."

One old man was running the big cigar he'd just bought under his nose. A Puerto Rican teenager was caught between a muscle mag and hand-packed half pint of vanilla-fudge ice cream, and the man behind the counter was wiping it with a slimy gray rag.

I don't know if any of them were listening. What did it matter? "I know you will," I said. Hoyt put the glass on the wet counter top, and we stepped outside. "Call me again in a day or two," I said.

He was still holding my wrist. I kissed him. He walked across the street and under the marquee. I watched for a blue suit to emerge from a dark corner and follow him down the block. No suits. Hoyt must have been seeing things, I thought.

I started home, the pirogen a lump in my stomach. Our conversation, another lump, rumbled through my mind. I was still somehow angry with him. I turned his accusation over—uptown downtown burn baby burn—to see if it smelled better on the other side. It didn't. I was wasting my time driving a cab. It made me angry because he was half right. But at the same time I was unwilling to do anything about it. I'd dropped out of City in '67 when everybody was dropping out. Then a few years later, when everybody was dropping back in, I barely noticed. I was too busy working in a day-care center during the day and typing articles at night for the underground alternative rag where I eventually collided with Hoyt. The day-care center—an old storefront—folded, the paper— an old storefront—folded, and to prevent my folding I started driving a cab. Those sound like economic necessities. In part they were. In part I stayed out of college, despite the ready availability of scholarships, because I never got along in school. I didn't have the patience to sit in classrooms or to spit back at the teachers what they wanted to hear. I wanted in the end to remain working-class, to remain my mother's daughter in a sense she'd never understand.

So the idea was that I'd work part time at cab-driving and spend the rest trying to find out if I could convince myself I was a writer. Several reams of paper neatly stacked above my desk and densely covered with type were still trying to convince me, and I was still driving a cab. I was still trying my luck, an impasse maybe, but trying your luck is supposed to be an honorable American pastime.

When I crossed the Bowery I saw a man in a blue suit looking in the window of the hardware store. He was staring at an eight-piece wrench set. He was obviously crazy about it. I stopped at the adjacent window and stared at the sign that said WE MAKE KEYS. It took a while, but the man finally got his fill of the wrenches and walked away.

I stole a look. His hair was brown and his back broad enough to suggest stockiness.

The phone was ringing again when I got home. Hoyt wanted to have lunch the day after tomorrow. Two combination p̶ ̶s. I'd have the shrimp with lobster sauce and he̶ ̶ the spareribs, and we'd share. That was the attitude. A̶ it turned out, I saw Hoyt the next day anyway, th̶e da̶ before our date, by accident.

3

At the shift change, the cabs fill the yard. They line up bumper to bumper to be fed at the pumps and pile on top of one another out of the yard in a ragged double column, backed up the long dismal block of warehouses and garages near the Hudson. Suddenly the yard and the street are yellow, solid heat-shimmering walls of yellow wherever you look. On the other side of the pumps is more yellow, with hoods and fenders still pulsing from the day's long, hard ride. Down the next block, pointing east toward the life of the city, shiny cab-length rows of yellow line both curbs, waiting for their new drivers. On Forty-eighth and Eleventh Avenue, at the traffic light painted a flat yellow, two more yellow lanes, four and five deep, jockey till the light changes.

In the late afternoon's palpable heat the yellow even tinges the dirty, sun-filtered air with a wretched enlivening glitter that hits me hard as I leave the gloom of the garage, where I've been sitting on a bench for the past two hours. Once it reminded me of the strange yellowish make-up I saw painted like a mask on my father's face when someone lifted me up to see him in the funeral home. "Say good-by to your daddy, Emma." His fingernails were shiny as if they had been painted too. The true and false cosmetic intensity of the yard and the thick air above it, of going to work one more time, of the way the yellow streaks the streets, bites into me. Such contradictions are too much work to resolve, so I just get into the cab and let the physical world take over.

According to my trip card, I clocked out at exactly 4:17, and according to the three transistor radios I passed on the way out of the garage there was exactly ninety-one-degrees worth of solidified air suspended over the brick-and-glass island. At 4:18, as I pulled up to the corner, a man stepped out into the sun. He'd been invisible under the shade of the green awning, like a frog under a rock. Instead of croaking he put an unlit cigarette to his lips. His expensive suit was greener than the faded awning. While lighting the cigarette, he peered at our yellow line of cabs throbbing at the corner, then spun a still-lit match straight up into the air with his fingertip without looking at it. I could tell he'd do the same thing in a tinder-dry forest if he felt like it. He knew it would hit the ground too dead to spark. The gesture made me smile. Naturally he caught me smiling. Naturally he'd think there was something more to it than there was. I quit smiling, but he passed up the three empty cabs in front of me just the same and got in mine. "Straight across town," he said.

I was hoping for uptown. You crawl crosstown this time of day. There's very little money in crawling. "You're lucky—you know that?" he said. He didn't wait for an answer. He expected to be listened to. "You think it was an accident I got into your cab, don't ya? That's where you're a hundred percent off. Two hundred percent. Those were all guys in front of you, right? I make it a point I see a girl cabbie I grab her. I always think I don't take her cab, maybe the next guy gets in Times Square somewhere could be a pervert, a rapist, a lowlife, who knows what. Is it even a job for a girl? That could be it's none of my business. You don't need my two cents to tell you if you want to put your life on the line. It's your business. One hundred percent, right? But if a pervert gets in, you've had it. I've seen examples of their handiwork. I could describe it. You want me to describe it?"

I glanced in the mirror. His small mouth was set. It would have been better to keep my mouth shut.

"I do all right," I said. "The perverts I pick up are well-behaved."

"A joking matter." In the mirror the lips were turned up slightly. It wasn't exactly a smile. "But you don't know. You don't know what scum will come off the street. No way. You want me to tell you about it?"

Probably he was harmless, like a chameleon. But I was glad he was on the other side of the plastic safety shield.

"No," I said, "I don't."

He shut up for a while.

When we crossed Lexington he tapped the shield to get my attention. "Stop near the phone booth," he said, "but don't pull the flag. We might be going farther, you and I."

I stopped: he stuffed himself into the booth. He jabbered a while at an increasing pace, slammed down the phone and got back in. "Why can't these goddamn monkeys do as they're told?" he asked.

I was going to ask, "What monkeys?" but I happened to glance at his face in the mirror. It was pasty and over-barbered. It gave me a sinking feeling. We were both white. We happened to be partners on this ride. That was just enough overlap. He might feel the freedom to vent his frustration.

"Take a run to Sixty-sixth," he said. I put my foot on the accelerator. "They couldn't tie their goddamn shoelaces without help." The shoelace theory had intrigued me in the past. I didn't pursue its implications this time. The light went yellow. "Catch the light, for Christ's sake," he said.

"You bet," I said and peeled onto Third. At Sixty-sixth I veered to the curb and braked hard. The beef in the back jumped a little. I put my hand up to shut off the meter.

"Not yet," he said. "I didn't say we were finished, did I? We're meeting someone here." Some fares entertain themselves by keeping you hanging. "He'll be here soon." I watched the cabs hustle up Third, thought of the cash being clocked on their meters. Every thirty seconds of waiting time when my meter turned over I made forty-nine percent of a dime. "Here he is," the monkey-hater said.

A stocky blue suit strolled off Sixty-sixth. I watched it get closer. The meter turned over. It was blue, it was a suit, and it was stocky. My fare met him with a complaint. "You didn't bust your ass getting here, Taylor."

"Wrong, Frederick. You don't appreciate the trial it was gauging the correct momentum." Taylor's head slid into the mirror. It was Frederick's on a little bigger scale. Every other mark of difference appeared to be a stab at denying evidence that the two issued from the same womb. Sweat beaded identically on their two foreheads. After leaving the tailor together they went to the same high-strung barber and took turns in his chair. Both wore trim cookie-dusters. Both had matched sideburns clamped to their jaws like book ends. An identical off-center clench to their lips was the most telling sign of their spiritual fraternity.

"I feel for you," Frederick said. "You aborted the project as requested?"

A pause. "In a word, not quite. There was a last-minute countermandation."

"How so?"

"I let it go ahead. It seems to appear we had a hitch-up."

"How so?"

"The secondary element I mentioned earlier?"

"Say something already."

"It has to be incorporated from the physical point of view."

"Has to be? Wait just a little minute. What about the potential risk, Taylor? It'll be our ass if this screws up. This was conceptualized as a demonstration project. So far we've only demonstrated our incompetence."

"Nothing to wet your pants about. Now's the time to wipe the plate clean and eat two birds with one fell swoop."

That statement deserved an interruption. I rapped on the shield. Four unexpectedly placid eyes lined up for roll call in the mirror.

"Where do we go next?" I asked.

Frederick answered. "I told you once, driver. Pier eighty-six. Did you hear me that time? Eighty-six."

"Halfway between Eighty-fifth and Eighty-seventh. Got it."

I shifted into drive. I wanted to get rid of these two. The peculiar way their diction slipped out of Business English 101 and into defective street smarts was getting on my nerves.

"At this very minute," Frederick said, the note of warning back in his voice, "we don't need a girl comedian."

"Girl?" Taylor said, "It's just another of them hippies. It better drive better than it jokes."

I turned onto Sixty-sixth, the fastest way back crosstown. I longed to ask them to get out, but Frederick had already run up a high fare. I'd lost the blind man's fare the last time, and I wasn't feeling lucky today. Anyway I was a little rattled as soon as I saw the blue suit come off Sixty-sixth. I kept trying to decide if it was exactly the same color. I decided it wasn't. Taylor wasn't the blue suit keen on eight-piece wrench sets.

At Park Avenue, increasingly impatient, I drove the cab halfway up over the curb to get around an oversized Pontiac, and then slithered back onto Sixty-sixth before north–south traffic could cut me off. A blue van double-parked halfway up the block reduced movement to a single lane. The cabbie ahead of me leaned on his horn.

I saw Frederick's head move out of the range of my mirror. He leaned forward, nosing the shield, his attention focused on the van.

Two men in gray coveralls were moving sealed cardboard cartons into a handsome granite-faced four-story building. Frederick cursed under his breath. I heard, "Those monkeys..."

Taylor rapped the shield. "Stay slow here. We might have to stop a second." Then he said conciliatingly to Frederick, "They should have delivered after dark but..." He interrupted himself. We'd just pulled past an empty van parked on the right curb. We were about three car lengths from the van being unloaded. I must have looked in the same direction as Taylor at about the same time. A man crouched on a stoop and partially hidden by a small cool-looking stone lion had a Super-8 movie camera held up to his face. He had a clear angle on the movers' action. I glanced into the mirror again. Taylor's slack jaw was slung even lower but his eyes glistened with a wet sheen. I looked back at the man with the camera—slim, full-mouthed, chestnut hair. I'd thought so the first time but didn't want to think about it. Hoyt lowered the camera for a moment. I jabbed my horn, quickly looking away from him. He was dressed in denims and a short-sleeve cotton polo that I bought him in a thrift store.

Taylor barked, "Pull up right here for a second." I pretended not to hear him and kept inching forward. We were about two car lengths from the moving van. "Right here, right here!" he yelled. He nudged his partner. "Look at that guy, Frederick!"

"Let's go be sociable. Keep the meter running, cabbie." They bolted from the cab, leaving the door open on the right side.

"Hey!" I yelled, and Hoyt, who'd just put the camera up to his eye again, twisted his stance as they rushed at him. Had they expected him to be there? Caught short he lowered the camera smoothly around to his back. I tried to read his expression to tell if he knew or recognized them. But the movement was too fast. Frederick grabbed his arm. I winced involuntarily. A red Fiat behind me started tooting its horn. I couldn't make out what they were saying except that it wasn't friendly. Frederick pointed to my cab. Hoyt's arm was flexed to pull loose, but Frederick held tight. Taylor grabbed his other arm. Taylor's suit looked very blue.

Hoyt said, "That's none of your business," in a harsh tone. The confab over, the trio approached the cab. Hoyt's heels scuffled along the concrete. Taylor bounced in first pulling Hoyt by the arm, then Frederick shoved in.

"Hey, listen," I said, "I don't want any trouble in this cab—buzz off, all three of you." Hoyt's head jerked up at the sound of my voice and he sent me a warning look through the shield. The Fiat was squalling like a two year old.

"Go on, girlie, don't hold up traffic. Get going—there'll be no trouble," Frederick said.

"Take your hands off him."

Startled that I was so vehement, they obeyed.

Taylor put out a hand. "Calm down, honey. Nothing's happening. We have some private questions to ask this gentleman."

Hoyt said, "It's all right—I'm here of my own free will. You can go on." His eyes begged me to shut up. I wondered if he knew free will wasn't what the nuns said it was. Did he really have a handle on what he was doing? I pulled around the van and out across Madison.

Frederick kept his voice low to keep me out of the action. Hoyt looked straight ahead. Frederick's lips appeared to be communing with his well-shaven cheek. "Listen, kid, normally our actions are pretested. We work out every exchange in scenarios that preempt failure." His last two words slurred into a dog's growl but Hoyt just grinned at them. Under my breath I said *you know better than that* to Hoyt. Frederick tried again. The cab was traversing

33

the park. "What you recorded with that box in your lap was only a one-term event."

Hoyt turned his head slightly toward Frederick. "Where'd you pick up that mumbo-jumbo?"

"Let's put it this way, whatever you might think, you can't slander my employer with that—"

"*Your* employer?"

"—not on the slim support of a one-shot deal."

Hoyt grinned again. "I can try," he said unpleasantly.

"Listen, kid, you don't understand the business—that's the trouble. You can't sell those pictures even if you diddle around with them to make them mean whatever you want them to. As evidence," he said contemptuously, "it's pure horseshit."

"So why get antsy about a little amateur moviemaking?"

"I'm doing you a favor just to set you straight, kid. And give you the chance to turn it over to the right personnel."

I was now facing Lincoln Center. The best I could make out of this spiel was that Hoyt had caught the van making an illegal delivery (of what?) and Frederick was trying to persuade him that his evidence wasn't strong enough to use.

Hoyt got snotty. "What if I'm not in the mood?"

"It might turn into a real headache for you," Frederick said with sympathetic menace. "I'll even put up the cost of the film just to square things."

"When I get it developed I'll send you a copy. You're probably right—it won't amount to anything."

Frederick sighed heavily. "That presents an unacceptable level of risk."

I bounced the cab down Ninth Avenue, hoping that all this hard talk was just men playing games.

Taylor spoke up impatiently, his voice in a high register. "Quit jerkin' around with the squirt. I'll show him the lay of the land." There was a sudden explosion of air and Hoyt's head slammed against the shield.

I made a fast wide turn around the corner of Forty-seventh. We were only three long blocks from the pier. As soon as I turned, I spotted the open fire hydrant on the right side halfway down the block. A dozen half-naked Puerto Rican boys were playing in the thick spray. One kid would carefully aim the high-pressure spray with his arm and send it high enough to hit passers-by on the other side of the street. I put my foot on the accelerator and bounced my hand on the horn. I figured it was my best chance. All the windows in the cab were wide open because of the oppressive heat. It was even money, knowing these kids, that they'd do their best to direct the force straight into the cab. It was one way to dampen the discussion in the back seat. I pushed hard and then jerkily on the brake. My timing was good. I skidded into the middle of the block, turning the wheel both ways for disorientation. Some of the kids scattered, but they could barely believe their good fortune, a sucker asking for it. The hard spray hit the right front fender. I skidded to a halt. The kids roared, "Taxi! Taxi!" The water hit the cab's back-seat interior full blast. I opened my door, rolled out and, crouching, threw open the back door. Taylor screamed to Frederick, "Get the window, schmuck!" I yanked his arm as hard as I could with both of mine and he fell over on top of me out of the cab. Frederick missed this action trying frantically to get the window up. I pulled my head up to catch Hoyt smashing Frederick on the neck to stun him and half-falling, half-stepping out over the two of us sprawled on the wet blacktop. Taylor was up on his knees and Hoyt, camera in hand, gave him a ferocious kick that spun him over. Then he saluted me, and I grinned and yelled, "Run, damn it!" Just so much street football to the kids. They went wild cheering and whistling as Hoyt sprinted away.

I watched his escape, forgetting about Frederick. But Frederick hadn't forgotten. He stumbled out of the back seat as I started to unpeel myself from the warm wet blacktop. He must have caught sight of Hoyt right away. I saw him begin to run after him and then think better of it. I grinned at the big slob and shivered. Taylor was moaning near the gutter. I thought it was all over and the good guys had won.

Frederick jumped into the driver's seat, put the car in gear and slammed the door. I lunged and grabbed for the door handle as he skidded away. Then a spray hit me and almost knocked me over. I yelled as loud as I could. The kids' uproar easily drowned me out. I started running. Hoyt was near the end of the block. The cab was faster. Frederick tried to brake. I saw the rear lights flash red, red, red. Hoyt turned before the cab jumped the curb and tried to dodge it. Frederick got the wet brakes pumping and swerved the wheel to avoid hitting him. The front end veered back toward the street. For a moment it looked as if Frederick had it under control. He didn't. It was still skidding. The rear left fender hit Hoyt almost full force before the cab finally stopped. Hoyt's body flew in an arc against a brick wall. At the same time a small black object flew even higher into the air and crashed against the brick wall close to the corner. Frederick staggered out of the cab, leaving the door open, fell on one knee, pushed himself up, and stepped toward the crumpled heap of Hoyt's body. Out of breath but still running, I felt a scream wrench itself from my chest. That startled Frederick—he looked toward me backing away from Hoyt and then took off. Before reaching the corner, he stopped and grabbed the camera. Then he was gone.

I stopped running. There was no blood yet leaking onto the sun-baked sidewalk. Hoyt's head leaned against the brick wall, one side of his face right up against it, hugging it. Blood did stream from one of his nostrils. He was very warm. Panting hard, I tried to arrange his limbs but it took too much effort. He weighed too much—much more than I remembered. His face slid away from the wall. That side had bits of red pebble embedded in his skin. I turned him over, and something hit the sidewalk with a brittle, plastic sound. I looked down. It was a movie cartridge. I picked it up. The face of it—where the film ran through it—said EXP. I put it in my shirt pocket. That was no reason to be killed I thought, angry at him. I couldn't close his eyes. Lids half shut, they stared at an indefinite point across the street in the empty parking lot. I stood up and leaned against the wall, dizzy for a second. A series of white stenciled signs read POST NO BILLS POST NO BILLS POST NO BILLS in a direct line.

Hoyt said to me once after an argument, his voice weary and shaken, "What I get most tired of is that there's no escape from the everlasting word, the everlasting motherfucking word." He was wrong. I looked back down the street. It was empty. There wasn't a human being or a vehicle on it, not a soul. But the hydrant still sprayed water onto the hot street.

It made no sense to me to look down again. The right-turn signal was still clicking on and off. I went over to the cab to drive it off the curb. I did, then pulled up to the corner and stopped. Now what? In the mirror I saw the flash of a cop car's overhead light. Ahead of me was a thick stream of cars and trucks. I knew vaguely that I didn't want to talk to any cops. I pulled around the corner and joined the traffic stream moving up Tenth.

4

There's no way to explain what doesn't have a reason. That's not an excuse. I'll try anyway. There was a red light flashing and spinning inside my head. My brain said, you don't have anything to say to the cops and that's not Hoyt any more.

I'm all right about talking to cops by now, almost your average citizen. But in 1974 I was just beginning to emerge from the phase where I wanted cheerfully to kill them all. That had been a keen clear desire on my part—as I say there's not a real reason to stick to it. I imagined their blue uniforms coming toward me where I stood (not being able to look at Hoyt any longer). So I knew I wouldn't have anything useful to say to them and, more than that, would just end up hurting myself and, I thought, would end up not helping Hoyt either. So these are not reasons—they're what I told myself as I held on to the wheel with both hands and turned and turned again and followed the traffic downtown.

No wino was sprawled across the doorway of my building. I was glad of that. There often was a body lying there, since the Bowery was only around the corner. The Italian bakery was closed. That was good too. It seemed an impossible thing for me to handle if someone were to bother me while I walked upstairs in my wet clothes.

I had the second-floor rear apartment. My neighbor across the hall was a friendly, selectively spaced-out hippie. On the other floors were an ex-Jesuit, a perpetually frightened old lady and her secretary daughter, a boatload of Sicilian immigrants, and a young gay accountant. None of us spoke exactly the same language so I didn't want to run into any of them either. For a while I sat quietly in the cab and tried to plan my physical movements. My body was stiff. I had a hunch that the second floor was very far away. I could imagine myself unlocking the gate in front of the door to my apartment, but it confused me to think what would happen after I opened the car door. A shower might be nice.

My apartment, once I managed to get myself into it, looked out of focus. Closing the door, I stood shakily in the kitchen gazing at the living room that doubled as my bedroom, with my bed that doubled as couch and two full-length windows framed by black painted shutters that doubled as gates to discourage junkies. The disorder of two overstuffed easy chairs, of too many books haphazardly stacked in white painted bookcases that disappeared into the white walls, of the two tables and dresser I'd scavenged off uptown streets while driving the cab, only made me more nervous. Instead of padding over to greet me, the cat slowly and warily uncurled from his sleep and stretched in his resting place, the unusable brick fireplace. I retreated to the bathroom.

I stepped into the shower, then had to step out of it. Most of my clothes were still on. I took off my jeans and sneakers. That was enough. There were two faucets to turn on. The young bare-chested Puerto Rican at the hydrant had smiled broadly, showing white teeth. The water poured over my head in a soft lukewarm spray. I know what I'm doing. You do? You'd be better at this than me. Hoyt had a boy's slim torso. Peculiar how memory tries to give back what's gone. I dropped the rest of what I wore into the shower while it hit me. Twice we'd made love here. I showered and stepped out. I grabbed a robe hooked on the back of the bathroom door and got it around me. I pulled the light string in the bathroom, and the light went out. That seemed like a startling demonstration of cause-and-effect, so I did it again.

In the living room I switched on the window fan. It blew the smell of yeast from the bakery downstairs into the room. My body ached everywhere, as if I'd been pushed around a lot. Well, I had been. A giant arm, stretching in answer to some unknown, unnamed need, had shoved me into a hole I didn't recognize. I sat up, suddenly afraid that if I didn't move right this second I wouldn't be able to later. The fan teased the pages of an open book on the chair. I hated the idea of the book moving of its own accord. I grabbed it and threw it. It skidded across the floor and hit the bookcase, breaking its spine so that pages ripped from the cheap glue. I wanted to pick it up but my body didn't.

Hoyt's body was so heavy. Two attendants in white are lifting it onto an ambulance stretcher. I heard a siren, a dull stupid sound. My fingers tingled. Wasn't that a symptom of shock? Wouldn't those two businessmen be trying to do business with me now? Maybe not. Maybe they don't know me. That giant arm pushed on them too.

Hoyt had reached for a slice of tomato smeared with cream cheese. He said something about Wincey and the Berndt death. Then the next minute, a day later, he's dead. He wasn't counting on that when he asked me to do his legwork. What difference could it make, Hoyt, who killed whom, who picked the lint out of who's pocket, who was squeezing whom? You needed some security—nothing wrong with that, an entry into real life, a stake in destiny, an illusion of influence. Those are the things you learn about in school. There are much worse things.

I heard the shower water running in the bathroom—

I'd forgotten to turn it off. He would have come here tomorrow, in a few hours. We would have made love and then showered, soaping each other's bodies, sliding in and out of each other's arms. He had his fantasies, but that was normal. You always want to know what to go on to. But I'd caught the fugitive look of panic drifting in the corners of his eyes. There was nothing I could do about that panic, I thought. I tried to fight it. But I didn't really have the tools. Maybe a part of me was infected with it. I knew I couldn't live with it.

He was only trying to get in control before those first tremors of panic gathered speed. So he made a choice while I chose to stay where I was—and as soon as he showed himself they came and got him and smashed him up against the wall.

I was in the bathroom again. The shower curtain was open. There was no one in there. On the shelf above the toilet there was a big glass bottle of green mouthwash Hoyt had left. He'd swig from it, rinse his mouth and, stepping toward me where I stood brushing my hair, say, half-taunting, "Now you're stuck. You have to kiss me," and put his hands on my shoulders. "You won't need that any more," I said out loud. I put my hand around it and dropped it into the tub. It shattered. Wide green rivulets ran toward the drain. I could find them, shove the shower head down their throats and turn on the hot tap full blast. They were just the mud somebody tracks in the door. I wanted to get past that door before it slammed shut after the somebody. He should get it in the neck too, and he should know why. I had to know why. Who. In a few moments I went looking for an address in the telephone book.

People flagged me all the way up First Avenue, even when I turned on the off-duty sign. Well, Hoyt, let's see if I'm any better at this. I parked in a taxi-stand near a Hofbrau on Eighty-sixth Street. The address I wanted was on Eighty-fourth in the heart of Yorktown, sometimes called Germantown. I was going to lie my way in the door, and I had nothing but reservations about it. If somebody asked me, I'd say the mother should be left to her memories.

Eighty-fourth looked as if it had been scrubbed and hung out to dry. The garbage cans had just been waxed and buffed. Nevertheless one relentless old woman was punishing her walk some more with an angry broom. The building I wanted was a tall, narrow affair with a shoe-repair shop a few steps from the sidewalk. In the store's plate-glass window an industrious cardboard cobbler sat hammering a cardboard nail into a man's cardboard boot. I watched that for a while, getting up my nerve. No matter how much he hammered, the nail never got any deeper into the cardboard leather. The cobbler didn't seem to care. You could tell from his fixed apple-cheeked smile he liked hammering for its own sake.

The inside door at the top of the stoop was unlocked. I climbed up the dark narrow steps looking for number six and finally found it on the third landing. Chimes played the first bar of Beethoven's Fifth when I pushed the button. Nothing happened, and I was about to go when the spooky music of a series of locks turning stopped me. The door opened a few inches, a chain lock stretched across it inside. I could see a segment of what was probably a small kitchen. I took another step toward the door.

"You have the wrong number?" the kitchen said in a thick German accent.

"Are you Mrs. Berndt? I'm Emma Hobart. I'm sure Evelyn must have mentioned me several times. I—" The door shut and opened. She wasn't as old as the woods, but she suspected she might be and was fighting it. She wore a short blond wig too big for her head, a lot of pancake make-up, penciled-in brunette eyebrows and a cotton print house dress depicting Parisian hot spots. She stood inspecting me as if I were damaged goods.

"I don't remember," she said. "But Evelyn . . ."

"I happen to be in town, so I thought I'd say hello and

see how you were getting on. Mind if I come in a moment?" She wasn't tall, and I fairly pushed her aside. She fell back near an old broom just her height. I could see how she had given Hoyt trouble. All the surfaces in the kitchen were very worn and very clean. "Evelyn used to talk about this apartment," I said.

"Did she? She always thought it was so tiny. She had a joke about it." She paused and then recited, "Fine for three people if two of them are dead."

I didn't think it was such a good joke. "I was so shocked," I said. "I wanted to see you to tell you so myself. Eve meant so much to me. I hope you don't think I'm being brash. When I got to the city, it was suddenly very important to me to meet her family."

She looked straight at me. "I don't meet many of Evelyn's friends. She didn't like to bring them here." There was a pause. "Maybe I could offer some coffee. Please go into the parlor. I bring something." She waved toward the next room. "Don't mind Papa. He likes quiet nowadays."

Except for a huge color TV in one corner, the parlor was like a page from a 1940's women's magazine. Overstuffed chairs with flowery slipcovers, dark-stained pale wallpaper with lilac bushes and gazebos, little tables with legs that curved into paws, lace doilies, antimacassars, crewelwork. Propped in a chaise longue in the angle of two full-length windows, Papa looked as if he'd about had it. Despite the heat his legs were shrouded in a woolen blanket. He fixed me with a stare that gave a brief glint to his gray mask.

"We have his pension," Mrs. Berndt said after serving me. I hadn't said a word about money. Bustling about the kitchen with the sun's last efforts streaming in the window, she'd been brooding on her dimming prospects. "With Eve we were doing good. Good enough. She was generous. Now not so good." She became downcast.

"But how could Eve have done so much? She was a secretary . . ."

"Well, you know Eve, she had her ways. Always a step ahead of the game, she was. That's why she made sure to go to Barnard with the rich girls. She worked for it—I'm not saying she didn't—but she was always a step ahead. Is that where you know my Eve?" she asked abruptly.

I nodded. "We had some classes together. I was out of the city for some time. I was so upset . . ." I wanted her to say something about the death without having to pinch any nerves.

"Of course, there was her insurance. But they are being bad about that. What can I do? I'm nothing to them."

She poured herself more coffee, her movements quick and accurate. She'd poured a cup for the old statue, but she didn't hand it to him. It stayed on the coffee table between us near a cut-glass bowl filled with mixed nuts. I caught a veiled movement of his eyes watching her. Something—an argument in progress before I rang?—was being enacted in a minor key before my eyes. Maybe this explained why she was being so obsessive about money—out of a desire to taunt her husband and his "pension." The mother wouldn't have scrupled using the daughter as a pawn in their arguments if she was always like this.

"I just don't understand how it could have happened," I said. Her eyes under the permanent surprise of her eyebrows flashed up just as she cracked the shell of a pecan. The noise seemed to emerge from the depthless brown eyes.

"We don't talk about it. It is not allowed to talk about."

She slid a nutmeat between her lips and chewed. I murmured an apology. She already had me a little cowed.

"We are going to be lucky now, are we not, Fritz?" She cocked her head to acknowledge the man in the chaise longue. He didn't stir, and she didn't wait long enough for an answer. "We have help."

"Did you apply for aid?" I asked.

"The congressman," she whispered, glancing slyly at

Fritz. "He wants us to be happy in our old age." A rising note of self-esteem entered her whisper.

The old man's hand fell like a club onto the table and brushed his cup of coffee onto the carpet, just missing his wife. She stood up. "Fritz, you clumsy fool, look at the mess." I glanced at him. He had fixed me with an impenetrable look. She trundled out to the kitchen, muttering in German.

As soon as she was out of the room, he leaned forward in his chair. The veins and tendons bulged in his neck. "I don't know who you are or who sent you here, young lady. Truth is I don't care. But you can tell them I don't want any more vultures in this house." It was a hoarse growl that cost him an immeasurable effort, but each word was uttered precisely with only a trace of an accent. By the time he got them out and fell back into his chair, his wife had swooped in with sponges and a plastic pail.

While she got on her knees to wipe out the offending stain, still muttering in German, I stared at him.

5

I took a number of fares after leaving Eighty-fourth Street, writing down their comings and goings on my trip card. The third fare tapped on the shield just after getting in. I looked back. "Is this yours?" she asked. She passed me Hoyt's wallet. I stuffed it into my bag and did not look at it again. I didn't need any more reminders. After about an hour, I got a fare down to Christopher Street, two men happily romancing each other in the back seat. I turned around on Hudson Street across Tenth and down Greenwich and stopped at a cabstand up Sixth Avenue, from Whelan's drugstore. I slid a roll of Super 8 film into a mailer, wrote the name and address of a friend on it and handed it over a row of vibrators to the sullen young Puerto Rican behind the counter.

"Deposit of a dollar."

I handed him the dollar. He tore off the receipt and handed that to me.

"When will the film be ready?"

He shrugged. I stood there. "Day after tomorrow in the afternoon, maybe."

"Thanks." I wondered what could be worth seeing on the square black cartridge.

I drove across Eighth Street, hoping for a fare to keep me from thinking. Hoyt lowered the camera and turned his head to see what the noise was about. I had no plan of action till morning, when I'd go try Wincey. I wasn't even thinking about how I'd manage to get to see him. The green lights turned on one by one on Broadway and then I was parked in front of my house again. In the stale little lobby I stopped long enough to slide the film receipt into my mailbox so I wouldn't forget where I put it. Go upstairs, I told myself, get some sleep or at least some rest and then you can drive till morning and make the money you need to live . . .

I entered my apartment and switched on the kitchen light. The two men were facing me. One of them was armed or pretending to be. I recoiled, snapping back my head. A car with washed-out brakes hadn't plowed into me but I felt as if it had just missed and was coming back to try again.

"You were expecting roaches maybe?" Frederick said.

Taylor quit fingering his mustache to answer for me. "You bet she was expecting roaches in this hellhole. I wouldn't even sit down in a place like this. They'd eat you alive."

They exchanged glances with each other, moving only their eyes as if their skulls were granite.

The last thing I wanted to do was show them how scared I was. "It must have been hard for you in the dark. Did you come here to pay me for the fare?"

"Yes, that's right," Frederick agreed. "We'd like to pay you. Here, this is all for you." He reached into a pocket, drew out a good leather wallet and fished a bill from it carefully, as if peeling off a piece of skin. "Keep the change." It fell onto my kitchen table next to a coffee mug. I had drunk from that mug this morning. A hundred-dollar bill was now sitting next to it. I should wash that mug.

"I'm not worth it," I said. "I have nothing to sell. I don't know anything."

Three denials should be better than one.

"Don't be modest. See how shy she is, Taylor? We want you to drive us somewhere. We like the way you drive, don't we, Taylor?"

Taylor nodded.

"You two don't know how to behave in a moving vehicle."

"While we were waiting we looked for something we misplaced. We thought you might have it around somewhere."

I glanced into the living room. It was a shambles.

"I have nothing that belongs to you."

They looked at me, saying nothing, waiting for me to give because they knew I had to and they weren't yet in a big hurry to prove it. A physical dread of their strength hit my body, a dread as specific as that swift moment before sudden nausea when the world feels as if it's going to convulse before your eyes.

"Get out. I'm tired and I need some rest."

They didn't respond. Two statues, bigger than life-size.

"Why don't you look for it? If you find it, it's yours. How's that?"

I carried the mug past Frederick to the sink. He turned aside to let me by. He looked amused.

"You know," I said, "you thugs look more like cops than businessmen. You have the beef for it."

Taylor sputtered, "Listen, girlie, if I was still in the TPF you wouldn'ta got by with any of this crap."

Frederick barked, "Shut yer face, stupid." It was too late. I turned the water on and kept my attention trained on the mug. Hard fast memories of the Tactical Police Force washed ashore in my brain. In the old days—the sixties—they were the elite corps specially assigned to cracking skulls in every antiwar demonstration. I turned off the cold tap, leaving the hot running.

While I still had my hand on the tap something pulled violently on the hair at the back of my head. My hand dropped into the sink around the lip of the mug. My eyes looked briefly at the water stains on the ceiling and then I was jerked around to look at Frederick close-up. He stood over me, his thick face lit harshly by the bare bulb over our heads. The thousand dark points of his beard looked like a mass meeting. Someone applied a vise to the back of my neck. It slowly tightened. "You have a choice—want to hear it?" His lips had the same mobile ferocity they had when he spoke to Hoyt in the back seat of my cab. I spit in his face, slammed my elbow into the gut behind me and my boot into the shoe below me. The vise loosened for a moment.

I pulled away while it was loose and threw the mug at Frederick's face. I missed because he was already coming toward me. It hit his shoulder. I ducked and squirmed around him and made for the door. They switched direction and lumbered toward me. I needed a gun in my hand. I wanted to watch them assume unhuman positions like Hoyt's. I shouldn't have hesitated. They might look as agile as bears, but they weren't. I grabbed for the door, knowing I'd never get it open. There was a loud knock. A voice I knew called my name. Someone pushed against the door. I pulled it open.

It was my neighbor across the hall, Tony Corrigenda. He was tall, thin, hairy, and except for a pair of pink sandals, naked. His appearance jolted Frederick and Taylor out of their momentum. Violence can be sapped by an equal and opposite force. They stared at Tony. Tony gave them his beatific grin—picked up from watching TV reruns of *The Song of Bernadette* while tripping. That held them like epoxy. He turned matter-of-factly to me.

"Sorry to bug you when you have guests, but Con Ed just cut my electrical connection to the cosmos. Could I . . . ?" He held the end of an extension cord that ran back down the hall into his kitchen. I nodded gratefully and took a step into the hallway as if to make room for him. Tony, frail as he was, blocked Frederick and Taylor's approach to me by bending down to the outlet just inside the door, presenting them with the hairy lineaments of his ass.

"You know," he said, "this will only be till tomorrow and then I'll call Con Ed and pretend I just moved in and they'll say, 'Oh, of course, Mr. Blank, sorry for the inconvenience, service will be restored within four hours.'" He straightened and turned toward them, scratching his balls with the hand that had inserted the plug. "Hot enough for you?" he asked them. His other hand, shielded from their view by his body, waved me away. I took another step, my fingers searching my pocket for my cab keys.

6

I drove the rest of the long hot night, earning money, trying to cruise out of the range of overt violence, thugs and ex-lovers. On green I moved, on red I stayed. What the Motor City generals smilingly call an accident could easily cancel my subscription to existence (as Tony would say). Beyond the smash-up—product turnover, that is—there was the smooth, subtle and attractive violence of the upper middle class emerging in scattered waves from show, theater, bar and other playgrounds. They raise their well-tailored arms so gracefully that no notice need be taken of how much room these few take up on this small island, no conception need be formed about what violence is required to secure them the wide elbowroom they think they deserve and delude themselves they have earned. They pay me one after the other and tip me and joke about the female hackie. If they don't tip me enough, I shout my own well-tailored curses out the window, hoping to embarrass them, to drive them in their brains to that uncomfortable nonexistent street where the luxury high rise faces the ghetto. Then when the doormen usher them safely away, I get the night shift late for work and cursing the heat, the whore cursing the cop, the drunken tourist cursing life. As I cruise, I see young men who look like Hoyt on Lexington, on Park, on Bleecker. I avoid the West Side. Once I refuse a fare to the West Forties.

Toward dawn I stop at a newsstand for the *News* and the *Times*. In neither is there any mention of a hit-and-run fatality on West Forty-seventh Street. I drive to the car wash on Twenty-third that opens at six A.M. and turn up the ramp. This is the first time in all the years I've driven I have ever bothered to get a cab washed. It is also the last.

As dawn breaks, I pay the dispatcher at my garage and go to a donut shop. For an hour or more I sit alone and drink coffee, wait for the buzz to go out of my ears, try to guess whether the tremor in my hands is from driving or from shock. I try to make plans, but I can't think more than two steps ahead.

Once in a while congressmen are in Congress, so there was more than a chance Wincey wouldn't be in his office. But he was campaigning, so there was more than a chance he would be in his district. The merchants of East Fourteenth Street were beginning to open their doors and roll out their shlock. The sole criterion of quality on East Fourteenth Street is that whatever is up for grabs—slacks, umbrellas, lamps, blouses, stereo components, radios, tablecloths or toiletries—must be shiny. The stores whose wares spill out on this street are really poor people's jewelry stores. In the total absence of quality, everything should have the luster of diamonds. Wincey's office on the north side of Fourteenth between Third and Fourth Avenues faced the glitter merchants.

At his storefront he was selling himself. It must have been too early because there was nobody buying. A six-foot poster photo of Wincey with a red, white and blue banner that boasted THAD'S DOING THAT JOB was carefully designed to give a balanced impression. Everybody's favorite uncle (as long as everybody's WASP) looked straight out (not at us but through us to a grand vision skulking on the horizon) with the suggestion of a smile (good-humored confidence or the narrow-minded craftiness of the master pol?). The eyes deep-set but narrow, the lips broad but thin—the message on the banner resolved these contradictions. I felt reassured. I pushed the door that said PULL FOR WINCEY.

Six gray steel desks, an all-weather carpet, pastel stacks of campaign literature. At the one occupied desk a woman sat reading a paperback. As I walked over to her, she looked up briefly, beamed me a smile, held up a finger that said, "Just a sec, hon," and dropped back into the book. Her eyes chased down the page. I looked at the title: *If You Feel Yes, Don't Let The World Say No: The Psychotherapy of Self-Realization*. After a while, she licked the finger, flipped the page and set the book down.

"Now then," she said, "what's the good word this morning?" Her carrot-colored modified Afro went with a chocolate form-fitting sleeveless top made of the kind of acetate that gives laboratory rats skin cancer within two weeks. Her arms were blue and goose-bumped.

"You should throw a sweater on before the frost gets you."

"The dumb thermostat's gone blooey again. Nothing to be done," she said fatalistically.

"I want to see the congressman first thing. He in yet?"

"Well, between you and me, not yet. What time's your appointment?" She was already opening the appointment calendar. "Here we are, August 25." When I didn't say anything, she looked up. "Well perhaps I could arrange an appointment in the near future, though, my goodness, he is booked up." The carrot head was down for that part of it and then bobbed up again. "What did you want to see him about?" Her affability seemed both too hard-won and too fragile to risk pushing it off the tracks.

"I'm a grad student in government at NYU and for my summer project I was considering volunteering. Wincey's been a good legislator and—" I stopped before the enthusiasm seeped out of my voice while gazing elaborately around the big cold empty room.

"He'll be tickled pink," she said. "He's a little short of volunteers this time around."

"Somehow I thought the place would be really hopping."

She sighed the arduous, heartfelt sigh of the woman who begrudges herself such shallow subjectivity. "The news media just wiped the floor with us, honey. That's all I can say." She looked at the floor, which was perfectly clean, and then at me. "All those filthy innuendos."

"It's not right," I said encouragingly.

"Not right? It's dirt. You've no idea how many sleazy characters slid under that door to try and get me to say something bad about the congressman." She blew out her rouged cheeks. "I'm not made like that."

"Well, I'm glad I came then," I said. "I certainly never thought Wincey"—I paused—"drove her to it." I thought I might be pushing too much, but I wasn't counting on her indignation.

"You should have seen the poor man. I had to field calls and those damned newsmen all morning while he got himself together."

"He was shaken by her death?" I was hoping for one more go-round before discretion overtook outrage.

"He kept saying, 'It's not possible, it's not possible. She couldn't have.' That's how shocked he was." Shaking her head in dismay, she pulled out a drawer, thumbed a file and handed me a sheet of paper. Given her gloom, it could have been a death warrant. "Here, honey. Fill this out. Maybe I can get you a few in-person minutes with the congressman when he comes in."

I sat at the nearest desk. After a minute or two of penciling lies, I tried again. "Did Evelyn Berndt start out as a volunteer?" I asked.

Interrupting some envelope-stuffing, she looked at me warily, not saying anything. "I'm sorry," I said. "Talking about her made me start thinking about it and how she must have gotten involved with the political life." I paused again. "I don't really know much about her except that she was young and pretty and died in her own bathtub." I said it slowly, keeping my eyes on the secretary even when they wanted to pull away. She softened visibly. If anything, I was exploiting the mother in her.

"Don't get morbid, hon. She was too much the go-getter to start out volunteering—no offense meant. She got recommendations from the top and was off and running. How did she start out?" She tapped her forehead to joggle an imperfect memory. "Doing research maybe. Don't worry, kid—she was the high-strung type. Things like that don't happen twice, bless the Lord."

I tried to look relieved. Evidently she didn't think me the high-strung type.

I picked up a pale-blue Thad Wincey Fact Sheet. Only forty-four, happily married, father of two, high ACLU rating, well-informed and energetic vice-chairman of subcommittee on labor racketeering, passionate sailor, recently an ardent jogger. Too many copywriter's adjectives. Could be Wincey didn't have the common touch. As if to contend this with me, a man answering to his description—but minus his poster's wise smile—gave a violent pull at the glass PULL FOR WINCEY door and entered the big room as if it were an arena. It was too early in the morning to go up against a competitor like him. But in a moment his secretary had him pointed in my direction.

"NYU?" he boomed. "Professor Halbird's one of my biggest fans. Know the old geezer?" He was shaking my hand. I can't remember how he got it or how I got it back. "Let's see the application," he said reaching for my tissue of lies. "Just a formality, you know. Weeds out the fly-by-nighters. I'm a speed reader anyhow, it won't take half a second."

I watched the gray eyes tear over the page and stop three-quarters down. The good-natured smile vanished.

Something was taking the wind out of the passionate sailor. Or was it ardent? He looked at me. No love in those eyes.

"Can't use you, Miss Hobart. That's the name, isn't it?" He handed me the application as if relieving himself of a great weight. "We have no place for you in my organization. Good morning." He left through another door, and the room shrank back to size.

I shrugged my shoulders at the secretary.

"Goodness, he's in a bad temper this morning," she said, clearly surprised by his behavior. "He just hasn't been himself since Evelyn . . . I'd put in a word for you, hon, but once his mind is made up . . ." She shrugged.

"Don't bother," I said, "I screwed up."

She nodded sympathetically, "Did you fill it out wrong somehow?"

"I'm not really an NYU student. I just wanted to talk to him."

"He'll never talk to you now." She pursed her lips. "You should have been more direct with me. Now you're sunk."

"Could you tell me your name?" I asked.

"Connie Fortini." She looked at me searchingly, perhaps hoping for an explanation.

"Well, Miss Fortini," I said, "I'm glad I met you." I carried the weight of my application outdoors into the ordinary heat, let my eyes travel down the inane questions and answers until they got close to the bottom. Next to "In the long history of the struggle for democracy who personally has influenced you the most?" I'd penciled in block letters, "Hoyt Erland."

7

The three women were younger than I, slimmer, and held their noses higher in the noontime heat. Sixty-sixth was suffused with a sweet perfume for them while I inhaled poisonous whiffs of oil, tar, carbon monoxide and dogshit. Too many hours spent loitering in air-conditioned boutiques had marked them with an indoor pallor. Their long legs sped down the street, slowed to a canter. At short intervals each of them climbed the sandstone steps, rang a bell, waited and was admitted.

The first, wearing a modish green visor cap, snatched a slip of paper from a slit in her pocketbook and matched the number, looking from the paper to the door of the building. The second, dressed like a sailor, walked right past the building and then with a sigh visible from where I stood on the corner of Madison Avenue, had to retrace her steps. Her stark-white middy blouse hurt my eyes. The laggard third, in silk and chiffon, clattered on narrow heels, the impractical sister, always charmingly tardy.

Watching them enter the place Hoyt had been caught filming had been a meditative experience. A brass plaque on the building read: Institute of Philosophical Healing. I decided I needed that kind of help and walked up the steps. I tried the door, then pushed an unmarked white button. A stout middle-aged woman in a flowery pants suit that clung to her for dear life opened the door, after peering for a moment through the glass. She wore thick-lensed butterfly-rimmed glasses that magnified her pale pink eyeballs. Her neutral voice said, "Follow me," and we went through a second door, were hit by a blast of cold air and went up a carpeted flight of stairs. We kept passing Japanese scrolls hung on the beige stairwall. They seemed to tell some kind of narrative about the tortuous life of a geisha. My guide's ponderous, silent tread made the climb endless. I began to identify with the geisha. When we finally got to the landing, she pushed another door open. I followed her meekly into a hall with recessed lighting and an antiseptic smell. Far away a woman dressed like a nurse passed across the hall carrying a small tray. I allowed notions of illegal abortions and giant hypodermics leaking heroin to cross with her. My new friend stopped at a door with a small wired window, the kind popular in modern asylums and prisons. She opened it and waited for me to go in without looking at me, or seeming to look at anything for that matter. I hesitated, went in. The door clicked shut behind me.

The room which smelled faintly of burnt chocolate and lavender perfume, contained the three women I'd seen from the street and a thin balding man in a white smock and white pants. Beneath the smock a striped business shirt and a conservative tie were visible. I decided he was a doctor. The four of them were giving me the eye.

"Sorry I'm late," I said demurely.

He looked at his watch, at me and then at a clipboard in his hand. "There shouldn't be four of you," he said doubtfully. His voice carried an undertone of complaint.

I tried to give the appearance of belonging, of waiting for him to make up his mind. He apparently could not bear such mute pressure. "I guess I can handle four. This particular experiment," he mumbled, consulting his clipboard, "doesn't require so many separate operations that I can't monitor all of you." He looked up. Like many scientists, if that's what he thought he was, he was not particularly observant. He didn't notice the gulf that distinguished me from the other three women, all of whom were much better dressed than I. The sailor cleared her throat. "Could we get down to business please? I only have a little over an hour." An assenting murmur came from one of the other two.

"Okay," he said. "Sorry to keep you waiting."

The three sat in low chairs that were a cross between a child's school-desk chair and an electric chair. I immediately began to regret the doctor's complacency. The silk-and-chiffon woman smiled sweetly at me but I didn't smile back. I took a seat in the row behind them, cautiously lowering myself into it, and then, like the others, slipped a metal ring attached to a wire onto the middle finger of each hand. The wires led down one leg of each chair and disappeared in a tiny slit in the carpet. The chairs were bolted to the floor. The pressure of conformity was sinking into me more directly than those bolts into the floor. I was having a rare attack of helplessness.

The doctor watched me hook up and came over. "You, uh, forgot the belt. The belt," he said pointing to one of the other women. A leather strap held each woman in her chair. I fastened mine, after some more confusion with the metal rings. I tried not to consider the consequences of what I was doing.

The doctor looked us all over. His nervous energy made me feel he was awaiting clearance before takeoff. He slid the metal ring farther down on my left hand. I noticed that his fingernails were bitten to the quick. He nodded with satisfaction, scribbled on his clipboard and taxied out of the room through the only door. The lights went out. In the total blackness one of the women whispered, "Did you take that medication this morning?"

An answer came, "I was afraid not to."

59

"Me too."

Split. Get out. Pull off the rings, unclasp the belt . . . An audible hum, like a refrigerator starting up, interrupted me. A loud glitch followed that and then a male robot voice. "Absolute silence is required throughout this experiment. Listen for the signal to begin. . . . Thirty seconds . . . fifteen . . . five . . . ready." The voice said each syllable with equal emphasis in a tone that was soothing and disembodied. I persuaded my muscles to unclench.

A shimmering beam of light hit a screen on the other end of the room. "Remember to concentrate on the image. Later you will be asked to recall your impressions. Focus on the image."

I tried to focus, but for several eternities nothing showed but an empty screen. I felt my eyes grow heavy. Maybe it was a stimulant they took this morning. I prevented myself from dozing by watching the dust motes float in the beam. Every so often I'd hear a click in the room, behind and above me, I thought, and a rapid wipe would blur across the screen. I invented images to fill the blank. On a kitchen table a juicy grapefruit half with a maraschino cherry in the center. A hand holding a spoon dug into the grapefruit, disappeared and then the spoon came back empty. After consuming each wedge of fruit in the same way and scraping the bottom for juice, the hand put the spoon down and disappeared. The cherry was still in the center. Then there were two hands sharpening a pencil with a kitchen knife. The shavings and graphite powdered a pure white surface, each uneven stroke of the knife came nearer to slicing the long tanned fingers holding the pencil. Then Hoyt was leaning over me in bed, his elbow holding up his head. His hair was cut short. He flicked cigarette ash into a bowl on the sheet between us. We'd shared a bowl of chocolate-chip ice cream in bed. He squashed the butt in the bowl and turned back to me. I looked at the curling hairs around his nipple and then down at the bowl, the gray ash and the squashed butt. The bowl was a devastated lunar landscape. Another click. Finally I saw something. A black-and-white slide appeared on the screen for a second: Johnny Carson, the talk-show comedian, his gray face caught in a smile, a cigarette in his hand and his head cocked as he mugged for the camera. There was a tingle in my fingers. Lights flashed on, startling our eyes.

Our experimenter stepped in, swinging the door behind him. The rug kept the door from closing. He dished out one machine-sharpened pencil and one legal-size sheet of paper to each of us. About to say something to me, he was distracted by a noise. Two men stood in the doorway watching us as if we were part of a diorama behind glass in the Museum of Natural History. One of them was stamped with a pinched, mildly pedantic look of ethnographic seriousness—gray hair, nubby gray suit, gray pipe set between thin gray lips. The man next to him was blond and tall and muscular so that he seemed ready to edge his companion out of the doorway at any moment.

It's good to have such contrasts offered to you from time to time. They can remind you why it feels good to be young, why it seems so inexplicable when you're not any longer. The blond male who filled the doorway while the older man occupied it said, "This a new setup?" His voice had a rippling quality, like a cold drink on a hot day.

Chiffon dug her heels into the carpet. Her hairdo didn't spill over onto her forehead but that didn't prevent her from brushing back what wasn't there with fingertips the color of juniper berries or magnolia or plum wine or the protruding tongues of poisoned rodents. I watched to see if the movement caught the eyes of the audience. It snagged the older man. He was slow in answering. It takes a while to get the hook out, especially when you already have a pipe in your mouth. "New. Yes." The pipe came out. "Just at the exploratory stage, in fact, Gil."

Gil waited for more. The situation flip-flopped so that they rather than we now seemed to be posing. I wanted to hear more about the trap I was in before it got any more strenuous, so I was rooting for Gil. The pipe, unsurprisingly, went back in. Looking down at the gray man, Gil said, "I'm sure you could give me a clue, Doctor."

Our experimenter stepped up to play his role. He leaned near the end of the open door, blocking our view. "We're just buzzing the variables out of this one," he said, looking at Gil. His hand reached blindly for the door knob, caught it and turned it back and forth, back and forth. "If you ask next month I'm sure Dr. Foals will have more to say in the specifics department." He shifted his weight. "Won't you, Doctor?"

Foals hesitated and when he spoke reluctance slurred his words. "Yesss—of course, Dr. Ridley."

"Suppose I watch and see if I can figure it out. How would that be?" Gil stepped around Ridley and gave us a once-over. Even Chiffon pretended he wasn't there, gazing away from him. I returned his stare. "Hi," he said. "What they got you hooked up to—a polygraph?"

"I hope not," I said. "I'm a born liar."

His wide-set blue eyes that made you want to tell the truth were leveled on me. He didn't smile. His look was quizzical, getting ready to frame a question.

Ridley said tentatively, "We're really sort of in the middle here."

Gil nodded, but kept looking at me. It could have gone either way then. I half-expected to be unmasked as an agent of reality.

"Come along to the Observation Room," Foals said.

Gil nodded again and said to me, "No, you're not."

I thought of the moment in front of B&H when I shook my head while saying yes, I'd share an egg cream. I was still thinking when the door closed again and we were back in the experiment.

The robot voice said, "Please fill out the forms quickly and accurately." Below a coded number, each three groups of ten lines were headed Adequate Description of Successive Images. The first image that occurred to me was fishbowl. I was one of the fish. An accidental victim of someone's sadomasochistic fantasy. I shifted in the uncomfortable chair, tugging against the belt. What was in Gil's expression? A question. What are you doing here? He realized I didn't quite fit.

"Did you feel anything?" said the woman in the green visor.

"No, of course not. I was numb," said Chiffon pronouncing it *num-buh* and rustling the chiffon as she giggled.

Much more of this and my skin would start to crawl. I left the form blank except to name the smug mocking face I saw at the last. Our worried white smock collected the sheets hurriedly, the beam went on. This time the screen was popping.

Women striding down crowded New York streets, in lines at Chock Full O'Nuts buying coffee and a donut, the uniformed attendant sullenly bagging the food; at newsstands, their gloved fingers extending a quarter; at lunch hour in Bloomingdale's and Alexander's, crowding at the purse and leather handbag counter. Women in garment district factories, row upon row, leaned over sewing machines, women in offices typing and filing, at computers and keypunches; nurses in hospitals administering medication. Women with money in their hands, opening change purses and wallets, signing a charge slip, in line at a bank, in line at a subway, a cafeteria, charging toward the Port Authority Bus Terminal. Women's hands grasping erasers, pencils, books, telephones, packages, their arms outstretched to take one bag after another. A woman handing another woman behind a counter a boy's swimsuit with the price tag still attached.

A swimming pool. Men relaxing around the pool on lounge chairs and on beach towels, their eyes squinted against the brilliant sun or shaded by sunglasses. The shapes and contours of the men's bodies slow and seductive, their crotches in tight swim suits. The right half of a torso, tanned rippling skin, muscular shoulder, a curly tuft of golden hair in the armpit, the arm raised and bent showing the size of the bicep, the veins on the inner arm, the thick wrist, outstretched fingers. As I focused on the big long-fingered hand my own fingers started to tingle and then I felt a shooting pain through my forearm.

A dull chain saw sliced across the nerves in my wrist. A direct jolt passed through the rings on my fingers and my brain burned out like the picture tube in a TV set. No images, no dreams, no ideas, only a gray and total silence the texture of elephant hide. The elephant sitting on my head very gradually shifted his weight and lumbered off to graze elsewhere, leaving me looking up from the bottom of a swamp. Something big and thickly muscled was moving in the mud. It was getting closer. I pulled away to avoid it, but it brushed against me, its wake trailing slime on my forehead. I gagged, and the big body slid back through the mist holding a damp towel to stuff down my throat. "This'll do the trick," a man's voice said. I put up my hand to block him. He was out of focus. A robot voice said in my ear, "Focus on the image." A small slice of white showed on the dark honey-colored surface of the robot's cheek. It turned into a crescent-shaped scar. Robots don't have scars.

I was lying on a high stretcher or table. Gil smiled at me. His teeth were dazzling.

"Your teeth are giving me a headache," I said.

He closed his mouth, looking at me curiously. "You gave our researchers quite a scare."

I said nothing, letting my eyes fall shut. He'd have to be part of the trap I'd gotten myself into.

"They say you weren't scheduled to be here."

"I didn't know where I wasn't scheduled to be." The place had seemed like, successively, a hospital, a school, a laboratory and a prison. Do all institutions exude negative possibilities depending on the color of the sky, the thickness of the walls, the number of watts in the light bulbs, the smell of the long hallways? I shrugged as people do when flat on their backs.

"I knew when I saw you with the others that you didn't belong. How'd you get into this?"

My eyes were still too heavy to keep open. I said, "That would take more explaining than I'm capable of right now. It's a fix you'd never get yourself into, I suppose." I wanted him to respond. It would prove I could still make myself understood.

"I might," he said, accepting my terms. "I've done some pretty dumb things. I mean if I was after something really important I'd—"

This speculation seemed awkward enough to be spontaneous. I'm not used to men whose thoughts are so near the surface they can't hide behind them. Maybe he wasn't part of the trap. I opened my eyes. "Is anything important enough? To take risks like that?" I remembered Hoyt pointing the little camera in the space between two wrought-iron rails recently painted black.

Gil seemed to be thinking about what I'd said while soaking the towel in a stainless-steel pan of water. He hesitated before he spoke. "Do you want to tell me what risk you're talking about? No, of course you don't. That's fine. I respect that."

He was as sincere as a public-service announcement, too sincere for me to tell him to come off it without shattering his good will. And I didn't want to complicate things. He was willing to take me seriously, which was already one up. "The truth is I'm a little afraid to talk about it here."

"You really don't have to be afraid," he said.

"It's not a matter of having to be."

He twisted the towel. "Yes. But if you could be a little less abstract about your aims . . ."

I shrugged again. "You mean in the abstract you understand my position, but I shouldn't expect anything from you unless I come across?" I struggled up on my elbows. The room started to move.

"I can help you sit up at least," he said. He reached over and touched my elbow. His fingers were wet.

"No, you can't," I snapped. He took a step back. The little crescent on his cheek heated to red. What good would it do me to give him a hard time? None probably, but he was clearly vacillating between his desire to help me and some inner necessity that forbade this impulse. Momentarily bewildered, he came back and helped me lie down on the stretcher again.

"Take it easy," he said, gently holding my shoulders.

"I'd like to," I said. "I'm one of those misfits that has a hard time getting used to being electrocuted."

He held me longer than he had to, and I submitted. His touch was soothing, connecting me to reality.

"Dr. Ridley had no way of knowing you weren't properly grounded."

"Dr. Ridley isn't properly grounded. Are all your people so competent?"

"You had no business being there in the first place," Gil pointed out. "He didn't check your chair because he wasn't expecting a fourth person. You flustered him."

"What was that experiment about anyway?"

He paused and then said, "Cognitive psychology." I was losing him. He went back to the towel, folded it in halves, then in quarters. Finally he looked at me again. It's your play his face said, not unkindly.

"Oh, I get it. You're in cahoots with them. You're only here to pet me up if I'm pissed."

He crumpled the towel. "You don't get it. I'm here because I was worried about you. They kept saying it was nothing, you'd come right out of it, but—"

"But you don't trust them either," I said, my voice rising.

He grinned, shifting around on his hind legs. "You're obviously much better now at any rate."

"How about a drink of water? I'm parched."

He looked around the room, grinned at me again and hurried out. Obviously he hadn't been in this room before, and this knowledge somehow made me feel a little better about him. Besides, his hesitant bewilderment gave him an air of vulnerability that sat well on his muscular body.

But speculation got me no closer to squeezing out of this trap. I tried to sit up, closing my eyes to keep from being too dizzy. I was in a sweat by the time I got there. I looked down at the floor. It was white-and-black checkerboard linoleum, I think. It was hard to tell because the whites and blacks were dancing cheek-to-cheek, and the dance floor was about a mile away. My feet were down near there too. That was luck. I sent a message down from my brain to my toes and waited for it to get there. My feet wriggled. So far so good. I edged my weight toward the precipice. With nothing to hold on to, to keep me steady, it was like pushing a piano off a cliff and going along for the ride. After a long time I was standing on the checkerboard, one foot on a white square and one on a black. The big boy should be here with that water I told myself.

When I got myself over to the door, it came as a blow that there was no door handle. The trapped sensation got hold of me. I had an inspiration and pushed the door. It moved, and I got a quick glimpse of the hallway before it slipped back. Soundproofing, recessed lighting, and a nurse crossing it holding a tray.

When I tried again the corridor was clear. I was at one end of it. To my left double doors with steel bars across them. EMERGENCY EXIT ONLY red letters warned. A white smock emerged from a room at the other end. It hesitated, studying a clipboard. Cognitive psychology. It startled itself by turning toward me.

"One moment, please!" Dr. Ridley called out in a tone

normally reserved for the psycho ward. The alarm didn't sound until I was at the steps on the way down.

I looked through the next set of doors and there was Pinky Eyeballs seated at a desk. Between her desk and where I stood was the door I entered many years ago for a session of philosophical healing. Now that I was so much better I wanted to leave. I pushed the door and walked perhaps a little groggily toward the exit, not ignoring my old friend but not looking her way either. She saw me soon enough. Her chair made a scraping noise that plowed a furrow into my brain. She got to the exit ahead of me and stood in front of it. I flashed a smile at her and said, "I'm leaving now, thank you so much."

"I'm sorry, miss," she said, not sounding at all regretful, "the doctors think you ought to rest a while before you try to travel. Shall I give you a hand back upstairs?" She reached out the hand she wanted to give me, I feinted and reached out mine and grabbed her glasses at the bridge. She lunged toward me. The glasses landed on a leather couch on the far wall and, bouncing, hit Dr. Ridley's leg as he burst through the emergency door.

"Where are they? Give them back! I can't see anything without them!"

There was panic in her voice. It was an awful transformation. She staggered past me, beginning to sob. I couldn't stand it, so I stepped around her.

8

A squat blue-suited man with a cough hacking his chest and a chauffeur's cap in his hand stood in my way at the foot of the sandstone stairs. He spit into the gutter as I passed him. The sound nearly set me retching. I crossed the street in front of a parked limo, concentrating on maintaining my balance. I kept my head at an even angle until I got around the corner on Madison. At the first open doorway, a pizzeria, I stopped and asked for a Coke. While the man drew it out of a tap I tried to catch what was playing on the radio. I wanted to know if my memory still worked.

Plastic cup to my lips, I watched a strong brown hand dusted with curly blond hairs set a glass of water on the Formica counter. The man behind the counter stared at it. He'd never seen glass before. When the Coke was gone, I set the cup next to the glass. "Thanks," I said, looking at Gil. The glass was heavy in my hand, as heavy as liquid mercury. I forced it to my lips and gulped down the water.

"You realize by now, I suppose, that you weren't being held against your will." His assurance had the same specific density as the glass and helped wash away some of my nervousness. "They just wanted to be sure you were all right."

"So did I, that's why I split."

"They were willing to take care of you. You know, these places are a little afraid of lawsuits. I think they were hoping to get a waiver out of you."

"Are you their lawyer?" I asked. I didn't want him to be—that would tar him with my distaste for institutions. Besides he would have to be very aggressive to be a lawyer at his age, and he wasn't.

"Hardly. My old man put up a lot of the money for the place." He stuck out his hand politely. "Gilbert B. Breakstone, Junior. At your service." I shook it and introduced myself. He inspected me as we sat down at a little table. I didn't get the feeling he was rating my attractiveness. I had another Coke in my hand. "You got me confused in there. What are you after?"

Somewhere along the line I'd heard enough from the radio to recognize that "Layla" was playing. With that music moaning insistently in the background, "What are you after?" seemed for a moment like an ultimate question. His too-blue eyes fastened on me. Things conspire sometimes to make you sentimental. I didn't answer him for a while, fighting off the wave of sentiment that seemed to be half evoked by the color of this stranger's eyes, even though Hoyt's eyes weren't blue. I decided on not a whole lot of evidence that he was the kind that gave back what he got, maybe not the kind that gave on his own initiative but at least a whole step better than nothing. "Yesterday a friend of mine was pushed into a cab right in front of the Institute and later smashed up against a wall." The last part was hard to say out loud and probably I showed that.

"In front of the Institute?" he asked, giving every indication of being shocked. "Was she badly hurt?"

"He's dead."

Gilbert Breakstone winced.

"My friend was gathering information about Evelyn Berndt's death. That's why they got him. I figure the Institute is connected with it somehow."

"I knew Evelyn."

"You did?" I wasn't really expecting to get anything out of this, and I certainly wasn't expecting it on a platter.

"She was my sister's roommate at school."

I asked the first question that came to me. "Was it your sister who got her the job with Wincey?"

His forefinger circled the rim of the half-empty plastic cup. "No—that—" He looked up. "She must have got it on her own. She was a real bright girl."

He should have said "she was a very bright woman," but I let it pass.

"Are you certain about your sister?" I asked.

"My sister," he said solemnly, "disappeared about seven years ago. Nobody knows what happened to her."

Somebody probably knows, I thought, but didn't say. "What was her name?"

"Josie Breakstone."

I let my mind wander back till it stuck in 1967. "I don't mean to be nosy but was she involved with the antiwar movement?"

He nodded. "Now you remember." He looked pleased. "The second day of what they called 'Stop the Draft Week,' December 1967. She'd stayed that night at the house and left before dawn. And that was it." His expression went blank. "Nothing. No message. No clues. No Josie."

His mention of "Stop the Draft Week" jogged my memory. At planning meetings we called the incident the Breakstone Red Herring and thought of it naturally as a police attempt to smear the movement. None of us had thought Josie Breakstone was really missing. But we were quick then to be short-sighted about some things. We knew from all the publicity that the family fortune came from the giant data-control corporation, Sypher-Breaks.

"I do remember her. We never really met, but we went to some of the same meetings. She was very intense." Actually I remembered her as too intense.

He nodded again, but it was tighter, a little more curt. "So we knew Evelyn somewhat."

"Could either of your parents have gotten her the job with Wincey?"

He considered. "Not likely."

"Could you get me an interview with them?"

"They've been burned a few times talking to strangers."

"Listen, Gil, my friend Hoyt Erland was investigating the Berndt death when he got it. It's odd that your family knew her and that his investigation should take him to a site paid for and supported by your family. Maybe your mother or father could help."

"They won't like it."

"You don't do things they don't like?" I asked incredulously.

"Sometimes."

"But not much or often."

"We get along."

"Maybe it's time you pushed yourself a little."

His biceps tensed under his shirt.

I'm from the wrong neighborhood to know much about respecting limits, and sometimes when it's too late to back up you floor it. "Tell me what you know about Evelyn Berndt."

"What? Oh . . . pretty, a logical mind, liked things her own way, took yoga classes, spoke German." He was being objective, or pretending to be.

My stomach was very tight. I took a sip of the Coke. "Did you ever sleep with her?"

The little crescent scar in his cheek fired up. "She was considerably older than I."

"I bet she wasn't as repressed."

A not entirely good-humored laugh broke in his throat. "That statement requires interpretation."

He didn't deserve to be needled but I didn't see any other way to get any further. "Was she ambitious?"

"She hated being poor and growing up in Yorktown eating Wonder bread and boloney."

"And yet you think she wouldn't ask your parents to help her get a job she wanted?"

"She might."

"Well?"

He squirmed, bouncing his fingers on the table. "You're goddamn . . ." He bounced some more. He had big hands, and the little table shook. "You don't . . . I'll call and see if they're home."

I patted his hand lightly. He looked away in discomfort. I was on my way toward formulating a theory about what parents are likely to do to the younger child when fate snatches away the elder. Or maybe it was a theory about how the younger becomes responsible to compensate for the elder's recklessness.

Mrs. Breakstone lived in two stories of a four-story renovated mansion on one of the rich streets off Fifth Avenue downtown. Gil had me at her front door in half an hour. He slapped his pockets for his key. Diagonally across the street was a black limo. A squat man got out of it and put his hand up to his mouth to cough as Gil ushered me in.

Tribal African carved wood-and-ivory figures with engorged genitals emerged in phalanxes from the hall walls—one side all male, the other all female. "At least your mother has a sense of humor," I said to Gil.

He said, "She doesn't think it's funny."

As we went down the stairs into the living room I could see why. Her house was colonized by the oppressed cultures of the Third World. Africa filled her hallway, and

Guatemala had taken over her living room except for a small silver-framed photo or two. Every available surface had some handwoven artifact on it—all the sleek, low-slung chairs and couches, the lamps, the walls, the windows, the ebony piano, the parquet floor and she herself.

The ancient, exquisitely embroidered dress she wore straddled the frail edge of time between the absolute beauty of peasant antiquity and the beginnings of disintegration. Looking up from her clothing, I saw a similar process at work in her face. Her ravaged features had achieved a dimension of character available only to rich and idle women conscious of their own absurdity. Her lack of height nearly dissipated a regal carriage, salvaged by hints of sarcasm in her constantly moving eyes. Silvered strands of hair escaped from the loose bun gathered high at the back of her head. These trademarks of sensitivity clashed with her son's purely physical presence. They looked at each other across a gap I couldn't measure.

"Really, Gil. You should be more considerate. I feel so disheveled."

"Well, you don't quite look an absolute mess, Mother. My friend Emma Hobart has a few questions to ask you."

She glanced coldly at me. My lack of visual style must have been offensive to her.

"I'm not in the mood for interrogations, but suppose we all sit so we don't get the idea we're in a bad movie," she said, somewhat ungraciously.

We settled into a couple of dark couches over which bolts of Guatemalan cloth were strewn. Now that I was here I was hesitant to begin. "This won't take too long," I said, unable not to apologize. "A close friend was in an accident and as a result I'm pursuing his investigation of the Evelyn Berndt suicide—"

She held up a hand to interrupt me. "Your preamble is unnecessary. My son would never bring you here under dubious circumstances." She obviously didn't like being overinformed.

"Then maybe you could tell me how well you knew Evelyn Berndt."

"Not at all." Gil, who was looking away, raised his head suddenly. "I was always in Europe or South America when my . . . when she was around. I met her, of course, but to be frank she never interested me." Her bored glance rested on her fingernails, coated a smoky red.

"When was the last time you saw her?"

"Years and years."

Since the invention of Silly Putty? Or is time even more malleable than that when it's all bought and paid for?

"All right, let me change the subject somewhat. Do you contribute large sums to Thad Wincey's congressional race?"

"Wincey? No, I don't. I think he's a fool or a crook, I don't know which. I tried to get Bella to run again for his seat. But she wouldn't hear of it. A good strong woman I could support—not a two-faced fence-straddler like Wincey. The name alone is enough to put you off him. He's never had an—"

"I suppose your husband feels the same way as you do?"

"My husband?" She looked at Gil quizzically. "Well, my ex-husband used to support him quite handsomely, I believe—I presume he still does. I don't know. I'm getting tired." Her gaze wandered over the room's sumptuous textures.

"You see," said Gil, speaking as if she'd already left us, "she hasn't much to tell you."

"Have you had any contact with a man named Hoyt Erland?"

She'd been holding on to an embroidered pillow, and now she came close to throwing it at me. She half-rose off the couch, her long earrings dangling.

"I should say I have. Don't ask me how he got my number. He started bombarding me with questions even more pointless than yours so I hung up on him. Then I was shopping in this wonderful crafts boutique down near South Street and this skinny little worm comes up to me and starts again with the questions. Well, I signaled for Eddie—that's my chauffeur—and had him led out. Imagine!"

"And you never saw him after that?"

"I wish to God I hadn't. He approached me again on my very doorstep. I had him taken care of."

"How?"

"Eddie."

"What does Eddie look like?"

One of her smoke-tipped hands waved vaguely in the air. "Like a chauffeur. Shortish, fattish. I have him wear a conservative blue suit and a cap." She turned to Gil, "So how did Saturday's softball go? How many home runs did you hit, slugger?"

Gil glanced at me. "Mother, I'm sure Emma still has a couple of questions."

She trained her made-to-order smile on me. A dark-skinned woman dressed like a maid passed through the highlands back of her couch. "Oh, I'm sorry."

"How did your daughter and Evelyn get to be roommates at college?"

Her eyes, that had kept sliding over to Gil, fixed on me. She said nothing. Her lips still seemed to have something of a smile carved on them. Gil leaned forward, his elbows resting on his thighs. "Are you all right, Mother?"

She ignored him. "You know," she said to me, "Josie had this incurable leveling streak since she was ten at least. I have a feeling just from looking at you that you'd understand that. Gilbert, my husband, and I used to try to tell her the way the world works, but she refused always to see things straight. No treatment helped. Thank God you weren't like that, Gil." She barely glanced at him. "Then when she went to Barnard she insisted on a dorm room. We gave up, hoping that a strong dose of reality would—"

"Kill or cure her," I finished.

"Yes. The Berndt girl was somewhat involved in the rubbishy brand of campus politics, but just at the periphery I understand. In a matter of weeks Josie was smack-dab in the middle of the stinking mess. Then she was barely civil to us any more, wore the most atrocious clothes. . . ." There was a pause while Mrs. Breakstone toyed with the large turquoise on her left hand. She caught me watching her. "It's a noble ring, isn't it?" She held the hand up. "Navaho."

"We'd better go," Gill said grimly and got to his feet. He looked at me, and we left the room without another word.

The small elevator going up in the mansion on Twelfth Street held just the two of us. Gil was staring intently at the door.

"Why are you so upset?" I asked.

"I should have said something about her. I didn't know how to. I generally avoid anything too real for her to handle." I saw he was angry at rather than sorry for her.

"Where are we going now?"

He'd pressed the button for the third floor. The elevator stopped. He put his hand over the CLOSE button.

"When they split up a while ago, my mother took over the first two floors, my father the top two."

He said this as if it were a natural arrangement. I didn't want to spoil it for him. He dropped his hand. The door opened onto a vestibule and immediately after a hallway a little bigger than my apartment. The high-ceilinged wall facing us was protected by three big paintings of Stalin in the style of Warhol's Mao portraits. Satellite to these were a number of smaller nonrepresentational paintings, all of which appeared to have been slapped together in the late sixties. Each of the Stalins was painted with a different set of exquisite colors. In one of them Uncle Joe's mustache was a warm turquoise.

"I didn't know Warhol did Stalin as well."

"He didn't. My father put some money behind a young painter who did. Until the market shapes up he's stuck with them."

The living room Gil led me into was studded with minimalist sculpture set off by black-and-white furniture, an ankle-deep white rug, all-white walls and a vaulted white ceiling. The world had been drained of color like a noxious swamp drained of water. "Wait here," Gil said in a hushed voice. Perhaps the severity of the room had something ecclesiastical about it. He was back before I got ready to smash anything.

"He'll be out in a moment."

"Have you figured out why you're bothering with all this? It can't be just because I'm a pushy type."

"Things happen to people and nobody takes the trouble to find out why and how. Or if they do, they give up too easily. Also"—he paused and caught my gaze—"I like you."

A balding middle-aged man in a brown golfer's shirt, dark-brown gabardine slacks and brown saddle shoes stepped from behind a ten-foot white box at the other end of the room. He faintly resembled a human roach scuttling around a sugar cube.

He trekked across the room to us and offered me his hand.

"Gil tells me I might be of some service to you, my dear." His voice was soothing. He folded himself into a soft black chair across a low glass table from Gil and me.

"A close friend of mine was killed yesterday. I want to

narrow down what he was doing in the few days before his death."

"Was his name Hoyt Erland?"

"Yes, did you know him?"

"He called my secretary several times to arrange an appointment. We were never able to get together, unfortunately. When I picked up the *Post* this afternoon, I remembered his name. A very strange accident. Hit and run, apparently. I hope they catch the cabbie that did it. It's bad for business. Of course that's not your concern. I wish I were able to help you a little more." He looked down at the table. There was a three-foot lead toothbrush on it, an *objet d'art* perfect for a big guy with radioactive teeth.

"Did you get Evelyn Berndt her job in Wincey's office?"

"What an odd question!" he said, and repeated it, looking up at the ceiling for the answer. "No, of course not. That's not a good principle in my opinion. I'm sure Evelyn got the position on her own hook. She always . . ."

". . . seemed to you a very capable girl. I know. Everyone in the city knows how capable she was. Except she didn't know how to take a bath well enough to keep from drowning in it."

"Accidents like that are often inexplicable. How many tragedies do we all know of in our personal lives that have never been explained? Of course there must be an explanation—I don't think it's all the hand of God, but—" He sat up and leaned forward, running his hand over the lead bristles of the toothbrush. I was changing my mind about his voice. Gil sat quietly.

I stood up, said, "Thanks for your time," and started out.

He looked astonished. "You came here to ask just those two questions?"

I passed a sculpture stand on which reclined a small Pop ceramic of a naked woman in lurid colors, exaggerated dimensions. "How do you know those deaths were accidental? Would it be accidental if I took this piece of clay and tossed it into the middle of that glass table?"

Breakstone got to his feet. "I'm sorry I annoyed you. Forgive me."

I was irritated with myself for wasting my time on him. But there was another rage I couldn't even name, let alone handle so easily, a rage at the ease with which he invisibly assimilated and turned to pure grace the privileges of his class. I hefted the ugly little sculpture by one of its spread legs and shook it at him. It, at least, was visible. "Fate has nothing to do with the way anybody dies—least of all Evelyn Berndt and Hoyt Erland." I put the ceramic back on its stand.

"You don't know what you're talking about," he said quietly. Gil rose. For the first time I noted a resemblance between them although they were not the same physical type. The energy that had congealed in the father to a syrupy shrewdness was still bursting in the son's body as muscular effort. Trying to minimize his nervousness, he crossed the room to me and carefully turned back to his father.

"Maybe not," he said, "but I remember your being very friendly with Evelyn at one time. What about that?"

His movements were exaggeratedly casual. The father looked as if he'd been slapped.

"That's a malicious thing for one's own son to say."

"Is it?" Gil's hand jerked out of his pocket and his elbow knocked against the stand, toppling the sculpture to the rug. Breakstone stood up again. We all looked at the floor as if a dead body were lying there. The sculpture's legs were severed at the hips, making the fat-lipped vagina even more prominent. Breakstone cursed under his breath. His smoothness was somewhat ruffled. He picked up one of the legs. "Sypher," he said, "my partner Sypher recommended Evelyn to Wincey, I believe." I took Gil's arm.

The elevator doors opened, and a darkly tanned woman

of perhaps forty stepped out. She eyed us sharply. Gil nodded to her. I wondered if she was his father's mistress. "Gil," Breakstone called out, "please call me later. I must talk to you." The doors were closing on us. "Please!" The voice was plaintive now. Gil looked straight ahead. When the elevator stopped, we were in the basement.

"I'll drive you home," he said. He started the car, pushed a button and the garage door opened. When we hit the street he said, "I apologize for butting in; I didn't help."

"Forget it. Was it Evelyn who told you he approached her?"

He nodded.

"Do you think she was telling you the truth?"

He looked at me in surprise, "I just assumed . . ."

"Are you going to call him?"

"Later. He'll be good and guilty in a few hours."

We pulled up in front of my house. In the open doorway of the bakery stood two dark-skinned Italian boys in sleeveless white undershirts and white pants, hands slid under the waistband thumbs up, giving the Granada a long hard look. They reminded me of the Puerto Rican boys at the hydrant.

"No doubt they're appraising its resale value," Gil said. "Open the glove compartment." I looked at him. "Open it."

I opened it and pulled out a Colt .32 automatic, with seven bullets in the magazine and one up.

"I'm not much for hardware," I said.

"You might need it now."

"What do you mean *now*?"

"You mentioned on the way to my parents' place that you're a cabdriver."

"I remember."

"You don't have to tell me about it, in fact don't, but my father did mention that your friend Hoyt . . ."

"A hit-and-run cabdriver. Don't leap to any conclusions."

"I'm not. I couldn't because it doesn't make sense. But I have this funny feeling you should be armed. Don't get pissed, but I don't like to see a woman in your position without some defenses."

I put the gun into my bag. "I get your point. Would you like some iced tea?"

He laughed. "I offer you a gun, and you offer me tea. I was coming up with you anyway. Two of us might scare away any action if we're lucky."

"Might."

The heat hit me hard after the air conditioning. One of the boys pulled out a red handkerchief and tied it around his forehead. There was no one in the hall, and my place was still the mess my playmates left it in. "Home is where the heart is," I said and switched on the fan. Gil started to pick up things from the floor.

"Are you always so helpful?" I asked him.

"Just trying to calm myself down with a little physical therapy."

After I put the kettle on I returned to the living room. Gil was setting things straight slowly, examining books, pictures, incidental ornaments. I could see him trying to read me from my disordered environment. He made this seem not a violation but a kind of compliment. Maybe he didn't know how to ask the things he wanted to know and this was his way of finding out. Aside from that, his awkwardness, which stemmed mostly from his size, changed the room for me and made me remember how long it had been since Hoyt had lived here. He didn't resemble Hoyt in the slightest, but he had a similar definite yet unaggressive way of using and moving around the space. For the first time I really looked at his body. He caught me looking.

"Mind if I put a record on?" he asked.

I shook my head. The kettle started whistling. The long day was darkening outside the windows. I realized then, and probably so did he, that we were attracted to each other. I switched on the light. I made the iced tea, sliced a lemon to squeeze into it, and we drank it sitting in front of the fan and talked. I said how tired I was, which was the truth. I asked him to close the gate on the way out. He leaned over to kiss me good-by. The heat had given his body a good strong smell. There are benefits in not being able to afford air conditioning.

9

Two monkeys beckoned to me while I was hitch-hiking on the narrow road to Chichicastenango. I left the road, the monkeys leading me into the sultry jungle. The birds spoke to one another in high-pitched German. In a clearing in the middle of the rain forest was a naked blond Tarzan with a long wet curly beard. I thought the monkeys were leading me to him. So did he, and we were all for it, but the more it rained the bigger the monkeys got and the tighter their grip on my wrists. I realized I was in jail. Tears soaked my gray wool blanket and started dripping off my bunk, hitting the taxi cab resting in the lower bunk. I looked down. The two monkeys in the cab were beating on someone. I tried to lean farther over to see who it was. A hairy arm jutted out the window and grabbed me. I held on to the bunk. The monkey pulled harder.

Someone was tugging on the sheet covering me. Frederick's face was split by a wide grin. "Morning, Sleeping Beauty." Startled, I lost my grip on the sheet. He yanked it away. It fell on the floor near the fireplace. When he saw that I was wearing something, a cotton nightgown, he quit grinning. "We're here to collect," he said.

Trying to create distance, I sat up, my back to the wall. Taylor stepped to the end of the bed. "Frederick and I are very busy today. We're wall-to-wall with appointments. But we have to collect."

There wasn't time to think. I had no jokes, no plans, no delaying tactics. "You do, I know you do." I managed to get that much out.

"You're learning," Frederick said. Taylor flanked one side of the bed, Frederick another, the wall a third, the window with the fan in it the fourth.

"I decided to give you the film."

"Did you?" Taylor said. "I wonder what were the major inputs to your decision-making process." He sat down on the end of the bed. "You don't mind if I sit?" He put his hand next to my ankle. His hand was bigger than my foot. My foot wanted to move away but I didn't let it. I didn't want to call attention to it.

"Taylor was getting edgy," Frederick said. "I had to persuade him that you were a rational-type person even despite what he called your erraticism."

"To be honest," I said, looking from one to the other, "there's a problem."

Taylor groaned. "A problem! I told you, Frederick. I was implicit about this, wasn't I?"

Frederick held up a hand to quiet him. "She's not thinking," he said and used the same hand to tap his temple. "She's not thinking about what happened to her boyfriend." He turned to me. He was wrong. That's what I was thinking about. "That was an accident. We were making a simple business request. You were along to exert extra pressure. You were the ace in the hole in case the boyfriend wanted to put on a martyr act. We had a cozy little spot near the pier all picked out. The good little cabdriver was going to drive us. And if things didn't square up by the time we got there, Taylor was going to show you some of his cruder talents. Well, it didn't quite come off that way. Win a few, right? But now we must resort to more stringent collection methods."

"For instance," Taylor said, "your ankle is definitely a breakable item."

I moved it but Taylor was faster. He gripped it between his thumb and forefinger with slowly increasing pressure. I dug my hands into the mattress in case he tried to pull me off the bed. Even while digging in I knew it was hopeless. I pushed my back harder against the wall. I tasted blood. I was biting the inside of my cheek.

"Inform us about your problem," he said.

"I don't have the film." They didn't move. They didn't say anything. My ankle hurt. I tried to move it. He held it steady, I couldn't even bend my knee. "But I can get it."

Frederick leaned over and tapped Taylor's shoulder. "You see. You're a worrywart." Taylor wasn't convinced. Neither his thumb nor his forefinger was convinced.

"I can have it by three this afternoon."

Frederick hit his shoulder again. "Aren't you ashamed?" he asked. Taylor didn't even look at him. He was busy looking at me. There was a pause. I held my breath. The pain seemed less sharp that way.

"Can?" Taylor asked, pulling harder on my leg.

"You sadistic bastard," I said. He wanted to see me wince or cry out. In another moment I would have. I tried to hold my ankle rigid. He twisted it like a doorknob that's sticking.

"You lack," Frederick said, "a proper respect for authority."

I hadn't heard that since the seventh grade. Despite pain and hate and tears behind my eyes I looked incredulously at Frederick. He was an ordinary guy who just happened to have a job that required more violence against people than against things. He shifted closer to Taylor. My desk, strewn with books and papers, became visible. The drawer, I knew, was so filled with stuff that I could barely open it.

"Okay," I said, looking intently at the desk. I paused so they would note my line of sight. "I'll give it to you." I looked at them and then again furtively at the desk. I didn't want to take a chance on their powers of observation. "Let me up, and I'll get it."

Taylor took the cue. He released my ankle, jumped for the desk, and pulled out the drawer. It crashed onto the floor. He followed it, on hands and knees. Distracted by the noise, Frederick half turned his back to me. Taylor started throwing the contents of the drawer onto the floor.

"I said I'd get it," I said. I hobbled over to one of the easy chairs. I couldn't remember which one was the right one. It was a tossup.

"It's not here," Taylor growled.

"I didn't say it was, did I?" I asked. I lifted the seat cushion. I'd guessed right. I turned back toward them, holding Gil's .32. "Here it is," I said.

Taylor looked up. "Don't be—"

Frederick said, "Amazing."

I agreed with him. My ankle was throbbing, so I shifted my weight. I wasn't sure if the safety catch was on or not. What if they realized that no matter how much I feared or loathed them it would take me hours to pull the trigger? Weren't they tipped off by the way I held the gun? But I was wrong. I was so jittery they were sure I would shoot. "Stand up," I said to Taylor. He obeyed me. That did wonders for my confidence. "Now, Taylor, hold his hands." I gestured to Frederick with the gun.

"What?"

I repeated myself. Taylor looked disgusted but they clasped hands. "Now sidestep slowly to the door as if you were dancing together. Go ahead."

"You're sick," Frederick said.

I gestured quickly with the gun. It worked again. They started to move, tripping over each other every few steps.

"You're not off the hook," Taylor said. "Get that film. Get it by three."

"Close the door after you," I said. I followed them with the gun, still very jittery.

The door closed. I walked over carefully and locked it. One of them rattled it from the other side. "By three," Taylor shouted. He put as much menace as he could into his voice, but underneath that I could hear some of the frustration of the six-year-old yelling at his mommy.

I put the gun on the kitchen table next to the sugar bowl. It didn't look quite right there. I sat down to massage my ankle. I needed the physical contact not just to relieve the pain but to make it clear that my body still belonged to someone I knew.

When I felt better I made some tea and then I tried calling Sypher. I got through the receptionist to a secretary who put me through to the executive secretary who informed me that Mr. Sypher was out of town on business. I put the phone down. It immediately rang three times. I picked up the receiver.

"Kit-Kat Auto Repair. Laight Street. Eleven thirty. Be on time." It hung up.

I didn't recognize the clipped voice. Somebody thought I'd show up on Laight Street on invitation. And they also thought I needed information or help or knowledge so badly that I'd even follow an anonymous summons. They were right.

I dressed, put the automatic in my shoulder bag and hit the street after locking the outside gate. There was a cop car parked on the other side of Houston. So far it seemed the cops hadn't connected Hoyt to the cab I drove that night. Puerto Rican kids don't much like talking to cops either.

I ate an omelet in B&H, sitting at the counter, looking out the window, trying to think and not doing too good a job of it. A black limousine rolled up to the corner. Eddie, the chauffeur with the delicate health, got out, walked out of sight, and came back carrying a newspaper. He looked through the window at me and climbed back in the car. The clock on the wall said 11:10. As I left, Eddie rolled down the window.

"Need a ride?" he asked. I knew if I got in I probably would be taken for a ride. Much as I wanted to say no, I also knew that my best chance lay in treating every implied threat as a possibility. I got in the back seat.

"Mrs. Breakstone says to me, 'Eddie you can take the car for a few hours if you like, I won't be needing it.' Fact is she doesn't use it much, shopping, shows once in a while. It's a pretty cushy job." He started the car noiselessly and glided into traffic. He drove with one stubby finger on the small steering wheel. "The furthest she goes once a month we drive out to this very exclusive little cemetery in Westchester. That's it. Ask me the whole Westchester is a very exclusive cemetery." He turned down Broadway. "Look at this traffic," he ordered waving a hand. "It's unbelievable the way they run this city."

"What grave does she visit?"

"Her daughter's—which is funny if you think about it because her daughter ain't buried there."

"Where's she buried then?"

"No place. They never found her body or a piece of it even."

"No idea what became of her?"

"Not a smell. She was never seen again after she went to one of those hippie war-protest things. One of them freaks must have picked her up and did something to her."

I could imagine Mrs. Breakstone bending over the grave with a spray of tropical blossoms in her hand. I thought of my own mother for a moment. Both women's lives had been despoiled by a sudden irrational event. I followed this thought for a while, getting more morose. When I looked up we were buried in Broadway traffic. Eddie scooted over to Varick and continued downtown. Then he made another right and a left up Hudson and a left on Laight. "How do you pronounce this street—Light or Late?"

"I don't know."

He stopped across the street from an open garage. Three hundred pigeons were feeding on the sidewalk and street in front of the garage. I leaned forward in the seat. Eddie picked up his hand and waved toward the garage without turning his thick neck. The motor was still running, but I couldn't hear it. The blood was drumming in my ears. Next to the garage there was a big picture window with a pink neon sign, KIT-KAT AUTO REPAIR.

"You know," I said, "when I was a kid going to school in Chicago, every school day this heavy-set guy would come on TV named Uncle Billy Wheeze, and he'd eat lunch with us and show us cartoons and joke with us. Then he got arrested for molesting a little girl, and that was that. He looked just like you."

Eddie didn't turn around and his neck didn't get any redder. "I ain't the guy."

"I didn't think you were."

I walked across the street toward the garage, the pigeons courteously clearing me a path. A black mechanic was wrestling with a tire straddled to one of those pneumatic machines. He ignored me. A big black van was parked nose in. A guy in greasy work clothes was barking into a phone in the little office with the neon sign. A well-dressed man was smoking and pacing near the overhead door. Every so often he'd glance at the big clock above the tires in the back. The clock said 11:30. Five or six brave pigeons were strutting about inside, although all the bread crumbs had been strewn outside. I looked toward the street, and a truck backed into the frame of the open doorway. A little guy danced alongside it, directing. Everybody seemed to have a reason to be there except me.

The guy at the telephone slammed the receiver down, rolled up his sleeve to look at his watch, stepped out of the office and pointed me to a big door at the back of the garage. A bright-eyed pigeon on the tire shelf watched me open it. That was odd I thought. Pigeons don't usually watch humans. There was a gray stairwell on the other side of it with very low ceilings. If you weren't careful, you'd bump your head on the landings.

I could have walked away. I decided not to. I wanted to know what had happened to Hoyt. And by now it wasn't only Hoyt, it was me. I went up two flights and tried a door. Nothing came of it, so I went up another flight. This door opened into a long cold room. Almost everything in it was gray: the walls, the thin carpet, the long steel table in the middle of the room and the steel chairs that came with the set.

At the far end not quite a city block away were three motionless men in quiet gray suits. One of them, the one seated at the very end of the table facing me, looked up after a while. He took something out of his suit coat pocket and one of the two flunkies flanking him lit it. It was a cigar, but it looked like a lighthouse beacon on a foggy night to me. I decided to walk over that way even though I knew the weather wouldn't be any better over there. I got about half way.

I saw the important one signal and the other flunky, the one with the slower reflexes, said sharply, "That's far enough." I took a seat on one of the steel chairs. Mr. Big puffed once more and nodded. My ankle hurt, and I was feeling queasy. I was sure I was about to be attacked. A flunky slid down my way on the other side of the table. He took something laminated and about four by five inches out of his pocket, leaned toward me and held it up so I could see it. It was a funny juxtaposition, his tough young face and my hack license. My picture on it was almost two years old, but I looked about the same—high cheekbones and long intolerant nose. He slid it back in his pocket and resumed his seat.

"You're an absent-minded young lady, but that appears to be the least of your faults I'm afraid," the man in the middle said. They had my license, but they obviously weren't cops. Maybe, I thought, it would be better if they were. At least with cops you have some idea what you're up against.

The man in the middle opened a folder and started reading: "Emma Hobart left her hack license in the cab she drove on the night of August 24, 1974. Subsequent investigation has confirmed that same taxi was used in the perpetration of a violent crime. Bits of brown hair, denim thread and blood were found to be adhering to the lower left rear bumper of the vehicle in question. When matched with similar substances found on the deceased person of one Hoyt Erland, the victim of a hit-and-run accident on the night of August 24, 1974, attested to by citizens of the four hundred block of West Forty-seventh Street, Manhattan, New York City, these substances were found to agree in blood type and composition, hair color and thickness, cloth color and fabric."

He stopped and looked at me over his glasses. "Are you paying attention to this, young lady?" He took off his glasses and looked harder at me.

Unless they got it from sweeping the floor of the Twenty-third Street car wash, the evidence, it was obvious, had been concocted. I relaxed a little. Although this fact-finding mission had so far yielded only lies, I had a feeling that the threat of violence in the air was just that, a threat. If not, why this elaborate setup?

"Any defense in this case is out of the question," the man in the middle said, as if to forestall a defense.

I obliged him. "What is the question?"

"So far this is not a police matter. The case lies entirely within the purview of the Hack Commission which has seen fit by special arrangement to turn over further displacement to me, that is, to union representatives. You're a very lucky lady."

This also could only be a fiction. The Hack Commission has no legal purview of apparent murder or manslaughter. "What do you want?" I asked.

"Only a signed statement. It's already prepared. I have

two witnesses to verify that everything is open and above board, and that's it. Not another word said. You go home with your license and keep your nose clean, and everything is taken care of. How's that sound?"

"Am I to take it that all this comes down to revoking my hack license?"

"Not at all. In fact"—he nudged one of his pals—"give it to her." The stooge handed it to me. "However, you must remember that you cannot pull the flag in this town without the union behind you."

We were back where we started. I stared at the license in my hand. The woman in the picture looked grim. She must have known what was coming. Somebody, not the police and not the Hack Commission but somebody with connections was trying to keep a lid on this. My stomach felt less queasy. There was something exhilarating about that fact. I was having an effect. I put the license down on the metal table, slid it fast and hard to the other end and made for the door. I had my hand on the knob when they caught me, one shoulder and one arm each, twisted just as many turns as possible without breaking anything. They picked me up in the air and planted me down facing the boss, who'd slowly come around the side of the table and was walking just as slowly toward me while they gave me sharp, painful little jabs. He finally got there. I stopped struggling. He was a head shorter than I and about sixty-five. He had a stupid look on his face. He could afford to have a stupid look on his face.

"You know," he said, "it's been a long time since I've had to deal with one of these unpleasant episodes. Years. But I got a special request to handle this personally. I'm giving you a chance to be a good girl. Quit while you're behind, and we'll let bygones be bygones."

I suddenly recognized him—he was a past president of the union, the man honored for leading the first organizing drive twenty years before. "I can't," I said. "I can't, and I won't."

He looked sleepily up at me, his head moving in an old man's tremor. "I've done my best, girl. All I said was I'd do my best. Give her back her picture."

He started back as if crossing the George Washington Bridge. The two goons let go of my arms.

The pigeons, still chasing every last crumb, reluctantly made room for me and quickly closed the space as I passed. I walked over to Church and took a bus up Sixth Avenue to Whelan's.

10

I started up the stairs of my building with fifty feet of tiny pictures, exactly 2240 of them, burning in my pocket. When the Puerto Rican boy handed me the envelope he'd said, "Just came in two minutes ago, you're in luck." I took the steps one at a time like an old lady, listening after each slow movement. On the fifth step I picked up a slight noise behind me. I stopped short, crouched and clapped my hand to my pocket. But in my building you don't need good reflexes because the pane of safety glass in the front door rattles in its frame. I sat on the step. Relax. You're in luck.

Through the dirty glass I could see the ordinary street and the ordinary Texaco across it. The Texaco wasn't quite ordinary since it usually didn't have any gas and the mechanic never took less than two weeks to repair a car. Still, being careful with your craft is only a misdemeanor in New York.

I started up the steps again. The guys on Laight Street held my livelihood, a four-by-five orange card, in their grip. Probably I'd never get it back. Despite my bravado in the garage, that wasn't negligible. I couldn't shrug it off as I'd shrugged off the pane of glass. I could do other things besides drive a cab, I told myself. I tried to think of one I could stand for more than a week. My head felt light and my feet leaden. I stopped again on the stairs. Since Hoyt died I'd tried to cast myself as a detective. I put my forehead against the cast-iron rail to cool it. These old tenements were built with cast-iron staircases so heavy that they sank over the years, twisting and turning the rest of the building with them. I raised my head. I had to keep moving or I'd sink.

I walked past my door to Tony Corrigenda's and knocked hard. I had only one close friend with movie equipment, and he was dead. But I had to see as soon as possible what was on that little strip of film.

Tony's door opened. "Come in before they hijack you," he said. He grabbed my arm and pulled me into the tiny hall, peering over the stair rail for the heavies he thought must be dogging my steps. He spun back to me. "It's okay—the coast is clear."

It was refreshing to find him even more paranoid than I was. "Those two gorillas stomped right over me to get at you," he murmured in awe. "Nudity ain't what it used to be. Used to be you could plotz most anyone with live dangling genitalia." He took one more gander down the stairs and set the three locks on his door. "Not that I've made a profession of it." He was shirtless and barefoot, dressed in denim cutoffs that had been patched in particolored crushed velvet, repatched, and despaired of. Even so he looked more solid now than he had holding his extension cord the other night.

"Listen," I began, "I am eternally grateful . . ."

He waved a hand to shut me up. "I can relate to that. The eternal. The infinite." His heavy-lidded eyes ascended to the ceiling, paused and drifted back down. "Sometime maybe you can spin out the myth you were living. But for now. . ." He was silent to let the vibes clear the air. "Put your ears on this." Without looking, he slid a forty-five onto his turntable.

I leaned back on some cushions waiting for a dollop of dreamy space-music to ooze from his system (as he referred to the dazzling audio setup that took up most of one wall). But I had to sit up right away. A woman's voice, hoarse and intense, barked out a song about working in a piss factory. The sound recording was ragged and unfinished and so was the rock band backing her rising chant. There was an almost hopeless defiance in her voice. Tony rolled a joint. When the record spun into the groove, he said, "You might think she sounds terrible but that kind of music will be the next hot scene. You watch."

I nodded distractedly. Tony lit the joint and held it out for me. I shook my head. He took a hit, and while holding his breath said, "Only problem is that there are more next-scene junkies than real ones, and they're more trouble." He put on an old Velvet Underground album.

"Would you do me another favor?" I asked with a reluctance I hoped was obvious. I didn't know him well enough to ask any favors.

In a moment his projector was ready to screen on a section of wall just stripped of its Indian print. He had a sense of the fragility of states of mind—except that he would have said "holiness," not fragility. He lowered the bamboo shades on his windows. The Velvets were chanting "White Light/White Heat." I took the roll of film out of my pocket, and slid it onto the sprocket. His soft voice said, "Ready, Emma?"

"Ready as I'll ever be."

He switched on the machine. The hum and dense projection of light reduced the room to a small sharp-edged rectangle. Somewhere Eisenstein says something about the ideal projected image being a square. Mysticism never appealed to me before and still didn't, but I was looking for the ideal projected image. I sat still as a buddha.

The first thing we see is a street sign. Where are we, Hoyt? On Sixty-sixth Street. The corner where I stood watching those women on their way to make an extra buck on their lunch hour. To pay for the silk dress on layaway in the boutique. Then rockily, with quick off-balance jerks, we follow and then lead young women like the ones who led me into the Institute. The Institute of Philosophical Healing opens its door to the women. I half expect to see myself approach that door. Only that wouldn't be possible.

Had Hoyt been content with this kind of footage? Spending time behind a camera couldn't have told him much about what was going on in the building. I wanted to pull him across the distance, pull him from behind the camera into the daylight flashing on the white wall. You'd be better at this than me. A wrist falls in front of the camera, very blurred, but I can tell it's Hoyt's. The hand disappears. A white van pulls up, blocking out the Institute. A uniformed man opens the rear door. Movers haul cartons on hand trucks from the van. I can be only minutes away. Frederick and Taylor are squabbling in the back seat of my cab. I can't tell whether they're businessmen or thugs, but I don't really mind because they're just a fare. The anonymous gray uniforms continue to haul. Hoyt shows no interest in trying to get their faces. The camera keeps swooping in on the cartons as they wheel past. Over and over again three or four cartons race across the rectangle on the wall. The flat rectangle makes it look as if uniforms, not men, are moving the cartons. The action is so repetitive that I can't remember what I've seen a minute after it disappears into the wall. One hand truck jumps too quickly over a curb and the stacked cartons spill. The camera jumps toward them as they fall, but they go so fast they are out of focus. Instantly we are in focus on the sidewalk where one carton is turned on its side, spilling its papery entrails over torn strips of masking tape. The spilled paper flaps. That means there's a breeze. I don't remember any breeze on that dead day. Maybe this is another day. The back of a gray uniform blocks the rectangle. My fingernails are digging into the palm of my hand.

"Tony, can you turn it back or something?"

He stopped the movement on another stack of cartons.

"How far, all the way?"

"No, just to the van."

The mover backs up to the van. The spilled carton jumps back into place. There is something servile, something smug about the reverse motion. At the right moment Tony put the action forward again. Once again the uniform pulls the hand truck up over the curb carelessly. The carton spills in the same place. The camera swoops toward it: we're very near the sidewalk. It comes clear, and I signaled Tony again and he stopped the machine. The spilled carton's stuffing is a crumpled colored sheet of paper about to be swept away by the breeze. A red, white and blue TH is visible on the paper, along with a photo of the top of a man's head. I heard Tony inhale the weed. THAD'S DOING THAT JOB. I nodded to Tony, and the crumpled sheet spins toward the gutter. The moving continues. What was Hoyt making of all this? No way to tell by what he was seeing. Seeing what he saw could never tell me what he thought. These cartons belonged to Wincey. Did Hoyt notice that or did he already know it? He crouches there with the camera in his hands. Frederick sees him. I keep going, have to stop. The rectangle on the wall shows two burly businessmen shoving out of a cab's back seat. Out of sight in the front seat a cabbie waits for them in the stalled traffic. The cab door hangs open. The men walk toward us, turn first into torsos and then into two meaty faces out of focus, as if a fog has suddenly settled over Sixty-sixth Street.

"Hey," Tony said, "Look at that. Movie stars."

I looked at the whole thing again. Then again. There was something else I hoped to see, but no matter how many times I looked it wasn't there. Frederick and Taylor wanted the film too much. I had to be missing something. Finally I put the film back in my pocket. Tony shrugged. "It won't win any awards."

"No," I said, "it won't."

Movies, I decided, don't tell you enough of what you need to know. They tantalize.

11

The cat squalled for the tuna long before I set the opener onto the lip of the can. For no reason I had a feeling I should try to feed him something other than tuna. Maybe the hard brown food that looks like tiny crucifixes. That would have been simple, obvious, no complications. Very concrete. A fed cat instead of a mewling nudging little fiend. But I set the opener onto the lip of the can with something like TUNA LUMPIES on the label. The cat, sensing my hesitation, hissed at me as I punctured it. I held it as far away from me as I could. Its smell was a little too much for me in this August heat. I made a circle with the machine, and the lid snapped as the circle closed. The cat still squalled at my elbow. I poured the food into his bowl. The cat dove into it. Thad's doing that job, I thought. They say you can smell trouble. The cat couldn't even taste it.

I rinsed my fingers and escaped to the living room. I dialed Wincey's office and got Connie Fortini's cheery voice.

"This is Emma Hobart. I was in the office early yesterday morning."

"You were? Oh, yes. I remember you. So many people come in your head spins sometimes. The student who wasn't. The congressman isn't in, dear, he's campaigning in the neighborhoods. Very busy day."

"If you'll allow me, there's something—"

"I don't want to be rude, hon, but—"

I broke in. "Was your office robbed recently?"

Silence. Then a sharp tone, "What are you after, young lady? You really don't look the type to—"

"That's right! You're right. I'm not the type, Miss Fortini. I just want to know about the robbery. For personal reasons. For reasons I can't explain over the phone. I'm not out to hurt the congressman or anything like that. I probably won't have any use for whatever you can tell me. But I might. It might be important. I know I'm being vague, but—"

"Who told you about the robbery? That was privileged information."

"I found out accidentally. Could you tell me maybe what kinds of things were stolen? Or anything about anything?"

"No, I really couldn't." She sounded upset now. "The congressman is still beside himself about it. No, I couldn't," she repeated, "I still don't see why you—"

"I might be able to help get the stuff back," I volunteered out of nowhere. "Especially if you could give me an idea—"

"Wait a minute," she said. "Oh goodness, I have to think. I can't say more right now. Call me back later, you hear? I've got to think." She hung up. I hoped she didn't think enough about it to speak to Wincey. I had a feeling that if she did I wouldn't get any help from her.

My canvas bag was lying on the bed. I rummaged through it until I found Hoyt's wallet. His jeans always bulged in the same pocket. This wallet had lived there a long time, molding to the curve of his right buttock. I passed my hand across the soft worn leather, following the curve. A more graphic print of his existence than the film. It had in it what wallets always have: old receipts, outdated documents, identifying papers, some money, no credit cards. Hoyt had no credit with institutions. There was a photo of the two of us, machine-made for fifty cents. We looked like derelicts on that cheap brownish paper. Tucked in one of the discolored folds was a single small sheet of yellow paper, one edge ragged where it had been wrenched from a long-gone pad. Four seven-digit numbers were scrawled on it in orange razor-point. Below the numbers it said: "E. B.'s last." The words were heavily written in blue ballpoint pen. The hand I recognized as Hoyt's had traced them over and over again, almost entirely obliterating the original orange until the words were barely readable, perhaps readable only to someone familiar with his hand. I still possessed letters and two poems in that hand, which veered from the cramped and careful to the cramped and careless.

Hoyt knew a guy who worked for the phone company, a rabbity electronic technoid. This guy was a quiet subversive. He wanted to sabotage the system, and his enemy was his employer. He could have gotten Hoyt these numbers in a flash.

The fan was blowing the papers from Hoyt's wallet all over the bed. I switched it off. It shuddered to a stop as I dialed the first number on the list. I heard steps on the staircase. The digital clock kicked over to 3:00 P.M. For an instant I thought of my mother who'd sent me the time machine for Christmas. Mother, tell them I'm not home.

I raced as quickly as possible to the bathroom. The cat, drinking from the leaky bathtub tap, leaped out of the room in one bound. I turned the shower on. I'd used a similar stratagem on my landlord once. Its purpose was to give me time to think. I edged noiselessly out of the bathroom and looked through the spyhole. Two distorted meaty faces and one meaty hand descending to knock.

The knock. "In the shower—be right out!" I screamed. "Hurry it up, kid," Taylor bellowed, just inches away.

I picked up the .32 from the kitchen table. A violent fantasy tore through my body on the way to a more receptive host. The clock kicked loudly over to 3:01. My mother never had much to spend on me. Taylor slugged the door again, rattled the doorknob. I stuffed the contents of Hoyt's wallet, the wallet, and the .32 into my canvas bag and crawled out the living-room window, the one without the fan, onto the roof of the bakery, between the bakery's giant exhaust fan and the skylight. Man does not live by bread alone, all men are mortal, and I am not a man therefore I must run. I got as far as the iron ladder that leads into the next lot, as far as clenching the sooty top rung. The sun was breaking through a film of smog. My brain started to kick in across my sweaty panic. There are only so many chances you're likely to get. Play the red, Emma. I stuck the gun under my belt like a victim of movie-style delusions, and Hoyt's wallet into my back pocket. I took out the film but changed my mind and left it in the canvas bag and the bag alongside the ladder. Let them get it. Everybody needs a little success now and then. Maybe it would get them off my back for a while. I stepped in through the window. A racket issued from my front door as if Frederick was using Taylor for a battering ram. Even these two wouldn't be hackneyed enough to search my closet again. Especially with the curtains dangling out the window and my bag slumped by the ladder. These two were the kind to take suggestions. So I slid the clothes on hangers in front of me, my heart not even racing now, possessed of the peculiar confidence that a plan, no matter how rudimentary, gives you, and waited for them to smash in.

They were getting more use out of my place than I was. I left the closet door open to encourage them not to look in it. I heard a definitive crack. My front door gave way to the superior strength of two armed men, two entrepreneurs, who like all good entrepreneurs would keep after me until they got what they wanted out of me.

I could see nothing but an old tennis shoe that once fit Hoyt's left foot. Noises, some verbal, in the kitchen. The shower curtain snapped. I flinched as if behind it. Then I got hold of myself and started cursing them under my breath. Taylor's voice came at me sounding only a few feet away: "Bitch foxed us."

"Check the roof. She might be out there waiting for us to turn tail." A scrabble of steps onto the roof. I could see the face Taylor was making without seeing it—afraid to soil his shiny black pumps on the hot tar. He cursed again. People do what you want them to at times. He'll find it now. In fifteen seconds Taylor's voice returned carbonated with victory.

"Found it! Found it!"

"Get in here," Frederick said. "That better be it or Breakstone'll chew our ass again."

That irreducible bit of information set my blood racing. I'd traded the last record of Hoyt's life for it. Knowledge was worth more than a record. The shock effects of adrenaline bathed my body in another sweat. I heard Taylor bounce back from the roof rattling the floor.

"Screw him," he muttered. "We got it, didn't we?"

There was some shuffling about for a while. Were they unrolling the film to look at it?

"Should we try and nail the kid?" Frederick's voice wondered.

A pause.

"Screw her. She's already scared shitless."

That's right, I thought, screw her. I was beginning to enjoy the sweaty life in my closet.

"The pictures in these goddamn things. So small you can't make out . . . Yeah, this must be it. It's it! Terrific, we got what we came for."

"All this extra exercise is giving me pangs of hunger," Taylor said.

"It's too late for lunch. The afternoon's practically over already."

"I gotta eat. My indigestion backs up on me if I don't get considerable solids."

Frederick grunted. "How about taking a chance on one of these Ukrainian joints over on Avenue A?"

In a moment they left, closing the remains of my door after them. That was considerate. Maybe they'd break it down, but they had the manners to shut it afterwards. I was beginning to appreciate their good qualities. I listened for their steps to fade, my heartbeat fading with each footfall. As I pushed away the clothes the cat sat looking at me from the closet doorway. He must have been there all along. He walked away now that he'd made his point. The spot he vacated was filled by the scrap of paper from Hoyt's wallet.

When my breathing returned to normal ten minutes later, I dialed the first number again and got only six long rings. Were these numbers in the order that Evelyn Berndt dialed them? I toyed with the dial, with Hoyt's list, with the ring on my finger, with a nail split from my recent stroll on the roof. The cat sat watching me. Several moments later I caught myself watching the cat. I picked up the list again. When the window is open you can see as far as a brick wall about thirty feet away. The cat walked silently across to the window, sprang onto the ledge, and stared at the brick wall. He was bored with me. I couldn't blame him. I blamed the city for a while, staring at the brick wall so long that the city and the wall seemed identical. Then I blamed myself for knowing too much about the city, as if I didn't live in it but watched it from a distance of thirty feet. I wanted to break through all that. At least I did now, since I'd left Hoyt near that brick wall.

12

I dialed the second number. I still don't know what the voice on the other end was saying when it answered in a rush of guttural syllables after the third ring. It was minutes before I could connect the German accent to Mrs. Berndt. She coughed into the receiver and then coughed again and said they were coming to get her.

"Who's coming to get you, Mrs. Berndt? Who do you mean?"

"They are coming right away. I cannot move without him I told them," she was coughing steadily now. "They have to come quick," she said between coughs. "The fire is creeping down already. I can smell it. The smoke is so thick he can't breathe. Please, Evelyn, come right away. They aren't going to come quick enough. Please come this time. I know you hate it, but it's burning." The phone slammed into my ear.

"Right away," I said into the receiver, wishing for a second that I could be Evelyn for her.

Moments later I hailed a cab on the Bowery. "East Eighty-fourth," I told the driver as I slid in. He nodded and unsheathed a ballpoint. A pink morsel of tongue flicked at the pen as he propped his clipboard in the fold of his double chin. His ears fluttered delicately as he scribbled on his trip card. I realized this wasn't going to be a quick trip.

At the moment the traffic signal paled to yellow, he finished his memoirs and punched the meter. The button needed more grease. He hit it again, and the meter grudgingly produced the metallic purr I heard fifty times a night when I drove. He pulled up to the light just as it went red. All over the cab were neatly lettered pithy little signs telling me what I could do with my gum, packages, cigarettes, leisure time, extra cash and love life presuming I was still interested in one by the time I left the cab. Mrs. Berndt's hysteria kept me on the edge of the seat, but I was extremely reluctant to tell another cabdriver how to do his job.

When I drove, I just beat hell out of the cab. I squeezed every last dollar out of my shift, but this guy owned his hack and kept finding new ways to pet it as we cantered uptown. I wanted to tell him to step on it, but I never got used to being a passenger.

It was the wrong time of day for a fast cab uptown anyway. Traffic was snarled on Third Avenue, four lanes abreast. When we finally got to Eighty-fourth, money from Hoyt's wallet paid the driver. Instead of making change, the driver tugged his ear lobe for half a minute. Maybe it was his way of counting. He tilted his bulk so far out the window I wasn't sure he'd make it back.

"Looks like some fire here," he said. "I didn't know you was on the way to a fire. It's all right though—I always make good time," and he passed me the change with such ceremony it broke my heart and I couldn't take it.

Mrs. Berndt thought I was Evelyn, and I used Hoyt's money to get to her. I took a cab to get there fast, and the subway would have been faster. I felt as I did when I had endless repetitive dreams about driving the cab back and forth on the same streets and thinking in the dream these streets are really my thoughts I'm driving through and these people I'm picking up over and over again are all the people I should be.

I walked past an empty blue squad car parked aslant that blocked the street. Beyond was a swarm of activity. Segments of people, cars, engines and squad cars were tied and scrambled by crisscrossing hoses and hastily drawn barricades. Firemen were pointing two or three of the hoses at the brick face of a building streaming with yellow smoke. Occasional vivid bursts of fire spurted like blood from a fresh wound.

The roof of a TV station's van supported a video cameraman zooming on a fireman racing up a ladder. An upper-story window burst, and flames spurted from the jagged opening. The fireman spun even while climbing and aimed at his adversary. My glance followed his hose down. A few steps below sidewalk level I caught sight of the cardboard cobbler. Unperturbed by the street din or the conflagration above him, he continued driving his cardboard nail into the cardboard boot. The example of too much perseverance can crush your initiative so I looked away.

On the other side of the street an ambulance screamed away. I thought that it must contain one or both of the old couple. I broke through the twisted knot looking for them, brushing past glassy-eyed spectators, pyromaniacs and survivors.

"The one near the river, the old Con Ed building, it burned blue at twilight and green later. Most beautiful fire I ever saw," said a middle-aged man.

A chubby woman wrapped in a housedress nudged her friend as they stared across the street, unruffled by smoke bursts, "So the kids and the wife went with. To see Daddy fight his last fire. He was set to retire the next day, you see." Her friend said, "You already told me that." "So he went up the ladder and waved to them from the roof. And they waved back. And then the roof fell in. They saw him die in that very instant." She shook her head. "A sad sight."

Her friend nodded. Their faces were as flat and hard as the sidewalk.

A few yards farther on I caught sight of the old man, upright in an aluminum garden chair directly facing the blazing building. His gaze didn't waver an inch as I approached. I didn't want to know just then what he was seeing or what he had seen. Above the chair stood Mrs. Berndt. A single sentry, a young fireman, protected them. I caught his eye. "You know them?" he asked aggressively. I nodded. He shook his head. "They sure was lucky. I found out it was the old lady called. She got a nose for smoke she says. They got out without a scratch, which is pretty lucky considering the old fart can barely walk. I got him that chair to lie in."

"Nice of you," I said. He seemed to expect a little more acknowledgment so I asked him where he got it, and he told me a story about extorting it from a garden shop on the corner. When we got to the end of that he looked a little dissatisfied with me. His story had no point except to show he'd done the right thing. I did my duty and congratulated him again; he nodded. "It was nothing," he said. He seemed to be trying to justify his fierce solicitude in standing guard over the old couple. If I hadn't happened along, he would have looked after them whether they wanted him to or not.

Mrs. Berndt's yellow wig was askew. Her make-up and mascara were caked, smudged and runny. She was trying to keep her end up, but despite the heat she was beginning to shiver. When I pointed this out to the fireman he nodded carefully and left in pursuit of a blanket. I waited till he returned to speak to her. She stared at the burning building without speaking. She had lost her homeland, her daughter, her home, but she was still standing. When the fireman returned with an old woolen blanket I wrapped it around her shoulders. She looked up at me briefly, no signal of recognition.

"My fault," she murmured. We stood in silence to watch

the building die. She steadied herself, gripping the back of the old man's chair, her knuckles white. "They came to me. I told them I didn't know where it was. Whatever."

"Two of them?" I asked, thinking of Frederick and Taylor. She nodded. "The kitchen linoleum was still wet from scrubbing. They walk over it back and forth in their big shoes leaving big dirty prints. Stupid men. I have nothing Eve gave me for them. They start pulling at everything. Drawers, cabinets, all the closets I have neat as a pin. Onto the floor, onto the rug. More mess. Always more mess. Eve pull out things, I would slap her little fingers. She cries, but she stops. She learn good when I teach. When she go to the college, only girl to keep everything apple pie." She paused, looked down, and then met my eyes. "Nowadays city people think it matters less who keeps clean. What do I know, just old lady, maybe it not matter. I am proud that Eve is not a mess like other girls, like the roommates." Her picture of Evelyn as her mother's daughter turned Evelyn into a schoolgirl, erasing the woman she became. "The flat is small, is old but always clean. The stupid men throw everything which way. I have nothing for them. They go away cursing their heads off and the lights go out. I screw new fuse. Fine. I go back to clean. There's always another mess. Eve called me about a mess."

This was so abrupt I almost missed it. "When did Eve call you?" I prompted, thinking of the files that might have been stolen from Wincey's office, of the frantic attempts to find something Evelyn might have left behind. Was Mrs. Berndt referring to a call from Evelyn the night she died? The mother looked at me again, took my forearm in her grip. She trusted me as a daughter, somebody's daughter. "You know," she said. "You were at school with Eve." She did remember me. "A police did a mess in Eve's after the other girl, the roommate, ran off. You remember." Finally I caught on; we were back in '67 when Evelyn and Josie Breakstone were roommates at Barnard.

"The other roommate, that pipsqueaker Paisley, would not help. So Eve call me."

"Paisley who?" I asked.

"You remember, Paisley Besame. Never lift a finger. Another mess. Worst mess. Three girls' things all thrown about. Stupid police bothering young girls. For nothing." She loosened her grip on the old man's chair, but she still held my arm. "For nothing, yes, Papa?" She tapped his shoulder. He ignored her, continuing to stare straight ahead. A deep-seated irritation came into her tearstained old face. "Papa angry," she said. "When the *schwein* go away, I start to clean. After putting in the fuse. Fire start in closet. Old wires in there. The fault of those bastards throwing everything around in my perfect closet. Not mine. Papa walk to kitchen where I scrub. Such dirt. He blame me. He blame me always. Blame me for Eve. Blame me for fire. Then the phone ring. He say, forget phone because we have fire in closet. So he angry. Yes, Papa," she asked, tapping him again, "angry still?" He didn't move so I did, to look closer at him, wondering if he would react to seeing me again. It was a move I'd been avoiding. But he wasn't going to react to anything.

Mrs. Berndt must have seen my expression change. She circled around the chair, pushing me aside. The blanket slid off her shoulders. A guttural Germanic sound tore from her breast. She looked angrily at the old man, unfazed by his motionless stare at the smoldering building. "They take you too, Papa. You let them take you." The tears started down her face again. I took her arm. She crumpled toward me. I led her a few steps away from the aluminum chair.

"Listen to me, Mrs. Berndt," I said very slowly. "Is there anyone we can call to help you out? Do you have the number of a relative or friend—anyone?"

She told me a number. "She has a good heart," she said without telling me who belonged to the number. I found a phone booth not far away. I'd been repeating to myself the number Mrs. Berndt gave me. It seemed familiar. It was. It matched one on Hoyt's list. Five rings and Connie Fortini answered.

"Just a sec—gotta turn down the box." It jarred me that at home she used the same cheery receptionist's voice. The phone rattled and I heard another smooth voice, this one male, suddenly strangled, the victim of volume control. "Sorry," she came back, loud and clear. "I don't even much like TV, but I have to turn it on to drown out my neighbors on both sides. If you can believe it. If only they'd watch the same show."

"This is Emma Hobart with the afternoon news," I said. Through the phone booth I could see black smoke crowding the sky. "It's pretty grim."

"Hey, listen now, you put me in a blue funk already today. I have a heavy date tonight, and I just can't handle any more downers."

"When I called you before, I tried to shake you up."

"You did. Now I don't know what to do. I know the congressman. Sometimes, only when absolutely necessary, he'll stretch the truth just a hair to the press. But he is always straight with me. If he says those files weren't stolen, then I have to back him up." The honey was melting but there was still a lot of it. "What news are you talking about?" she asked suddenly.

I told her.

There was a sharp intake of breath on the other end. "You should have told me right off," she scolded. "She can't handle this all by herself. I'm coming over there. I'm already there. You march right back to her and tell her I'll be right with her. That date would've only got me into a lumpy bed anyhow." The voice was almost gritty now—nothing receptionist about it. "And believe me, hon, lumps aren't the half of it."

Acrid soot-filled air crept around me as I slid open the door to the booth. Starting back, relieved but edgy, I caught sight of the young fireman. I didn't want to catch sight of him, but there he was. He was helping somebody else now. He had a boy's white tee-shirted shoulder in his black-gloved hand and he was shaking it. The boy was looking up at him, his smudged face twisted.

There was no other way back to Mrs. Berndt except past them. I didn't like the glove on the boy's shoulder. I identify too easily. Probably the boy deserved what he was getting, but it didn't make any difference.

The fireman said, "You know what you did, don't you? Do you know how close you came to getting hurt? An eyelash, that's how close. Don't you know it's your duty to help the fire department, your duty as a citizen, don't you? Don't you?"

He was still shaking the kid, only harder. He kept it up, but the kid never did answer—just looked mercilessly up at him, his young face emptied of all thought, reason or emotion, except defiance.

13

As soon as Connie put her arms around Mrs. Berndt I left, aching to get off that street, still another I never wanted to set foot on again. As I turned away the roof of the building caved in, like a part of Mrs. Berndt's mind. Those twin disciples of disorder, Frederick and Taylor, hectoring the old lady and tearing her closets asunder, had set the spark that set the fire. They did everything just wrong enough to break down the precarious equilibrium of people's lives. They didn't exactly kill Hoyt. They hadn't exactly killed old Mr. Berndt. They gave disorder the ambition it needed to turn into chaos.

I started down Third Avenue on foot, unwilling to pay another cab fare, unable to handle a bus or subway's close quarters with the taste of smoke on my parched lips. With the grime and smell of ashes in my clothing, I felt a part of the fire. All my responses slowed. Mr. Berndt's implacable face, holding the world responsible for his fate, dragged at my heels, making it hard to look at the ordinary faces rushing past me as if they were forging their own destinies.

As I left Eighty-fourth Street, Hoyt's suddenly dead face overlaid Mr. Berndt's death mask. Cabs rushed up

Third Avenue as if defying gravity. What killed Hoyt was a cab temporarily out of human control, a blind object following the laws of motion. What set it in motion? Telephone calls, half-articulate threats, a three-minute Super-8 cartridge, a possible theft, an odd suicide. And so far I had one name uniting them all—Breakstone, Breakstone as reflected by his hirelings: Frederick and Taylor, a retired labor exec who apparently owed him a favor, a U.S. congressman out for reelection, a scientific institute with elastic notions of science.

I tried to look at the shop windows. The new fall fashions, so different from the fashions I hadn't bought last fall, paraded in front of me. If you stare at a thing long enough your eyes go out of focus. The last two days would go out of focus if I stared at them too long. I decided I'd imitate Frederick and Taylor. They never stared. They just went ahead and stirred up trouble.

I found myself across the street from the Institute. After a while a doorman came out of the nearest building and asked why I was standing around. "Plain-clothes," I snapped, and he faded fast.

People started leaving the Institute one by one, their faces momentarily dazed by the light and heat. Last of all came Dr. Ridley, his balding head bowed. He made his way east on foot.

I followed him onto the Lexington Avenue subway, the Hunter College platform. He walked to an iron post and stood quietly next to it until his train came, taking no notice of anything around him. I thought he must make enough at the Institute torturing people to be able to take cabs, but I was grateful to him for being frugal. Now I could dog his heels without too much hassle. We rocked and screeched downtown holding on to steel straps at opposite ends of the same airless, crowded car. I stared at him the entire way. He stayed in focus. He left the car at my stop, Bleecker Street. When he walked east on Bleecker and turned down my block, I began to wonder who was being followed. Maybe he'd sublet my apartment. As if following my suggestion, he turned when he got to the bakery. He looked as if he was going to walk in my door. He didn't. He put his shoe on the cracked step and leaned over to tie it. His apparently unconscious mockery of me now complete, he continued across Houston another two blocks. I trailed half a block behind.

He approached a crowd that overflowed one corner of Spring Street, and then the crowd gulped him into its shifting maw. I moved faster, trying to keep track of the point of his disappearance. At first I didn't notice either the posters or the strained air of festivity on the street. Then I realized we'd stumbled into a local rally for Thad Wincey, the people's friend. Then I realized that maybe we hadn't just stumbled into it.

The hot summer crowd throbbed around me, swirling, snatching bits of conversation and hurling them at me in Spanish, Italian, wino and street languages. Above them, mastering them, organizing them, was Wincey's artificially amplified baritone talking about the working man, the working stiff as he called him. He wasn't actually talking about the working stiff either, but about Wincey's sympathy for him, about how much Wincey would do for the stiff if he was allowed to.

There were a lot of red gas balloons bobbing above the crowd with THAD'S DOING THAT JOB printed on them. Wincey himself looked like a pretty good imitation of a grass-roots pol with his suit coat off and his sleeves rolled up to the elbow, his tie loose and his hair tousled. His shiny slogan button was pinned to his shirt and caught the glint of the sun now and then. His voice was a slight problem, and what it had to say was another. But the energy was there.

Ridley was a ringer. I picked him out and kept a loose eye on him. He didn't move much; he kept his eye on Wincey. That was easy to do. Wincey was standing on the roof of his limousine. He pointed an accusing arm at the burned-out shell of the tenement behind him. "We're gonna . . . rebuild . . . the vital Lower East Side. Our priorities have . . . got . . . to change. There's no future in preparing for . . . war. We must prepare for . . . peace."

On the crowd's borders a few photographers and a video camera crew were riding the low crest of the media wave. Wincey tended to talk in the direction of the media truck. "I want the . . . citizens of the great Lower East Side to let their needs be known . . ., to trumpet them to the powers that be in Washington. This is the process of democracy and it will help make . . . me a more a more effective . . ., more responsive congressman." He raised his trumpet a little higher for the crescendo. "Let your needs be known."

His plea, fabricated or not, looked heartfelt twenty yards away. His insistence demanded applause. When he got it he beamed. But the crowd tired of beating their hands together and quit. Enough was enough. Ridley chose that moment to speak from his place in the crowd. His normally mild voice was too loud and sounded squeaky after Wincey's well-modulated tones. For that reason, despite the obvious fact that this wasn't his neighborhood, he sounded authentic. "What are you doing, congressman, about the crying need for new medical facilities and clinics for the poor and aged in this part of the city?"

The beam in Wincey's face short-circuited. He stared hard at his interrogator. Heads in the crowd swung from Wincey to Ridley and back. Wincey started slowly. "I'm glad you asked that question, sir, it's a good one, one of the best in fact. Health! The activity and involvement of our citizenry is . . . based . . . founded . . . on its health. I presume you are directing your question to pending legislation on continued support of research . . . scientific research . . . into the health of our citizenry. I support that research, in fact, I was one of the authors of the original bill. I can give you the facts and figures if you'll see me after this splendid gathering. Any other questions? I'll take all comers."

A few more questions were answered with equal candor. The rally wheezed to an end as Ridley edged over to Wincey's limousine.

Wincey broke smoothly away from the handshakes of straggling well-wishers, a few of whom might even have been registered to vote. I tried to get close enough to gauge the attitudes of the two men as they approached each other. Wincey took Ridley's arm in a wary but confidential gesture, too confidential to be glad-handing. The doctor threw up his free arm. Wincey's head went back as he listened, and then even harder words flew at Ridley. It would have been good pantomime if I'd known the script. Wincey opened a door of the limousine with the studied definition of an angry man. His chauffeur, settling into the driver's seat, glanced back. Changing his mind, Wincey turned from the door to Ridley and carved a horizontal bar in the air with his open hand. Would this settle it? Ridley paused, shrugged, looked at the curb for inspiration, said a few words that I could guess to be of one syllable each, turned on his heel and broke through the frayed remnants of the crowd. The silent litany of power relations they'd enacted invigorated me. Wincey laid a manicured hand on the open door of the limousine. He watched Ridley stalk off. A little girl who'd been dawdling nearby took up the slack, shoving a pink plastic-covered autograph book into the field of his attention. He took the book but continued to watch Ridley. Absent-mindedly, he moved to slide into the limousine. The girl protested, moving between the door and the curb. Wincey looked up, puzzled to see her standing so close to him, blocking his exit. For a moment it looked as if he might push her out of the way. Her finger pointed at the autograph book.

I crossed the street, skirting a police prowl car, as

Wincey signed the pink pad without speaking to the girl. As she ran away with her treasure, Wincey swung back into the seat, closed the door and signaled the driver.

I pulled open the near street-side door and bounced in beside the congressman. He gave me a look of ripe distaste I could remember encountering only once before. That time it came from a red-faced Texas marshall at two in the morning during federal dispersal of the march on the Pentagon in '67. Only Wincey smelled of soft leather, linen starched in a Chinese laundry and sweet mint breath-freshener, and the marshall had reeked of tobacco juice, sweaty socks and fear. I said, "I'd say that Doctor Ridley is in your employ. How many people at the Institute know that?"

The look was still there. "Do I know you?"

"I'm a rejected volunteer."

The limousine pulled away from the curb. Another free ride. He nodded, tight-lipped. "Erland," he said. There was a pause. I thought maybe he might have something to offer. He did. "Where can I drop you?" That wasn't what I had in mind.

"A van delivered Evelyn Berndt's stolen files to the Institute three days ago. That's no news. Ridley didn't care for it? Used up too much research space? He seemed upset."

The narrow mouth stretched into a grim smile. "Stolen files? No files have been stolen."

"You mean you arranged to have them lifted?"

"You're reading too much of this Watergate crap. Evelyn's files, such as they are, are just piles of press releases and outdated subcommittee notes, that sort of thing. It would take great ingenuity to find anything in them worth stealing."

I shrugged. "Well, somebody cared enough to deliver them to the Institute. What do you make of that?"

He offered a shade more politely to drop me somewhere. Ridley, not so dumb, had come after Wincey in the street, suspecting he would be vulnerable only there in the open, where it was his business to be.

"You know about the fire?"

He was looking out the window. The Bowery was becoming Third Avenue, a seamless transit in two blocks from rat-infested tenements patrolled by prostitutes to high rises terraced with hibachis and guard dogs, another New York miracle. "What fire?" he said without relinquishing his gaze.

"The Berndts' apartment house went up, and the old man died of the shock."

The muscles above his shirt collar tightened. He turned to me with full attention. "No," he said. "The poor old lady." He sounded genuinely upset. I felt a certain sympathy for him, but I wanted to avoid complicating my responses. I reminded myself that I was sitting in a limousine for the second, maybe last time in my life, and that what was for me an extraordinary ride was his subway.

"What a tragedy," he murmured and reached over to a small inlaid bar in front of him for a glass of iced Perrier. "Is someone caring for her?"

I nodded. "Somehow I hadn't expected you to be so moved."

"Perhaps you stereotype politicians too readily. Your friend Erland did. There's nothing odd about being upset about the old lady. She's a tough one, but enough is enough."

"Thoughtful of you to be contributing to the Berndts' monetary welfare."

"Whatever gave you that idea?" He brushed imaginary lint off his knee. I watched his manicured hands. Suddenly I understood how Evelyn could have been attracted to the man. The authority of those fingers on her body. The seduction of power made wholly carnal.

I realized that Wincey was incapable of telling me anything useful—it was the nature of his profession. So I told him something.

"Ridley wasn't supposed to meet you in public. He was panicked and he wanted you to do something about it. You were alarmed that he had the nerve to come to you. After all, you'd picked him for this job because he's a bundle of little fears. You didn't want him sticking his neck out—you just wanted somebody in the Institute keeping an eye open. Now things seem to be screwing up. Evelyn is dead, people like me are nosing around where they don't belong, there's a fire at the Berndts'."

"That's right," he said.

The limousine stopped. We were in front of a Park Avenue apartment house. The doorman opened my door. He was smiling. Wincey was smiling. "When you figure out the rest let me know," he said. "Take the young lady home, Walter." He got out and sauntered up the walk. The doorman leaped to open the door.

Walter, never letting a word spill from his lips, dropped me downtown. The glass of Perrier, smoothly fitting the depression in a silver tray, never let anything spill from its lip either. Soon the ice melted, and the bubbles disappeared. By the time Walter let me out it looked like an ordinary glass of water. There was a lesson in that, but I couldn't think what it was.

I walked into a Ukrainian coffee shop, still brooding, and ordered a bowl of pea soup. It was served in a beige crockery bowl with a white crockery saucer under it.

"What kind bread?" the waitress asked.

"Black," I said, "to match my mood."

This shop always relaxed me because nothing in it matched. The two abrupt, almost speechless waitresses were careful to wear different colored uniforms, pastel green and pastel yellow. The white-haired man who'd been standing at the ancient register for the last thirty years always wore a white jacket. The waitress slid the black bread onto the counter. The dish was pale blue.

After I finished the soup I tried the third number on Hoyt's list. A male voice said curtly, "Hello, who is it?"

It was unmistakably Wincey's baritone. Startled, I said nothing. "Who is it?" he repeated. "Christ," he muttered under his breath and I could feel the receiver pulling away from his ear.

"Wait a second, it's Emma Hobart."

The baritone came at me again. "How did you get my number? If Connie—"

"Your secretary had nothing to do with it. A phone-freak pal of Hoyt Erland got it for him. Why did Evelyn Berndt call you the night she died?"

He sighed. "I'm hanging up now, Miss Hobart. I've had enough of you for one day."

"Go ahead, but I'm going to keep coming at you until I find out."

"I do rather get the idea you don't give up easily," he said. "Tell me, Miss Hobart, are you a constituent of mine?"

"I live in your district. Why do you ask?"

"Just that in a sense you have a right to the truth. From your congressman, I mean."

I closed my eyes and waited.

He said, "Evelyn called me only to say she was going to take a few days off. Now leave me in peace in the God-given privacy of my own home, please."

"Was she leaving because she wanted to or because you wanted her to?"

"I've answered that question," he said and hung up.

He hadn't really told me anything, but I'd managed to get him to talk, which meant I could get him to talk again. That made me feel good enough to order another bowl of soup. It was set in front of me steaming. I looked at it and went back to the phone booth. I dialed the fourth number on Hoyt's list.

"Good evening, Sypher residence," said a voice from the previous century.

"Mr. Sypher, please," I said trying not to let down the repartee.

"Mr. Sypher is out of town, madam. May I take a message?"

"When is Mr. Sypher's return expected?" I asked, letting my voice lilt to get into the swing of things.

"May I ask who is calling?" The nineteenth century grew a little more distant.

I made one more try. "This is Congressman Wincey's appointment secretary. Congressman Wincey wishes to confirm an appointment for later this week. He understood that Mr. Sypher might be out of town."

"Mr. Sypher will return tomorrow evening at the latest. May I have your name, Madam?"

"Tell Mr. Sypher that Emma Hobart called and will call again. Tell him that something slightly tawdry has turned up tying him to Evelyn Berndt. Tell him another woman in a desperate situation has to speak to him. But warn him that she's not about to commit suicide."

I hung up wishing there was a mirror in the dingy booth so I could see how tough I looked.

14

I sat stiffly in the booth, nickels and dimes spread randomly in front of me. A burst of nerve had carried me through the phone call. But it was the last fizz, and now I wanted to go home. I didn't want to go home alone. I found Gil's number on the inside cover of my address book. There were numbers scrawled or scratched all over the booth by earlier occupants who didn't want to go home alone either. Earlier occupants, heroes in their own stories.

I was busy assembling the parts of a story, and when I had all the parts in place, I'd know something. At least I'd know how to tell the story. I'd know why Hoyt was not now breathing. I might be able to mitigate my accidental relationship to his death. Maybe I could alter my all-too-accidental relationship to my own life. I dialed, and Gil answered on the second ring. "Where have you been? I've been trying you for hours."

"All over. I'll tell you about it. If you're free tonight I can use your help."

"Name it. I'm at your disposal."

I askèd him to meet me in the Ukraine. I was pushing a bet maybe. But he'd been fine about it. I drank cup after cup of black coffee waiting for him to show up. Soon I was wired into each second that passed on the big clock over the counter. There was no polite way to tell Gil his father had hired Frederick and Taylor. "Listen, Gil, your daddy, who I'm sure in every other respect is a really great guy, gets two thugs to do his dirty work for him." No impolite way either. I kept glancing up at the big clock and pushing what I knew about his father over to tomorrow.

He didn't know what a hard time I'd been giving him when he wasn't there so I didn't give him a hard time when he was. I was nice for a change.

"I've got to get out of here," I said smiling, "before I turn into a cup of coffee."

"Where to?" he asked, elbow on the counter. He made it look as if he always hung out in Ukrainian coffee shops.

"I need somebody to run interference for me."

He stood up. We were both trying not to be uncomfortable. As we walked out to the still-simmering darkness, his hand closed over my elbow. I hoped we didn't pass anyone I knew. I'd asked for protection, now I'd have to sit still and be protected. When we turned a corner, I found a smooth way to slide out of his grip, gesturing at the sky to note a rare appearance of stars over the city. I narrated bits of my day, half telling a story, letting a part of my brain go numb. He steered through the selective amnesia, caught my mood.

"That film sounds very ordinary. You sure you weren't missing something? Some dumb little thing that shouldn't have been there but by some accident or another was? Because it makes too little sense that your friend Hoyt would hold on to it if there wasn't something worth holding on to."

"Hoyt held on to it because that was his job. He took the job seriously, more seriously than the job took him. He said to me, 'I have to know what real life is like.'"

"Real life? Wasn't he living a real life?"

I'm not good at explaining close distinctions. There is

no difference between life and real life. "You wouldn't . . ." understand, I started to say, but quit before insulting him. "It's as if all the other jobs he'd had were garden varieties of shit work. Or minimal pay because you're committed to the idea, the politics of the thing."

He waited patiently for more. I'd thought I'd explained. But I was asking him to cross from Fifth Avenue to East Fifth Street in one graceful leap. "You don't know that much about politics?" Asking it, I knew that it wasn't just a class boundary he had to leap, it was across generations. He wasn't a sixties kid. He could make me feel my age.

He shook his head as if discouraging a fly, puzzled but certain he'd catch on any second now. Maybe when you're used to having change rattle in your pocket you don't think many things are out of your reach. "I did go to some lectures at the New School on the confrontation politics of the sixties. But it was too rhetorical. And it made it all seem so far away—like the thirties. Big gap in my education, I suppose."

"I suppose," I said. "Well, Hoyt came out of the sixties. So he didn't care that much about making a lot of money. But he had skills, and he thought he should be able to use them to make his life instead of sacrificing his life in order to use them."

Gil trained his patient eyes on me.

"It's complicated," I said, feeling my throat tighten.

"But he wanted to make money, didn't he?" he said.

"He did—but he wasn't ready to exploit anybody in the process."

Gil nodded. "Like my old man, you mean."

"Right. He'd spent at least ten years subsisting, in order to do political work of one kind or another. Radical newspapers, that kind of thing. Finally he got very tired of it. Partly because of the money angle—and partly because nothing seemed to be changing."

"So he found a better job."

"He thought it would be better. But it seems he couldn't leave well enough alone. He'd had ten years of training. So now he's dead."

"So now you're trying to dig up what he was after."

"Sort of."

We approached my block. Above the cornice of the men's shelter there was a plaster statue of the Sacred Heart of Jesus. They always lit it at night to remind the winos they were children of God—even if they didn't smell like it. Jesus was holding his hand out to us. We turned the corner. No mugs in three-piece suits held out their hands to us.

"Give me your key," Gil said. "I'll play advance man this time. Walk slowly down the block while I see if the coast is clear."

I nodded, grateful not to have to figure out what to do for once and how to do it. I stopped to watch the birds in the little storefront aviary off the corner. You never heard them sing, the glass was too thick. And you could barely see them during the day, the glass was too dirty. So if you walked past in a hurry you might think they were specimens in a taxidermist's window. Then all of a sudden you'd see them leap from perch to perch and realize there was life behind the dirty window.

The sound of approaching footsteps running fast on the pavement made me jump. I cut past a parked car onto the street where there was more light. The steps were louder, with a slapping noise on every two. I panicked and started running toward Houston in the direction of my building. I turned after a few steps and saw an Italian boy dribble a basketball across Bleecker past Jesus. I stopped and inhaled, glad that both the Texaco and the bakery were closed. I turned back expecting to see Gil come out of my doorway. Instead there was a flash of brights. A double bank of lights bore down on me through the narrow street. I remembered Hoyt flying against that wall. Something wrenched my arm out of its socket, my hip bounced off the fender of the car parked closest to me. Something strong jerked me over it, grabbing my arm with a vise grip. I flinched, saw a pigeon skitter crazily to the sidewalk, and fell back against Gil's chest. He said without alarm, whispering to me, "Close call." I saw the red taillights of the car, the right one blinking, recede down Bleecker.

"I had to wrench you out of the way. Did it hurt? Are you all right?"

"I'm fine. I mean I'm blind, almost deaf, bone tired, and my hip feels like it's going numb, but all right, really. How're things at home?"

"The hall light is out, but there's no one around who looks bloodthirsty."

We made it all the way upstairs and in my shaky door without encountering resistance. But just to be on the safe side we looked under the bed. Gil did, that is.

"Home free," he said and sneezed.

"A little dusty under there?"

"No, no, just allergies," he said before sneezing again. Then his big broad face puckered once more.

I went into the bathroom, put a facecloth under the cold tap, wrung it out and brought it back. "Sit down," I said. He perched on the edge of my bed-that-doubles-as-couch looking pretty silly, but it impressed me that a man his size could suggest a bird. Another sneeze spoiled the effect. "Close your eyes," I said. He closed them. So far he'd done everything I'd asked him to. I massaged his face with the damp cloth.

"Feels good," he murmured, letting his head drop a little farther back.

"In a minute you're going to be purring, aren't you?"

He stood up then, taking the cloth away from his face. "You must be hot," he said. We stood too close to each other so I took a step back. He stopped me. His arms caught my shoulders. He pulled me to him. The cold damp cloth at my back made me shiver. There was a second cold shock when he slid the cloth under my shirt and kissed me. I felt my body give in a little. He kept kissing me. He held the cloth tight so that cool drops of moisture slid down my back. The feel of those individual drops made me arch my back involuntarily. He lowered his embrace. I pushed him back a little. He was easy to push. He wasn't planted on his feet. As his tongue slid to touch mine, we turned slowly so that he now faced the bed. He kissed my eyelids. "Lie down," he said, "I'll cool you off." I thought he'd turn on the window fan. He didn't.

He left the room and came back with a bowl of cool water and the cloth. I didn't lie down. I stayed up on my elbows to watch him. He leaned over the bed and kissed the hollow of my neck. I had some resistance to continuing this, but it was mental. He was measured, his touch light, he didn't push. He sponged my head with cool water and kissed it in each place he sponged. He made me realize I'd had a headache all day and that the pain was slowly ebbing. His lips were sponging it away.

Some lovemaking is therapeutic. But there are many kinds of therapy. Gil's was almost completely physical, almost thoughtless, as if sex wasn't mental at all. His shirt was open, his pants half unzipped. He hadn't done that, I had. His kisses were becoming longer and sharper, lowering to my breasts. He freed my breasts, lifted me toward him from the bed, toward his parted lips, raw and red now from contact with my flesh.

I don't usually like a man on top of me at first. I pushed against the golden hair of his sunburned chest, and he slid back easily, his head against the pillow. He was breathing hard and sweating. His hands went to gather my torso to him. I slid away and grabbed the bowl of cool water. I poured a little over my head so that it ran down in rivulets over my chest. He tried to sit up, reaching for my nipples. I laughed, edged away and poured the rest of the water down his chest, soaking the bed and his clothes. He laughed too.

I stepped off the bed to help him slide out of his clothes. "Another species," I said. I'd already pulled off my wet shirt, and he maneuvered to slip off my jeans, running his hand between my legs. I hadn't given him room yet to get his pants all the way down. "Let me just pull them off," he said, anxious to get at me unimpeded. Then he looked at me and quit pulling. He smiled, lips shut, put his hands behind his head and leaned back on the pillow, naked to the knees. I surveyed his long hard muscles, now that I could see them in their natural state. I caressed him lingeringly. The fan was in reach so I switched it on. It ruffled his chest hair as we fucked.

Somewhat later, in the kitchen, we toasted English muffins, spread them with spicy mustard and thin slabs of white Cheddar. Gil stood naked at the wooden cutting board I kept over the lid of the washing machine. He was paring a MacIntosh apple. "Don't take this wrong," he said in such a way that I almost surely would, "but you remind me a lot of my sister." I passed over several insults and contented myself with stabbing him in the back with a steak knife without drawing blood. "I knew you'd take it wrong," he said and then disarmed me. The knife fell to the floor between our bare scrambled legs. We made a truce with our lips.

"I know it sounds stupid," he said to my neck, "but as I reached puberty she was the older, mysterious female in my life. She always seemed to be wandering around half dressed."

"Not really a sister then but a sexual ideal," I said.

He gave me the thoughtful look people sometimes get before burping and then said, "Right." I knew nostalgia was rummaging in the half-lit attic of his brain. I retrieved the last can of beer from my larder, and we sat down to eat.

"Of course I never fucked Josie. To put it politely.'" He looked at me for a response, holding on to the beer can. I'd have to answer before he'd allow himself a swallow.

"Except in your dreams." His slightly swollen lips gulped the beer.

"Except in my imagination."

We ate a little. The cat nibbled a tiny sliver of cheese on the floor. "How old were you when she disappeared?"

"A fairly protected fifteen."

"When was the last time you saw her?"

He put the beer down as if permanently renouncing alcohol. "The night she disappeared."

I realized that he wanted very much to talk about it. It was the kind of thing most men could discuss only with a woman, perhaps only after establishing intimacy. Later I thought that maybe he'd never talked about it to anyone before, and I wondered why he'd chosen me. It took me a while to work that out.

"I don't know how late it was—very—the night of the 7th of December." Pearl Harbor Day, I noted automatically. "I'd been asleep in my room. I woke up to find her sitting alongside me on the bed. Looking down at me. You know the feeling of being awakened from a deep sleep? As if you're being pulled into quicksand. Her face was wet. 'Is it snowing out?' I asked, and she said 'No,' and hugged me. By now I was a little more awake. Still dazed but awake and getting scared. Her arms were around me. This wasn't her normal behavior. I think she sobbed a little. Still touching my face and my shoulders— she'd never been so physical with me—She whispered, 'I'll have to explain to you another time. But I wanted to tell you. I'm never coming back to this house again. I couldn't. I'd feel like a criminal if I did. I'd be an accomplice.' She sounded horrible, but I couldn't make anything out of what she was saying except how serious she was. I was numb. 'I just had to let you know,' she said. 'Be sure to call me at the dorm tomorrow. We'll arrange a time to talk. I'll explain the whole disgusting mess to you.' She started to pull away. I didn't want her to go like that. I freed my arms from the blankets. I held her face in my hands and kissed her. I remember exactly how her hair smelled." He paused. "I know all the useful words for an obsession with your sister. Very unhealthy. The words don't apply. Anyway, naturally I wouldn't be so concerned with her except that I never saw her again after that."

"Did she say anything else that night?"

"That was about it."

"So you don't know what she was upset about?"

"I've made guesses."

I waited for the guesses. Not the guesses of a fifteen-year-old but of an affecting, awkward, naked male.

"I said nothing about it to my parents—they were still living together then. Josie asked me not to. But the next day the old man went on a rampage at breakfast over some papers that were missing from his study. He started a great inquisition. I was late for school that morning."

I put a few dishes in the sink and cleared the table while he spoke. He watched me, watched my body automatically make its movements. I stopped in front of him. "Were the papers ever found?"

"He apologized to everyone when he found them in his office safe a few days later."

"I'm still waiting for your guess."

"Josie was freaked out about something in the house. Maybe she read those papers in the old man's study. The study was supposed to be off-limits for us. She could have been poking around. Who knows?" He shrugged.

"So?"

"My guess is that she might have found some Sypher-Breaks defense contracts."

"She didn't know Sypher-Breaks had them? Nearly every big corporation did during the war."

"True, but I remember her once asking the old man point-blank—and he told her Sypher-Breaks wasn't involved. He didn't want to upset her."

"So the company did have defense contracts?"

"Correct, but Sypher-Breaks's were only harmless data control projects."

"How do you know?"

"The old man laid it out to me."

"You're not fifteen any more, Gil."

"No, I'm not. I'm not fifteen. And when I was . . . well, Josie couldn't ever handle knowing that her father had anything to do with the war, however remote."

"But you seem as if you've handled it all right." If the loss of Josie had hit him hard, what was happening at the same instant six thousand miles away seemed barely to register.

"No I haven't, Emma, you're mistaken. But if that's what disturbed Josie I think she should have dealt with it. I don't think she should have run away."

"Is that what happened?"

"I think so. Anyway, you're wrong to think that I don't take these things seriously. Very wrong." He looked at me hard, expecting a response.

"Okay, I don't mind being wrong."

His eyes traveled down my body. I had been about to take a shower. "I'm going to take a shower now," I said. "Not now," he said. His hands covered my hips. I closed my eyes. He caressed my belly, kissed it softly and slid his tongue into my navel. I held his head in my hands. I pulled his hair to get him away from me. Instead his head moved lower. "You don't mind?" he said. I didn't mind. His hand slid down my hips. I tangled his soft hair in my hands. He raked my back with his fingernails and guided my hips into his groin. We began to rock gently in the kitchen chair. The cat padded out of the room.

I wanted to destroy again for a few moments the accumulated horror of the past two days. We said nothing this time while we fucked, making the noises of animals meeting in delicate combat on a hot plain at midnight.

Not much later I took a quick shower. When I got out,

Gil was already half-asleep in my bed. In repose he looked even more boyish. His body turned and he pulled me into bed alongside him. I fell asleep immediately, with his hand on my belly. It was the first real sleep I'd had for days.

15

It didn't last all night. Something woke me, the cat maybe on his way out to prowl, or a door closing. When you wake in the middle of the night in New York City you're always afraid there might be a good reason, apart from your own pattern of sleep. I woke warily and listened. I'd forgotten that Gil existed, that he was a few inches away from me. I fell back into the timeless condition of being alone in the room, in the apartment, in the hot grip of forces beyond my reckoning. I never surrender to fear in such situations. I just listen, as if I were camping in the wilds and listening for the telltale footsteps of marauders. It was the neighborhood I lived in that determined this response, but I had no wish to change my neighborhood. This was what I was used to, and here at least I understood the struggles of those around me. They were my own struggles. So I lay still for a long moment listening and heard nothing abnormal—a stray cat's howl, the clipped moan of the bakery machines, some traffic, a siren, my breathing. My loins felt good as I stretched, and I remembered Gil. I turned over to look at him.

He wasn't there. All the lights were out. I called him. No answer. I got up. "Where are you?" I said aloud. His clothes were gone. No note in the kitchen. I stepped into the bathroom and out again, listening to the machines downstairs. They sound louder in the kitchen and bathroom, thrusting not moaning. Why would he leave without even scribbling a note? Something made me step back into the bathroom again. I pulled the light cord. My face resembled itself in the mirror. It had nothing new to tell me.

I had no intention of taking another shower. The curtain was drawn. Goldfish with open mouths and half-shut eyelids swam without moving in front of me, row after row. I had left the curtain open but Gil could have . . . Drowned in a pool of tepid water on the other side of the curtain? I shuddered that faint possibility away. His clothes were gone, and he didn't leave a note. He gave no signs of a suicidal disposition. I am too often the victim of an overworked imagination. I decided to call its bluff. I drew the curtain aside. Gil wasn't there, of course, but I didn't feel any better. If anything, I felt worse. Dr. Ridley was staring impassively at me, his worn, tense body stiffening fast. It was very warm in the bathroom, but I shivered anyway. The body in my tub didn't seem at all fresh or vital. It was definitely another species. I went into the kitchen and sat down. I was glad that I'd cleared the table last night. The sight of food would have been too much. I made the tactical error of looking at the floor. The cat's half-nibbled sliver of Cheddar cheese was still there and two roaches were keeping it company. I looked briefly at them and then walked quickly to the sink. I got there in time.

After that was over, I got more serious. Outside my windows it was still pitch-black night and there was still an uninvited body in my bathtub, clothed in a sleeveless white undershirt (like the Italian boys, but Ridley had only a flabby, pasty body to show off), gabardine slacks, a pair of sandals. Dr. Ridley's house call left me with an outstanding problem. I approached the phone to call the police. In real life people don't dispose of bodies themselves—they call the cops. Then I remembered: this is not real life, this is a design of which you are a more or less unwilling part. Once you call the police you put yourself in their power, you mark yourself for their action, you give yourself a chance to spend a lot of time under their thumb, you suffer the print of their existence.

I threw on some clothes. From the shelf in the one closet I grabbed an old wool blanket covered with cat hair. I returned to the bathroom. The doctor was still in. He was a thin little man, that much was in my favor. I needed something in my favor, and that would have to do. The only way I could manage this was to work fast and not to think about what it was I was moving.

I threw the blanket over him, apologizing to him under my breath. He deserved better treatment. Anybody did, except the practical jokers who put him here. But I didn't want to touch any part of him. I cursed myself, filled myself with hatred, and started to move.

In fifteen minutes, with slowly decreasing strength, I'd got my one-hundred-thirty-pound package all the way to the nearest living-room window. The hard work had been getting it out of the tub. I was drenched with sweat and trembling from the effort. I'd scraped my knuckles on every available surface. I'm not a big woman or a particularly strong one, but if someone had asked me I'd have thought I was at least twice as strong as I seemed to be. But now I'd have to move even faster. I couldn't be caught on the roof as the light came up. It would be embarrassing.

With a lot of maneuvering I got the package a little better than halfway out the window, headfirst. The blanket kept falling off Ridley's head, as if he objected to being smothered. I found some twine to tie it down. Then I removed the fan from the other window and stepped onto the roof. There were two lights on in the windows of the surrounding buildings. They weren't close, but they were a chance I'd have to take. There was no one at either of them.

The machines were still kneading Italian bread downstairs. I hoped they'd keep at it a while longer, because I needed a bit of time to slide my package over the side into the narrow empty lot where people have been tossing their garbage ever since I've been a tenant. I grabbed my package. It thudded out of my hands onto the roof. I froze, closed my eyes and waited. Nothing happened, so I picked the body up again, grabbing it around the middle. The edge of the wall was miles away, but I had to give it a try. I started to pull and realized I couldn't move another inch. I was dead, ready to cry.

There are moments when life is not a through street. I breathed deeply, crouched and started to spin my package end over end. After every other spin I stopped to look at the two lit windows. Each time they looked empty. Each second I got nearer to collapse. At last I reached the edge of the roof. I had to lift the body once more to get it out of my sight forever. I lifted one end first, propping it on the railing. I reached for the other end, lifted it and watched the whole thing topple back. I looked at it lying on the roof. It was fated to follow me around. Nothing seemed to give me that last burst of adrenaline I needed to finish the job. They had me. A head would poke out of the window and scream. Then the machines in the bakery stopped. The silence frightened me. It was like a judgment. I picked up Ridley and heaved him over. I very nearly heaved myself over with him. When he landed there was a noise like any other heavy bit of garbage landing amid rubble.

I stood up and checked the two windows. No one, not even a shadow. Holding on to the iron railing, I looked over the edge. Ridley's body had half spilled out of my blanket. I gripped the railing as tight as I could—my blanket, with my cat's hairs all over it. I might as well have stuck my cab license in his pocket. I was dizzy for a moment, my fingers and toes tingling. I knew I had to climb down. I put my foot on the rung after checking the windows once again. I almost wished someone would see me so this could come to an end.

At the bottom I had to jump to avoid stepping on Ridley. The twine around the blanket had broken. I tried to roll him off the blanket. He wouldn't move. I picked up one edge and yanked. He rolled over. I yanked again. He slid off suddenly, and I fell back onto a mound of garbage. A cloud of flies blackened the air above me. I scrambled away, dragging the blanket along and grabbed the ladder. Ridley had rolled into a shallow ravine. I kicked some newspapers so they partially covered him. It was as much as I could manage without screaming. I ascended the ladder, every fiber of my body, every bit of skin, feeling as if it was crawling with vermin. I stumbled back through my window, half expecting to find another corpse tucked under the sheet.

I sat without moving on the edge of the bed. I was too tired to lie down. Every so often my arms twitched of their own accord. My fingers were too swollen to touch my palms. Beads of sweat rolled down my forehead. With many hesitations and false starts I washed, changed my clothes and hid the blanket under the linen in the closet.

My apartment had a grotesque appearance of normality, or rather normality suddenly seemed grotesque to me. I was beginning to have trouble figuring out why people did things like get up in the morning to go to work, or go to a movie, or sit in subways. I didn't pursue this train of thought too long. The phone rang, and my pulse throbbed in my ears again. Caught. I answered it.

"Here's the way it looks, kid. You've got a serious drainage problem in your bathroom. And we're sending some people in uniforms to come take a look. We thought we'd give you a minute or two to prepare yourself first." It was Frederick's voice, as expectant as the new dawn. I looked out the window. It was getting light, as mornings often do. They thought I'd still be sleeping, that they'd enhance my misery by giving me a few seconds to discover the trouble I was in, and who was responsible for it.

I cleared my throat. "I appreciate the way you're looking after me. I'll be sure to put in a good word for you with the police when they get here."

"Don't bother, kid. They won't listen. And why should they when they've got you and the goods in the john?" He put raucous emphasis on "the goods in the john." It was his punch line. He'd stayed up all night just to deliver it.

"I'm really not that swift, Frederick. How 'bout if I put Ridley on the line? Maybe he'll get it."

Before I hung up I savored the odor of confusion wafting from the receiver. I stuffed an extra blouse and a few toiletries in my canvas bag, and removed the last of my cash from its resting place between the pages of the first volume of *How Things Work*. I was nearly a block away before I heard the sirens. My body was stiff, but it moved faster when I heard them. Three flashing red lights rounded my street and poured themselves into the dawn. A few windows opened on the upper floors of the tenements and sleepy heads poked out. Several uniforms entered by the door I'd just left ajar. I stopped to watch a moment. I'd had too little sleep and I was exhausted, but I watched because it still seemed not quite credible that these uniforms were now strutting around my apartment, opening drawers and examining bits of paper. The violation bewildered me.

I made it to a coffee shop on Broadway and bought the *Times* and breakfast special number three. I didn't think about how they were ransacking my house, legal thugs this time instead of the illegal brand. I wondered how long it would take them to discover Ridley's body.

I knew what I should do now—call a friend, tell her I needed a place to stay, go there, shower in her modern stall shower and nap in her bed. This knowledge almost overpowered me. I knew which friend to call, what to say. The waitress filled my coffee cup to fortify me for my decision. Broadway was dense with Puerto Ricans rushing out of the subways on the way to the garment sweatshops. I watched them for a few minutes as they swarmed toward their jobs. Body after body streamed past the window in orderly procession. How could they keep going in the knowledge that the day ahead would be exactly like all the days before? Or maybe there wasn't any choice.

After a while, the numbers thinned. They were working now, bent over machines, producing more shoddy or useless junk. I couldn't call my friend. It would represent a return to normalcy. I never wanted to be normal again, to have a defined regular position in the ordinary lunacy of events. I preferred having a .32 in my canvas bag and living on the edge of the fantasy that I'd chosen after Hoyt smashed against the long brick wall on Forty-seventh Street. I knew that these events wouldn't last much longer, a few days perhaps, and then I'd be forced to accept my daily life again, to live inside my contradictions and struggle once more to play them out.

But for now I didn't have to recall why I was living—I'd pushed this bizarre situation far enough that I had to act. I had no reason to murder anyone, not even Frederick and Taylor, but I could see why some people did murder others. What I couldn't see was why there wasn't constant mayhem on the streets.

16

I took the Seventh Avenue line uptown. There were seats, but I held on to a pole. After a while I noticed that I was gripping the pole like a lifeline. My stomach lurched in time to the car. That was all right because you expect the IRT to treat you that way. The harder part was climbing the steps after I got off. My legs kept reminding me that I'd exploited them. My body was beginning to rebel, warning me to return to routine or face a gimpy future. I hobbled up toward daylight.

The thick, pasty air was a blessing when I emerged from the subway. It was almost breathable. The high rise in which Connie Fortini lived, a warren exclusively for single rabbits, was ten years old and already showing the stress marks of overcrowding and overcirculation. One of the flocked mirrors in the cramped lobby was chipped, and the carpet, though clean, was worn thin on the path from exit to elevator. Like laboratory rabbits, the building's inhabitants seldom broke with their fate—they hopped in a straight line from point to point. Taped to the elevator's Formica-paneled wall a Xeroxed sheet announced a cold-beer T.G.I.F. party on the eleventh floor hosted by Rick and Wade. I made it to the tenth floor.

Mrs. Berndt answered my ring as if she'd been waiting for me to show up. "Yes, yes," she said, grabbed my forearm and pulled me through a hall into a room that was only a little wider.

I was all right as long as I didn't have to climb.

Connie's living room was a near-replica of my mother's, with newer furniture, less clutter, less memorabilia. A portable color TV on an end table next to a large ivory lamp composed of a pair of glazed plaster dice was tuned to a game show. Periodically a wave of applause and screaming washed over us.

But the coffee table, white polyethylene with lethal edges sharp enough to thin-slice bologna, took up all our attention. It was stacked with crisp wads of ten- and twenty-dollar bills. They looked phony. Mrs. Berndt stood over the coffee table, making it even more phony. "Fifteen thousand exact," she said. She picked up a single stack and riffled it. Her movements were a good deal more vigorous now than they had been yesterday. Money can be a surer stimulant than a blood transfusion. She picked up a second stack and snapped that at me.

"Give me a hint," I said.

"Fifteen thousand exact," she said.

I believed her. I knew she could count. She was born counting. I took the stack out of her grip and put it back on the pile. Then I sat down on the couch next to the coffee table. The old lady remained standing on the other side.

I looked at the money. There was some screaming on the set. Someone had won and was crying hysterically. Colored lights were flashing behind the winner. The faces of the lamp dice showed five black dots and two black dots.

"Eve give it me," Mrs. Berndt said to draw me back. When I looked at her this time I noticed that the wig and penciled eyebrows had flown the coop. She'd gained ten years in age since yesterday, but at the moment they seemed to be ten years of strength.

"Connie help also."

"Not Wincey? He said he'd help you, didn't he?"

"Ach, Wincey," she waved him out the window. Everything was flying away in the wind whipping around the tenth floor of Connie's building, everything except the cash. "Words, big heaps of words he bury you in. But Connie have all the heart."

"What did Connie do?"

"I have key weeks already. Connie helps me find money. Connie is smart cookie."

It took a while, but with a number of detours and a few dead ends she navigated her way through the whole story. Connie had had Mrs. Berndt take a Valium the night before. In the morning, still worrying about the old lady, she called in to Wincey and told him not to expect her for a few hours. Then she tried to pry loose some basic financial information from her guest. It was slow in coming, and when it did come it was all of the kind that would have made a Gray Panther smile bitterly: insurance policies that had lapsed or been redeemed, a small inheritance saved for twenty-five years that the old man's hip operation had eaten away, a few valuables sold to pay for Evelyn's funeral. Connie had pressed her: There's nothing left, nothing you're forgetting? There was fire, the old lady said—I get nothing but my pocketbook, and pointed to it, a humble black bag sitting on the coffee table. Connie reached for it and dumped its contents on the couch between them. The two of them rummaged through the litter. "What's this?" Connie asked, picking up a small key. It was stamped with a bank's name, a three-digit number, and a warning: DO NOT COPY. The old lady glanced at the key. Eve had sent her that key. When? She called me about it the night she died, told me she was sending it. What did she tell you about the key? Nothing, except to hold on to it for her. Had Mrs. Berndt ever heard of a safety deposit box? A what?

In ten minutes the two were out the door; in thirty, they were walking into the bank. "So Eve be good to me. I could count on her." Fifteen thousand times over.

"Anything else in the box? Or just the money?"

"*Just* money? How can you say *just* money?"

Good question. "Was it empty otherwise?"

"I think that's all. Connie look for me. I am too crazy thinking of fire *und* Papa to think."

"Where is Connie?"

She glanced up at me, her eyes as seared by the money as they'd been yesterday by the fire. I still liked her, mostly because she was so tough, but I'd liked her a little more yesterday. If suffering didn't break her, money might. "She go to office. What you think I do with money? When I scold Eve as child, I call her slobby teenager, she say, 'Don't worry, Mama, someday I'm going to clean up.' And she laugh." Mrs. Berndt laughed. Her hoarse crabbed voice had all the merriment of a broom handle cracking.

"Did Connie take anything out of the box?"

"I didn't see. There were many many of these safety deposited shelfs in the room. Row, row, row. I think if each little shelf have fifteen thousand in, then how much?"

Her first purchase ought to be a calculator. "So Connie didn't take anything else out of box?" I said it just like that, my speech patterns becoming defective.

The old lady shook her head vigorously, certainly. "Young lady, there was nothing."

I sensed now how gimpy my future was likely to be.

Mrs. Berndt said, "She take my shopping bag I always keep in this part, see," and she showed me a folded plastic item peaking out of her handbag. "She unfolds it and we dump the money in and go, that's it." She started moving the stacks of green bills around.

"Didn't you count it?"

"I not counting. I know exact number. I was looking for receipt."

"What receipt?"

"Connie maybe put it in pocket. All right, I don't need it extra."

"What receipt?"

"I didn't pay attention. It was under the money I think maybe."

"It was in the box?"

"Yes, under money."

I picked up Connie's phone and dialed Wincey's office. When she answered I told her where I was and that I was coming down to see her. "I want to see the receipt you collected from Mrs. Berndt."

"Don't come by for that, Emma. It don't mean a thing, honey." She seemed to mean it, and I tended to believe her, but beggars can't be choosers.

I said good-by to Mrs. Berndt. She took my arm affectionately. "What you think about money?" she said.

I shrugged. It was beginning to be my favorite response. If Tony Corrigenda was the programmer for life's gestures, he'd ask, Is your shrug cosmic? The old lady was still waiting for an answer. "Don't save it," I recommended.

I took the IRT and the BMT downtown. Klein's square neon ruler was facing me when I climbed out of the subway. A few moments later I pulled the door that said PULL FOR WINCEY. The room was even more frigid than the last time. On the other side of the carpeted tundra Connie Fortini glanced up from her desk. Unlike the other day she was wearing a sweater. I took it as a sign she might keep herself under wraps this time.

"Mrs. Berndt got fifteen grand. What did you get?"

"I'm an honest person. You shouldn't talk like that," she said.

"I didn't mean to offend you," I said. "But I'm looking for something, and it might be only a scrap of paper."

She looked at me doubtfully. "Mmmm," she said. "I can't help it. It's the way my mother brought me up to be aboveboard and expect others to be aboveboard in return."

Aboveboard. How do we test our actions? The nearest ruler is the standard of morality. She wanted me to say something first, because from her corner there was nothing doubtful about her. There was sense in that. I didn't have any protective coloration and I'd already been caught in a semi-lie in her presence. But I wanted to try once more anyway. I stood over her desk. "What came out of the box?"

She was adamant; not unfriendly, just adamant. "No, I don't know the first thing about you."

I nodded. "I'll keep it short, Connie. A close friend of mine was murdered a couple of days ago. What happened to Evelyn Berndt had some connection or other to it. Maybe she didn't really kill herself. Maybe she knew something somebody didn't want her to know, and maybe they killed her for it. Maybe, in other words, she died from an overdose of knowledge. I have to find out. What did you get out of the box?"

"The congressman had nothing to do with it, you were wrong about that," her voice firm.

"Somebody did."

Her eyes raced right and left on her desk. Her index finger traced the profile of a pop-psych guru printed like a Roman coin on the cover of a paperback. She was a slow, careful reader. Did she believe what she read? Did she feel yes? Apart from making love I could almost count the number of times I felt yes. "Suppose I give you the receipt and you go away."

"Don't you want to know what it's about—or if it's about anything?"

"You don't understand. My job is ultraimportant to me. My boss has always treated me with consideration." Her eyes couldn't have been wider.

"But suppose he was . . ."

She was already shaking her Afro. "I can't suppose right now. I have to do what I think is right. And that's it."

She took a small folded piece of paper from her desk drawer. It was a slow operation. Each move contested a hundred hesitations, all chanting "What can I do? What can I do?" I didn't want to put the transaction on this level. It would have been better if she had wanted to know what was happening.

She held out the paper as if it burned her fingers. It was a big buildup and a big letdown. I unfolded the paper. It was a receipt, all right, made out to Wincey, but it was a retail store receipt. Electra Electric. $79.95 plus 7% tax, $5.60, total $85.55. That was it, except for one detail. A two-line unsigned note in a neat, angular hand:

> Is it snake eyes, Connie?
> Or my ace in the hole??

Connie was watching me. I read it three times before I asked. "Well, which is it?"

"You gotta believe me because I am a truthful person."

"Cross my heart."

"I haven't the foggiest."

I was hoping for something a little more definite, something even slightly definite, a date, a name, a place, animal, vegetable, mineral. I asked her all the questions you can think of, and she wrestled with them, and every time they floored her.

"The best I can do," she said, when we'd gone round

the bend for the fifth time, "is ask the congressman does he remember what he bought. But I know he won't, 'cause I don't think he bought it whatever it was because she—Evelyn, God rest her soul—probably did in his name."

"Maybe we should call Electra Electric."

"I already did. No soap."

They say everything has its price tag, but here was the tag and no telling what was the thing unless Evelyn's cryptic message meant something. I read it a few more times trying to break through her handwriting to her mind. She had an either/or, make it or break it, win-or-lose mind. You throw the dice and if you crap out. . . . I stuck there, Connie looking at me, while I stared straight through her trying to dislodge whatever it was that was nudging me, trying to shake it off while it leaned on me. I walked around the big empty room, ending up sitting on a gray steel desk.

"I should call Mrs. Berndt. See if she's okay," Connie muttered.

I got up and put my hand over hers while she was still dialing. "I'm surprised you don't have touch-tone," I said, as she looked up, a little surprised herself.

"I do at home," she said uncertainly.

"I noticed. Did Evelyn give you anything to keep for her in the last year?"

She shook her head, "She did give me a present for my birthday."

"When?"

"Oh, six weeks now. I'm a Cancer, a full-fledged crab."

"What did she give you?"

"You probably saw it when you were up. A lamp, the one near the TV."

I put the receipt in my pocket. "Tell Mrs. Berndt I'm on my way."

She nodded and went back to dialing. When I got to the glass door she said, "Good luck."

After I got back, Mrs. Berndt hovered near me saying,

"Connie said to tell you something." I was standing near the TV. I turned it off. "She said my Evelyn said it was something someone bought for her housewarming when she moved into her flat, and it didn't fit her colors, and could she use it and not to say another word about its being expensive and not to mention it to you know who. Who is you know who?"

"I couldn't say," I said.

The five and the two faced me so I looked on the other side. One black dot in the center of each ivory die. Snake eyes. It didn't fit Connie's colors either. I turned it on and then off and pulled the plug. It was an ordinary ugly overly expensive lamp, the kind Electra Electric probably sells five plus two times a day. I put it on its side.

Mrs. Berndt held her tongue watching me.

The underside of the base was covered with burlap. A white seam was double-stitched across the middle "Did you ever teach Evelyn to sew?" I asked Mrs. Berndt.

"She learn. She hate it. She say if it rip, throw it out and start over."

That sounded like Evelyn. I ripped the burlap. There was something stuffed inside in a small envelope.

Mrs. Berndt looked back and forth from me to the lamp. "Money?" she asked. I switched on the TV for her.

17

I sat in a chain donut shop booth. Outside the sun was deep-frying New York City. The papers, still a little crumpled, were beside my coffee cup. I still hadn't figured out Connie Fortini. It had been all right that Mrs. Berndt's greedy side had resurfaced. You can like old ladies with the courage to be awful. But you want a younger woman to come through. She'd practically begged me to let her off the hook even though she wasn't on the hook. She'd seen Wincey's name on the receipt, and that was enough for her. Then again, if my choices were among a heavy date, a rabbit warren and a good boss, I'd have to make the same choice.

I had the papers. Whatever Evelyn Berndt was after, they would be likely to tell me. There were five sheets of paper, two photocopies and three originals. The photocopies were dated August '67 and November '67, the originals June and July of '74. All five were documents from SBI, Sypher-Breaks Inc., the giant data-control organization.

Headed by SBI's logo, the earliest page began midsentence and ended midsentence. It appeared to me at first to be part of an abstract of a medical report, its language a hybrid of medical, scientific and businessese.

Physical alteration of (enemy) subject response, stress due to serial interrogation techniques, effects of chemical additives upon subjects in prior circumstances of extreme restraint, narrowed cost of failure in stress factors, interrogation styles plotted (see Fig. 18A) against cost in man-hours, purposive vs. random data net, chemical grid evinces new horizons of response, differential response along racial curve. It wasn't hard for me to look at this, even without seeing the curves and figures or testing the additives, and connect it to my last conversation with Gil about his father's business and its harmless data-control projects for the government. Crisp black letters formed into columns and marched down the page. My guess was that they were really dried-out bits of flesh, the flesh of native hostiles bearing the toothmarks of the great predatory reptile whose logo swam on the white paper.

I sipped some coffee before turning to the next page. How did Evelyn get this? Why was she hiding it? I moved up to November '67. A boldface heading read "Recommended By-Product Followup Study," on tissue-thin paper unlike any made in this country:

> Paralysis of central nervous system functions due to experimental chemical influence leaves brain response operational in subjects to date, with oral communicative skills intact; suggest further research for stateside usability potential. Subject antagonism muted by repeated application. Have strongly urged authorities to suspend other severe interrogation techniques without result. Scientific observation at a standstill. Any stateside support system available to secure authorities' cooperation?

The signature was illegible, but typed under the scrawl was the name R. E. Ridley, M.D. Below that: November 4, 1967, Hue.

I read this message from the dead several times. Ridley was a real company man, even as a practitioner of torture in Southeast Asia, stumbling on additives with such useful side effects, and he couldn't wait to write home with the news. Only yesterday he'd succumbed to a taste of his own medicine.

I was about to try page three when a paper coffee cup and a paper plate garnished with a donut were set on the table. I looked up. An elderly gent pushed wire-rimmed spectacles up higher on the bridge of his lean nose and gave me the faintest of smiles. I pushed together the papers spread on the table. Compact and neatly dressed in a work shirt buttoned up to the neck and old woolen trousers held up by suspenders, he took out the *Post* folded under his arm, thought better of it, and dropped it onto the seat as he maneuvered stiffly into the booth. He looked at me again with that whisper of a smile, and I murmured an apology.

"Think nothing of it. I wouldn'ta disturbed your studying there except this was the last table left, as you can see for yourself." In the last half-hour the shop had filled up with the early lunch trade.

"So I see," I said, smiling politely.

He broke his donut into four parts. "My four-course lunch," he said, and then he leaned toward me confidentially. "The thing about it is this: I hate to disturb someone so involved like you there because it's probably something very important you're working on . . ." he stopped speaking, but his mouth and jaw were still working. The hollows under his cheekbones trembled. He had more to say. It was aching to get out but he was keeping a leash on it to allow me time to reward his speculation.

"It's not much of anything really—just some old papers."

He nodded and then pushed his spectacles higher again. "The kind of news there is today—enough to make you puke." He popped a bit of donut into his mouth and talked through it. "You could half expect to find an ordinary person like yourself"—he unfurled his fist in my direction—"or even an old warhorse like myself"—the gnarled hand returned to its owner—"with another set of Pentagon papers or some other pile of secret bullshit, excuse my French." By now I'd folded the papers in half. "You want my opinion, all these conspiracy ideas aren't worth the paper they're printed on. The big guys just invent the whole thing so us fuddy-duddies on Social Security have something to think about while they pick our pockets."

"I have to get a move on." I edged over to get up. "But I think you're pretty right."

"Here, take my paper. You don't have to read it right away. Wait till you're outside or something."

"You keep it. I'm not really in the mood." I was standing now.

"Take it," he ordered, "use it to keep the flies away." He held it out while staring at me as if there was a fly on my nose.

I followed his directions and waited till I was back on the street to unfold the paper. I glanced at the headlines as I rounded the corner and then tossed it into the nearest trashcan. Traffic held me at the corner. I glanced back to face a rare breeze. The paper, thrown atop the heap of trash, peeled away its front page. My hack picture ran across two columns at the bottom of page three. The small headline read: WHERE IS SHE? I retrieved the paper. The story beside the picture said I was wanted for questioning in one, possibly two killings. The facts were either misstated or incorrect, but there was no questioning the fact that I was wanted. The traffic lights changed. The WALK sign flashed, so I started walking. I saw somebody reading the *Post*, and I started walking faster. Every so often I looked back. I'd been checking the newspapers. This was the first to call me by name.

I would have looked back more often except there was so much in front of me to watch out for. Every person that bothered to look at me was, I knew, about to scream,

"It's her! It's her! The killer!" The old man had kept pushing at his spectacles to be sure it was me—but he knew. I walked a block, three blocks, just to test if I'd be picked out, each second tensed to run. Whenever I approached a cop I stopped breathing. Every corner had the sinister, fraudulently empty look of a spider's web. I stopped into a shop and bought cheap sunglasses. But I didn't wear them because they made me look as if I was hiding something. I walked a little farther.

No romantic ideas about being an outlaw pursued me. I ran through a list of possible hiding places, another list of friends who would help, a third list of how to go underground. I didn't bother making a list of my delusions about American justice. It would be too short. They could hang at least one killing on me if they felt like it. They. I sounded like the anticonspiratorial old man in the donut shop. I had some information—they had knowledge. I'd processed some data—they had control of it. I was on the street—they were after me.

18

I detoured into a row of phone booths. I needed protection for a while from Broadway's swollen stream of sudden enemies. And the alluring syllables of Paisley Besame's name kept flowing through me at odd moments. That, and the fact that she was Evelyn Berndt's roommate, made me want to check her out.

The decor in the first booth must have been too "moderne" for a previous occupant, so he'd baroqued it with spray paint the passionate color of cherry popsicles. With instinctive restraint he'd left the phone box a stark black to offset his chef-d'oeuvre, the pure cherry receiver. The aesthetic pleasure was so intense I barely noticed that the directory was missing.

When you've found the perfect phone booth it can be a little raw to reenter reality. I stumbled into the next booth. The half-chewed corpse of the phone book, layered with scorch marks and grime, lay cringing on the floor.

The next booth had been visited by an impatient dog. The one after that had the right look and smell and a directory. No Besame, P. That was all right. I didn't let it upset me. I put a dime in the phone and waited for the tone. I got what sounded like Radio Iceland with authentic static but no tone. I didn't get the dime back either. I was about to waltz on to my next partner when I heard it drop.

It was a sucker play, and I was the sucker. I put two fingers in the slot. Probably there was a dime in there, but there was something else too because it grabbed my fingers. You know how it's hard sometimes to figure out where to put your chewed gum? It didn't take more than seven or eight minutes to wipe off the slack crud, thanks to the pages I ripped out of the directory.

Twenty minutes later I'd called Barnard and three other places. I hadn't lost that much change, and I'd found out where Paisley Besame hung her hat. Living up near Columbia, pursuing the academic life I'd avoided, Paisley Besame was a graduate teaching assistant in anthropology.

As I ambled down into the IRT, trying to look like an average citizen, a fuzzy loudspeaker announced there'd been an accident on the line. That meant another of the ancient cars had broken down in the tunnel. The trains would be running slow. I wanted desperately to take a cab, but I wanted even more to preserve the cash I had left. While I might be stopped at any moment, I might also be forced to wander in the streets for a day or two. My future was the next few hours.

I stood waiting on the uptown platform holding the *Post* in front of my face. Soon I'd worn the tabloid down to the sports pages. I read an inspirational interview with a southpaw who called on God to guide every breaking pitch. "He made me a pretty fair reliever," he said. "I get hoots now and then from the cynics but I made a pact with the Almighty not to ask His help with any of my other problems if He just be good to me on the mound." So far God hadn't let him down. The caption ran, "God's Jumpin' Screwball." Number 7 screamed around the corner.

On the ride uptown I ducked my head and unfolded the SBI documents. The next sheet was a summary report of experiments at the Institute. Oral ingestion of a chemical agent not dissimilar in composition to monosodium glutamate resulted experimentally in gross temporary impairment of central nervous system functions (in a broadly delimited area) with simultaneous stimulation of certain areas of the brain. An agent, no longer an additive. You see how drugs move up in the world. Stamped "confidential," this overview signed by Ridley was sprinkled with algebraic equations. The next page allowed itself a high-flown or agent-induced vision. "Relieve the human brain of the physical requirements of its host and its capability subsumes, in the abstract, any computer technology. Subject for further task-force research."

I would never have guessed Ridley to be such a dreamer, but I should have. I'd done time in the Institute. Such a drug, purified of adverse side effects, could have wide practical applications for a corporate dragon the size of Sypher-Breaks, and Ridley knew it. It had only been a matter of a few refinements to move from torturing native hostiles like the Vietnamese to torturing hostile natives like me. A few refinements—eight or nine years of work. Progress is our most important product. Had a vision of a brain freed of the physical encumberment of the body coursed through Ridley's cranium when the moment came to die? My pity for the man ebbed.

I read the last page quickly. It was P.R.-style rhetoric about market projections for the knowledge drug. Evelyn Berndt apparently thought such knowledge salable. The question was—Who was her last customer? Who helped her take her last bath? Or did she do it all alone, disgusted and depressed with her progress through the world, degraded by contact with men like Ridley, who reduce even their own effort and sweat to sordid grappling and blackmail and still end up in a bathtub? It must be possible to draw a line through these papers to Ridley to his connection with Evelyn. I just didn't know where to start drawing.

These half-baked ideas got me to Paisley Besame's building, which was a rundown six-story near Amsterdam. This was a neighborhood I knew only from my cab by night, endless side streets and scowling brownstones. "Besame" was typed on mailbox 4F with "Mastbaum" printed below it. I climbed the four flights, each step a little slower. Odors of Spanish cooking lingered in hallways lit on each landing by a single yellow bulb. People lived behind these doors in their separated apartments, living their separated lives. If she lived up to her billing, Paisley would subscribe to the *Times* and would never dirty her fingers on the *Post* except to check when *The Seventh Seal* played the Thalia, an uptown art theater. So I didn't fear her recognizing me. I knocked.

A mechanical doll answered. Carrying around Ridley's batty schemes to chemically engineer the brain into a more predictable and reliable machine made me susceptible to simulations of robot life. Paisley Besame's way of moving scared me a little at first. It made it worse somehow that she had prematurely gray hair, as if the little doll's withered brain cells not only had betrayed her by draining her of color but had condemned her to live through a second shrunken girlhood atoning for some unknown mistake. Take the gray away, and she'd look eleven years old. A black tube top and tight designer jeans with flower-embroidered pockets fit her like summer style-setters in Barbie's newest collection. But her voice was clipped and businesslike. I could only guess that the package libeled the product.

"I'm really sorry. The flat's already taken. Try the super on the second floor. He might know of something available on the block. You aren't likely"—she dipped slightly as if curtseying and swung gracefully sideways to allow me a peek at her apartment—"to find quite as nice a place, but there's a lot of really adequate housing on this block. One Hundred Ninth isn't bad either. There's one bombed-out mess at the end of the block near Columbus but . . ."

"I'm not keen on your apartment."

"You're not?" she said doubtfully. "You'd be the first that wasn't. I've had, oh"—she bounced a step to the kitchen table and picked up a legal pad on which I could see a long list headed name, address, offer—"better than thirty today who are dying for it, figuratively speaking." Her wide black eyes were immovable in their plaster frame. She compensated by batting her lids at high speed. The mannerism gave her a look of permanent amazement.

"Oh, your apartment looks adorable. I could imagine spending the next forty years in it. But I didn't come up to look at it."

"You didn't?"

I shook my head. "I'm a journalist. I'm doing an article—or a series actually—for the *Post* on the transition that young women are making from the sixties to the seventies, the choices they're making, the compromises, if any, with the intransigence of the last decade. One of my interview contacts gave me your name as an interesting woman to talk to."

"Oh, really?" she said, cranking out a smile. "Who was that?" The phone rang. It was a wall phone within arm's reach, even her arm, but she didn't reach for it, she jabbed at it as if seizing an unruly puppy by the collar. "Mastbaum," she said, and after a pause, "No, it's taken, it's T-A-K-E-N, yes, well, I was asking for offers over eight hundred dollars. Uh-huh." She gestured for me to sit at the handmade kitchen table.

It wasn't really a table, it was more like Plato's Idea of a Table, so when I sat down I tried not to touch it. There was no way I could measure up.

Paisley hung up, bit her lip and glanced at me. "With the housing crunch as it is in this city, I have a sort of principle against what I'm doing. But Sasha just killed himself over this place, and it wouldn't be fair. It just wouldn't be fair just to let it go. He broke his back to make it perfect."

I looked at the place. Nervous or not, she was right. It was so perfect I'd have taken a bet Sasha was cooling his heels in Bellevue for the summer. The walls he'd straightened had the religious whiteness of cocaine. The forest of his imagination was all natural oak, lots of it, and no other material substance, fashioned, planed, petted and placed exactly right with exact force. In other words, I didn't see any nails. Sasha was at least nonviolent. And there were ferns, rows of them, the same kind, the same size, in the same hanging pots. They were a necessary touch—life itself.

"So who was it gave you my name?" she asked, checking her references.

"Well, it was some weeks ago." I paged through my address book. "Her name was, here it is, Evelyn Berndt. She died unfortunately a few weeks after I saw her."

Paisley's hand twitched and while it was in the air she used it to fluff her hair. I wasn't sure whether she was always nervous because she had to be so aggressive or so aggressive because she couldn't help being nervous. "I didn't see too much of Evelyn. It was sweet of her to give you my name."

"I didn't spend much time with her, of course, but she didn't seem the depressive type to me. I could be wrong."

"You aren't. Evelyn didn't have a suicidal bone in her body. She'd never give up." She plucked a Gauloise from the pack lying on the table. "I do research also," she said. "I'm an urban anthropologist. I'm into documenting the synchronic patterns of city life, the structural and cultural patterns that are the essential motors for urbanism. Are you into anthro at all? You know, like what does everybody do on their lunch hour? How do people typically interact on the subway to and from work? What are the most popular jokes during Happy Hour? That kind of thing."

"Sounds interesting. At the moment I'm into history."

"History. I can't get into that. It's too temporal." She crinkled her nose. "The blessing of anthro is that it's timeless. That's what I'm into most—timelessness."

"Evelyn Berndt talked a lot about her Barnard experience. It seems to have changed her life. She said that the only real difficult time came during the Josie Breakstone episode."

She brushed some cigarette ash into a clam shell stamped Atlantic City. Her movements were either perky or taut. "That was hard. We really suffered over that. The press, excuse me, and the cops. Especially the cops. But we got real close over it. That was the by-product."

"Since I interviewed her I've been thinking of making Evelyn more of a focus for my research. Maybe you could fill me in a little bit on her early years. You know what I mean, like was she a good roommate?"

"She's a wonder. Was a wonder." She raked her hair again. "Neat. The German in her, I guess."

"The place must have been a real wreck after the cops tore it up—when Josie disappeared I mean."

"Josie," she said. "I barely ever saw the girl. Always at one meeting after another. They said she disappeared and I said, naw, she's just at a meeting." She looked through me. "Seven years is a long meeting."

"Evelyn cleaned up that time?"

She nodded. "She always cleaned. In the paper they said her place was a wreck. Has to be something wrong there. She was neater than a pin." She stubbed the cigarette in the shell. It was half smoked. "I have to get out of here."

"This'll just take a moment," I said.

"No, I mean I'm moving out of the city to do my thesis. They gave me a thesis grant, and I have to go out of the city to write about it. Ironic?"

The phone rang again. She started to get to her feet, then stopped. "Let it ring. I must have had thirty calls before nine A.M. And people streaming through here endlessly. I have to collate these offers. I'm telling people it's taken, just because I can't handle any more."

"What are you going to get for the place?"

"At least twelve."

"Twelve?"

"Twelve hundred. I know that's awfully high for a three-room place, but everything is built-ins. You can see that. Sasha killed himself over it."

I wondered what method he used. Maybe he Varathaned himself to death. "You must hate having to turn down people without money."

The wide black eyes showed amazement, but anything could have been happening behind them. "I do. I hate it. Something should be done about it. But where can you start without screwing yourself first? That's the question."

"I want to give you time to add up everything before you're too exhausted, so let me just ask you a couple more questions about Evelyn, and then I won't need to bother you personally at all for my research."

She lit up again. "That sounds fair."

"Tell me, as long as we're talking about your Barnard experience, how did Evelyn and you manage to deal with the press and police during the Breakstone upset?"

"The last cop was the worst," she said. "Let me tell you, for somebody like me who always lives in the present, I have a holistic memory. He just dumped the place. He was very neat personally, of course, a little beefy, sweat on the least provocation. But he just pulled the place apart. He was TPF, which was a little odd. Brown hair. Used language poorly."

"How so?"

"Scrambled words. Tried to sound intelligent by using four-syllable words and kept muffing them. Evelyn and I did imitations of him after he left." She gave an abrupt laugh.

"Did he find what he was looking for?"

"No. He gave Evelyn a number to call in case she came across something. You're really into this case, aren't you?"

"I have a friend who's still investigating it."

"Good. It should be investigated. You want to know the sort of truth? I'm leaving the city because I'm scared. It's very weird to me, this Berndt thing. I didn't see Evelyn or anything—except to run into now and then. But that she's dead, that they got her, I can't take it. I've got to get out. It's too sick."

"Yes, that's what my friend thinks too. Except she thinks maybe she can find out who was responsible."

She puffed on another Gauloise, a cloud around her head. "Maybe, but then what?" She pulled at her hair again. "It still scares me. You know, I always think I went gray so young because of what happened to Josie. My hair was black as the ace of spades until then. I was only nineteen, you know."

The phone rang again, a harsh sound in the perfect little apartment.

19

AN hour later I was in a movie theater on Forty-second Street. I sat in an aisle seat and piled refuse from the floor on the seat beside me to discourage adventurers. I was too edgy to watch the movie. I watched the crowd, mostly black, mostly male. Not a well-dressed or with-it person in the house. As the shifting light played over their upturned faces, the crowd jumped, sprawled, leaned, romanced, felt-up, laughed, screamed and catcalled everything it could think of to make the movie come to life. In response the movie shot off loud guns and explosives every few minutes. At every burst of gunfire the audience rallied and rippled with outraged noise until the movie meekly faded to the level of chitchat. Then the contest began again.

I was beginning to feel like some of the rubbish piled next to me. Ignoring nods and invitations I slogged up the aisle, my shoes sticking to the soda-and-candy-caked floor. Alone in the turquoise room marked LADIES, I washed and changed my blouse. I stood before the mirror trying to smooth the wrinkles from the bright-blue cotton. The turquoise walls reflected behind me jangled like my nerves. The orange hot dog I'd gulped a while ago kept reminding me I'd eaten it as I brushed my hair and changed my earrings to match my blouse. This is what a homeless person must put up with I reminded the hot dog.

I trekked down the wide steps of the crumbling movie palace and dialed Gil's number at a pay phone. My third try. I was beginning to anticipate a long hard night. This time he answered.

"This is trouble on the other end," I said.

"That picture in the *Post* makes you look as if you were born to be bad."

"Still on page three?"

"Yep. At least until the *News* comes out. It says here—let me look—that you were arrested for disorderly conduct in 1970."

"1971. Very disorderly. During a day-care demonstration at City Hall. This cop was backing his scooter into a group of our kids. So I gave him a shove. Two minutes later four cops had me pinned over a squad car."

"Well, when are you going to give yourself up this time?"

"When I make the top ten."

"When?"

"I'm stuck. I have to get at least a little unstuck before I let them catch me. I figure I might have only tonight. I need some help with an idea I have. Come and pick me up."

I told him where to find me and returned to my seat. There was a chance he might call the cops. A woman with a gun in her hand was shooting at the audience. They loved it, yelling, "Aim this time, sister!" I closed my eyes. Who knows how much later I felt a tap at my shoulder. I jumped.

Gil, crouched in the aisle, whispered in my ear, "I've never been in one of these theaters before."

"A serious gap in your education."

"Let's run. The car's parked right in front."

We ran. As we hit the lobby, I saw a police towaway truck slide behind Gil's Granada.

"Stay here," he said. I wasn't about to move. He ran out to stop the officer from writing up a ticket. His clothes were fresh and clean and fit him perfectly. I tried to straighten my blouse again. It had been in my bag too long. As the truck pulled away, Gil motioned to me. I hopped in.

"We'll go around the corner and stop at the first convenient place."

We stopped in front of a deli with a pink neon sign that said HEROS. I looked at it. I thought that if that sign had been in a story I wrote when I was still writing stories, I would have had the neon H be dimmed or broken so that the sign carried a meaningful ambiguity. You can see why I had so much trouble writing.

A cool breeze blew in my face from the air-conditioner vent. Gil was looking at me expectantly. For no good reason the scar on his cheek irritated me.

"I bet you got that scar playing lacrosse or polo or chess." I used a tone appropriate for addressing Eichmann so that he couldn't be so well-bred as to ignore it. He hesitated.

"I've done something to annoy you," he said, chewing on his lip.

"Wrong. Your scar annoys me. It doesn't belong on your unspoiled innocent face. You shouldn't have any blemishes. They don't belong . . . Bad idea to leave like that, Gil. Not the kind of thing that cements a trusting relationship."

"But we made a clean getaway. Once I got rid of the tow."

"Sure we did." I watched his fingers play on the steering wheel. They stopped moving when he noticed me watching them. "But I meant last night."

"Last night. Right. That was pretty sneaky. You didn't think my note explained it at all?"

One hand touched my shoulder. I pushed it away and turned my body to face him. "What note?"

He scratched his temple. "You didn't see it? You must have. I left it under the salt shaker. Your cat doesn't eat paper, does she?"

"He."

"Does he? I'd made a very early date way out on the Island with some friends. It skipped my mind—for obvious reasons. It was too late to break it, and I didn't think it was right to wake you. So I left a note on the kitchen table."

I was thinking. "When Frederick and Taylor delivered Ridley, they must have grabbed your note. For some reason," I said.

"Then they did dump Ridley on you. That's about what I figured from the paper. How did you manage to get rid of him? Never mind, tell me later. But it figures. They want to hang Ridley on you—better remove the note."

Through the tinted windshield I saw Eighth Avenue on a random night in August with random pedestrians crossing the wide avenue. If I'd worked tonight I'd be dropping theatergoers at this corner just about now. I'd been a little more angry at Gil then he deserved. Maybe to protect myself from his reaction to the other things I had to say to him.

"I should have told you yesterday but I chickened out. Those two goons do their dirty work at the bidding of your father."

He stared at me. "What gave you that idea?" A touch of condescension.

"It's not an idea. I heard them say so when they thought I was no longer within earshot."

He banged the steering wheel with the heels of his hands. His face tightened, screwed up. In a minute he had the banging into a steady rhythm alternating with distorted cries of, "I knew it. I knew it. I knew it."

"How did you know, Gil?" I said it three or four times before I could get an answer. I put my hand on his wrists to stop the banging. "How did you know?"

Finally the steering wheel had got all that was coming to it. He didn't look at me but at the stream of cars heading up toward Columbus Circle. "You described them to me. But I didn't bother to think it out." Now he looked at me. "I don't like talking about this stuff."

"Don't." Whatever he had to say would be stained around the edges with self-pity. I regretted the times I'd encouraged men to quit pretending to be self-contained. I'd liked sleeping with Gil, but I couldn't handle another man's disordered emotions right now.

I looked out the window. The vent still blew cold air at me. My skin was going numb so I shut it. It was at least thirty seconds before he started speaking.

"My family's been fucked-up ever since Josie disappeared. You saw how off-the-beam my mother was. My father's worse. For a couple of years he was convinced that Josie'd been kidnapped by quote unquote radical revolutionaries. Once in the middle of a Vietnam documentary he kicked in the picture tube of the TV set. He pretty much withdrew from the business and after the divorce he started seeing a shrink three times a week. Bit by bit he's gotten better. But he's never been one hundred percent since. He blames himself for Josie's disappearance."

"Was he to blame?"

He shook his head. "No, and he offered huge rewards, hounded the police and FBI, he even, well, he kept at it." He shrugged and looked out his window.

"He even what?"

"He got Sypher to agree to break loose some of the company's security men to search for her."

"Was Sypher reluctant?"

"Sypher thinks Josie's dead. He didn't want to waste manpower."

"How many men did Sypher agree to waste?"

"One at first and then another part-time. I saw them once in my father's study."

"Frederick and Taylor?"

He nodded. "From your description."

Someone had turned up all the neon on Eighth Avenue as the sun faded. Cars and pedestrians streamed endlessly toward the theaters. We could have parked there for seven years next to the HEROS sign, and cars and pedestrians would still be streaming. Nothing ever changes in this city.

A silence was punctuated only by Gil's finger repetitively tapping the steering wheel. Finally he said, "Looks like you got your man." His voice was muffled, like the sounds of traffic.

Another gap was forming as I pushed forward. Another person was accidentally hurt as I crossed another street. Like most people he preferred seeing his father as just his father, certainly not as a rapacious character who would even kill to get what he wanted. And I was making that happen. I regretted not telling him yesterday what I knew.

"Maybe," I said. I was certain now that Breakstone had hired Frederick and Taylor. The knots in my stomach were drawn tighter than ever. "He'd be home right now, wouldn't he?"

"Probably he's at the Institute tonight."

I glanced at Gil. He was staring through the windshield.

"Dad keeps an office on the top floor. Sypher still handles most of the business end, but Dad is trying to interest himself in the activities of the Institute. He needs something to do besides collecting."

"Collecting?" My notion of someone who collects is a bill collector.

"Art. Anyway he's usually there every night till ten at least." Gil's speech was clipped.

"You want to say what's bothering you, Gil?"

He shook his head. "No." The chasm between us was now wider than Eighth Avenue.

"Listen, even knowing that much about your father only makes all this more confusing."

He glared at me. "Confusing? It sounds pretty clear to me."

"Nothing is nailed down. Evelyn Berndt had a safe-deposit box and in the box were some documents. How did she get them? On a guess—and I really like guessing—I'd say she got them from your sister."

Finally he stopped tapping. "What kind of papers?"

"They document the nature of Sypher-Breaks Inc.'s involvement in the war. There was nothing harmless about it, Gil. There are references to torture and to the use of drugs on prisoners as ways to facilitate communication—to be euphemistic about it. Light reading."

"Torture? Do you mean actual torture?"

I nodded.

"Sypher-Breaks is about paper," he said, "words on sheets of white paper. How could . . . ?" He trailed off, too startled to make the connection that ran, or marched, between his old man, his secure family life and the native hostiles thousands of miles away experimentally (rationally, scientifically, forcibly) undergoing behavior modification.

I pursued it before he got too thoughtful to talk. "Do you think they could be the papers Josie saw the night she left your house? The papers your father said disappeared and then said he found a day or two later?"

His body leaned toward me. "Maybe—but how would Evelyn end up with them seven years later?"

"I don't know, but she did."

He sat there a moment, about to say something, stopping himself, looking at me, then away. He stretched his legs and then brought them back up. "Let's go up to the Institute and talk to him. He'll be able to explain. I'm sure he will. You're too keen on diabolical explanations."

I slapped his arm lightly. "The point is I don't have an explanation."

"Let's go see him." We pulled into the slow stream of traffic and made it up Eighth in two stops. I knew how to make it all the way up straight through Columbus Circle without missing a light. But I restrained myself.

"Did you find out anything else of interest in your wanderings?" he asked.

"Some details," I answered. "You're going to take Sixty-fifth through the park, aren't you?"

He made a tight smile. "The cabdriver. What details?"

"I saw Evelyn and Josie's old roommate." He turned to cross the park. It was like diving into a black pit after all the lights on Eighth Avenue. My heart beat faster as we coasted through the desolation. "She mentioned a police visit after Josie disappeared."

"The cops kept hoping one of them would remember something."

"Evidently. But this was an odd visit. A TPF officer. I'm reasonably sure it was Taylor."

His head swung to look at me. As if he could confirm my statement by reading my expression. I know that faces lie. "That's impossible." We hit the lights of Fifth a block from the Institute.

"Maybe. How are we going to get in this late?"

"I've got a key. Taylor wouldn't have anything to do with all that."

We circled around on Park Avenue, and he pulled into an illegal space near a hydrant. "You'll be towed if you leave it here."

He turned off the ignition. "Emma, you'd better do this alone. Whatever part my father has in this mess, I don't think he'd admit to anything while I'm standing there." He reached for his keys.

"Gil, I don't want to say this, but I have to. I don't know that he'd let me out of the place. He's been after me one way or the other since all this started."

He nodded and pulled a key off the ring. "You're right. I realize I'm not seeing this very clearly from your point of view. Tell him I'm waiting for you outside. Tell him to look out the window. Tell him if you don't come out, I'm coming in after you."

I stared at him.

He tried again. "There's nobody in there but him—and he's incapable of hurting a fly without help. If he was going to do anything he'd have his flunkies take you. But he can't. His hands are tied." He held out the key. "Go around to the side and down three steps. This will open the first door you come to. Just inside there's a service elevator. Take it to the top floor."

I took the key.

20

Warm night air grabbed me by the throat. The key started to sweat in my hand as I walked the few steps to the Institute's side door. "Let's go after him," Gil had said, and then sat there playing with his keys.

Inside, there was a vestibule, its walls decorated with notices of grants, job offers, chances to study abroad, new technology, conferences. I closed the door behind me. The fear of the unknown started to drain away as I approached the elevator. This place was all too recognizable, all too much like any other work place—a small self-referential world from which you can go either up or down depending on which button you push.

I pushed up. The doors opened. I couldn't detect any video cameras, concealed or otherwise. They thought the workers were self-disciplined—and who else would be using the service elevator?

In a few seconds the doors opened onto another vestibule, bare, anonymous and empty except for a clean canister ashtray. No cameras hovered in the ceiling corners. I dropped my Forty-second Street theater stub in the ashtray. That would be evidence someone had been here until the morning maintenance crew swept through.

A pair of oak doors faced me. I raised my hand to knock at one, stopped and tried turning the knob instead. No dice. I tried the other. It turned. I wanted the slight advantage of surprise. I stepped inside, closing the door behind me. Total darkness—not much of an advantage. I waited for my eyes to adjust. They didn't no matter how much time I gave them. I started feeling the wall. No switch where the switch should be. I took a step forward and advanced six inches at a time.

A hot-white light bounced off the floor ahead of me in the form of two stilettos and punctured my sight. I recoiled, ducking, and tried to blink it away. Finally the light simmered into a square shape a few feet ahead. Bookshelves filled with books lined the room it dimly lit. I didn't move. I was sure they were coming after me. I thought of the harmless little schoolchair with the funny little wires leading from it. The floor light must have a source. I listened and heard nothing. I edged over to the light. My shoes sounded to me like sledgehammers.

A hole in the floor, a steel spiral stairway glossily painted black with a curving rail extending up into the room, handy to catapult over in the darkness. I'd been maybe five steps from it when the light went on. The room below—what I could see of it—was also stuffed with books, bound volumes of magazines and pamphlets. Between two black steps and a brown walnut surface, a hand flipped the pages of a large volume. Only pictures, photos or diagrams stayed the hand even momentarily.

I crouched lower, changed my angle slightly, and could see a single corner of the volume's red-edged jacket and much more of the oak surface with a burning cigarette in an ashtray. A hand unseen before picked up the cigarette. I crouched still lower and saw a gray cloud dissipate before the face of Taylor. It was to Taylor's credit that he could give a good imitation of the act of reading. I backed away from the stairs. I supposed he could give an equally good imitation of the act of ascending a staircase.

I noticed another door on the other side of the room. If all was right with the world, it would be unlocked. But it would be impossible to get that far. I slid along the perimeter near the books. I heard Taylor slap his book shut. Not enough pictures in that one for Taylor. He'd have to go after another. Suppose he'd looked at all the pictures on that floor. My eye buzzed across nearby titles. Out of the comparative gloom rose gothic curiosities like *The History of Germ Warfare, Biochemical Malthusianism, The Use of Pharmacological Agents in Social Conflict Situations.* Just the kind of thing that might amuse Taylor.

I edged closer to the door and heard the unmistakable sound of a shoe meeting steel. My hand went for the door handle and turned it. I should clear out the way I came. But that long route lay across an open sea. A voice said roughly, "What are you doin' here? I been looking all over." It was Frederick.

"I get goddamn bored waiting for you to type your goddamn reports."

"Here, make your mark below my signature, perfesser."

I heard Taylor step off the spiral. I pushed the door with my shoulder, hoping it wouldn't creak. It opened onto a rooftop park. I guess they call it a roof garden, but in scale it was a park. I sat on the nearest bench and looked at the sky. If Taylor had heard the door or caught a glimpse of light as I opened it, I might as well wait for him to catch up with me. The gray surface above me looked like just another high ceiling in a poorly lit room. In about ten seconds I'd had my fill of nature. At the end of the garden path I sighted a long glass wall. An equally long heavy white curtain hid the room beyond the glass. Retreat now out of the question, I advanced. A sliding glass panel formed part of the wall. There the curtain parted. I pressed my nose to the glass and saw a huge reproduction of this country's flag, only in green instead of red, white and blue. In a moment the flag disappeared and was replaced by a panel from "Orphan Annie." Another slide show, this one maybe a little more edifying than the last. At least my hand didn't tingle. I tried the sliding door. It slid and I stepped in.

The slide projector sat alone on a small table, automatically changing slides every twenty seconds. The beam hit a wall that turned white when the carrousel was advancing. Otherwise the room was unlit except for a small alcove at the far end of the glass wall. When I pulled the door closed the room was silent but for the projector's warm hum and a regular click every twenty seconds as a new slide came into view. I watched the show. Maybe twenty paintings slid past me, modern, well-done, tasteful work.

The carrousel stuck between slides showing a smudgy slice of white on the far wall. Every second it clicked, trying to force the slide back into its slot, making a noise like a dog's paw endlessly scratching at the door. I went over to see if I could relieve its frustration. I was tugging its ears when Breakstone appeared from the alcove's security on the same errand of mercy. I froze. He glanced at the wall the beam hit and shook his balding head. "Same slide always gums the works. For some reason they cut the Ryman too big." He stood looking at the wall, which I now realized was not blank white but filled by a slide of an all-white painting. "Anyway, Mariana," he said, "take that one out and try to cut it down just a hair. It's a key slide for the lecture." He turned his back to me and started padding out of the room in his slippers. He didn't get far. When he turned around, he said calmly, "Mariana, of course, left a while ago. Who would you be?"

"A friend of Gil's."

He squinted to get a better view. Near-sighted and too

vain to wear glasses. "Gil isn't here just now. Can I be of some assistance?" Apparently the squint didn't help. Either he'd genuinely forgotten, or he was one of those snobs whose memory automatically weeds out the less favored.

"Yes, you can."

He stepped toward me. He had a hitch in his walk that made him seem to take three steps for every two. The machine clicked between us, offering the Ryman white on white. The combination of the two hesitations was almost hypnotic. I had to blurt something out before he got too close.

"You can start by calling off your dogs."

He stopped several feet away on the other side of the machine. He was wearing a beautifully tailored off-white summer suit. He slipped his hand gracefully into the pocket. I had just enough grace to keep myself from jumping. I should have realized he wouldn't spoil the lines of the suit by wearing a gun. "I offer my apologies. I forgot you. I've been preparing this little lecture on my collection for the past two days, and I've let every other thought—every thought of the real world—wither on the vine. Have you progressed any farther in your knowledge of the Erland tragedy?"

"Tragedy, that's almost as good a word as fate. You offered your assistance. I'd like you to call off your dogs."

He said nothing, but his appraising eyes measured me. I became conscious again of how rumpled I was and that I must smell of old popcorn and stale Spanish cooking. He pulled the Ryman slide out. The machine hiccoughed and brought forth another slide. "I don't keep dogs, Miss Hobart. But I have a sense I'm not following you. Shall we go sit in my study? Maybe we can work this out, whatever it is that's bothering you." He turned off the machine. "If we could understand each other," he said in the darkness, his voice meditative, "I'm sure we could straighten this out."

He sat down at a big oak desk lit by a small green lamp. I sat across from him. Behind him on a narrow table a slide file was lit from inside so that the slides on it glowed evenly. These were the only sources of light. Breakstone's face was impenetrable.

"You know what I mean by dogs," I said.

There was a pause. He must have gone to the same finishing school for Dramatic Pauses as Wincey. Only I think he got better grades.

"After you left so precipitously with Gil in tow—I sensed your power over him, I was impressed by it—after you left I considered several options. I thought you too much the rebel type. I'm sorry if that seems unfair. Unhealthy rebellion disturbs me. If it is too near, I can't even digest my food. I wish to be honest with you, however. I might have been more ruthless if this lecture weren't coming up. It's been all-consuming."

"You love art so much you sic your attack dogs on me."

"That's an extreme description. I did very little really. I'll be specific. For many years I have owned a taxi fleet. Some years ago, before your time, I made it possible for a taxi-drivers' union to come into being in this town. Not something I like to be known for, but I think that in general unionism is not a bad thing. So your little episode downtown, that short confrontation with the semiretired union official was, I admit, at my instigation. I understand that you faced that one down. So now where are the dogs to which you refer?"

"Downstairs."

He leaned forward and rubbed his lips with an index finger, a classic pose of the transfixed art-lover. The fingernail was carefully manicured.

"You are disconcertingly terse, young lady."

"They are, or were a few moments ago, on the floor below, writing you a report to fill you in on all the salient details of the last few days. In suitably circumspect language, I'm sure. It wouldn't do to be offensive. Two well-dressed dogs. Frederick and Taylor."

For thirty seconds there was silence. It occurred to me that he wasn't used to thinking on his feet and maybe Gil was right, he couldn't be directly violent. It was the kind of thing he'd have to pass down the line. He turned to his desk and dialed a three-digit number on his telephone. "Jim? I'm sorry to disturb you. Are Frederick and Taylor somewhere in the building? Fine. No. Tell them to step up here for a moment, will you? Then you can go. I'm staying late again tonight."

I sprang up to look for another way out. He dropped the phone to the carpet.

"Don't be alarmed, I beg you," he said.

"Gil is downstairs in his car waiting for me. If anything happens to me, your son will know it this time. You lost a daughter. Don't take a chance on your son."

"You're quite right," he said. "When my two dogs come up here, I am going to put a muzzle on them. You'll have no more to fear from either of them. I promise you." He found the receiver and returned it to its cradle. "I'll set it straight."

We didn't speak. We waited. My two friends materialized out of the darkness, nodding to me with all the interest they'd show a rusty doorknob.

"Sir," Frederick addressed Breakstone, "you wanted a word with us?"

Breakstone didn't ask them to sit down. "Miss Hobart tells me you two have been harassing her." Taylor made an aggressive gesture in my direction and started to speak. Breakstone said, "Let me finish. Whatever is the case, I must ask you to desist in your endeavors in regard to Miss

Hobart. If that is clear enough, and I think it should be, further discussion is unnecessary." Frederick grabbed Taylor's elbow. Taylor pulled it back.

"As you say, sir," Frederick said.

They dematerialized.

Breakstone was fiddling with another carrousel, choosing more slides for his lecture. "The hounds are off the scent," he said quietly.

"You have the power to turn loose battalions of dogs from this pen. You expect me just to fade—knowing what you did to Hoyt and probably did to Evelyn Berndt, knowing that you planted a dead body in my bathtub?"

Very calmly he put a slide back on the tray upside down. "You've got a few things mixed up. But I'm a little too busy now to explain it to you."

I stood up. He jumped after me.

"What's the matter," I said, "afraid I'll stomp on some more of your art?"

"I can't say what you'd do. You're too quick to take appearance for reality. I have my own tendencies in that direction." He smoothed his hair. "Please sit down again."

"You'd better have something to say." I sat down.

When he spoke, he was emphatic. "I intervened in your activities once only, down on Laight Street. I had nothing to do with Frederick and Taylor. Until you told me, I had no idea they were concerned in this mess in any way. They are, as I understand it, on retainer for some services they render the security division of Sypher-Breaks, and it is in that capacity that I became aware of their existence. If they have been harassing you, I am sorry, but I am at a loss to explain it. I know they have certain spillover duties at the Institute on a contractual basis, but . . ."

"They used your name. They broke into my place, swiped a film I was keeping from them and said, 'This'll keep Breakstone off our backs.'"

"They were leading you on."

"They thought they were alone."

"Then they were mistaken. I've had no dealings with them—until a few minutes ago. You'll have to take my word."

"Your word leaves me high and dry. You hired them to get something. You hired them to get it from Evelyn Berndt and when they couldn't get it you hired them to kill her."

He waved his hand at me. It was an involuntary gesture. He was warding something off. "You're living in a fantasy world."

"Let's put it this way. I have what Evelyn died holding on to. If you want it, you'll have to come across."

"You've lost me. Totally lost me." He turned back to his slide tray.

"Evelyn was holding on to some documents she got from your daughter."

He stopped moving, seemed to stop breathing. The soft off-white suit coat stretched across his shoulders. Without turning back, he said, "From Josie? What are you talking about?"

"Evelyn had papers that linked Sypher-Breaks to an American-sponsored program of physical torture in Vietnam. Maybe she found them in your daughter's room after she disappeared. However she got them, she held on to them. How much did she get you for?"

His back was still turned. "She never came to me."

"Your son thinks differently. He thinks you had an arrangement."

He didn't speak.

"He thinks you got Frederick and Taylor to do your dirty work."

"He told you this?"

I waited. Finally he turned around. He was paler than the suit. I nodded.

"Why didn't he come up with you, then?" Looking at

me he put the carrousel on the edge of the table. It fell and spilled to the floor. Slides spun out of their slots onto the carpet. He didn't even look down.

"He couldn't handle it. It's no fun seeing your old man as a rich thug."

Breakstone rose, stepping on one of the slides as he left the room. I didn't want him out of sight so I followed him past a litter of modern sculpture. At the far wall he wrenched a curtain aside. It made a long moaning noise and slid rapidly away. The floor-to-ceiling window faced the street. Breakstone looked through it. "Point him out to me," he said listlessly, "I don't see him."

I hesitated until Breakstone stepped away from the window. I was still not sure how much of this could be an act.

Gil's car was gone and there was no sign of Gil. "He must be waiting around the corner," I said, sure he wasn't.

"He's not waiting around the corner. He's deserted you." Breakstone spoke with utter certainty. "Let's sit down again, Miss Hobart. I'm very tired." I followed him across the room to the alcove, the hesitation in his walk more exaggerated from behind.

"He's been a good boy, a good son. Whatever wrong he's done, it's been unintentional. I know that." He sat down stiffly, as if he had Novocaine for blood.

"He's less indulgent in his attitude to you," I said. I said it to hear myself speak. I'd lost my bearings. The walk back through the sculpture had made me dizzy. "He blames you for Josie's disappearance."

He rocked his head. "Gil blames everyone for what happened to Josie. Mostly he blames himself. For a long time when he was younger we had him in therapy. He improved a lot. There were some bad episodes. Once he kicked in a TV set because Josie was mentioned on it as a casualty of the sixties. But I know he's much better now."

Each Breakstone agreed that the other was much better now.

"The night Josie left your house she took some documents along with her . . ."

"Not possible. I found those documents two days later in my office safe."

"Evelyn had copies—and she had originals of other documents circulated between the Institute and Sypher-Breaks. According to them, drugs used in Vietnam have been refined extensively in the last few years. The fragments I read made me think. Sypher-Breaks isn't only a data-control corporation—its on its way to forging profitable links between data control and mind control."

"Perhaps you have some interesting material, Miss Hobart. More likely you have an overworked imagination. Let me fill you in on something. Sypher-Breaks used to be known more simply as Breaks Inc. But at one point, a serious one in our financial history, we latched onto a much smaller electronics firm with a few intriguing patents. Sypher was the president of that firm. He's a very shrewd man, and his price was a full merger, to which obviously I agreed. The last five years or so my active involvement in the business has been extremely limited. No doubt Sypher-Breaks will become just Sypher one day. The programs presently being developed by the company that bears my name are not under my initiative. If you want to talk business, go see Sypher." He leaned over to retrieve the carrousel.

"I don't want to talk business. I'm interested in talking about what your business is doing in the name of profit."

He put the carrousel back on the table and put up a hand to stop me. "Please. I'm not interested in a dated appeal for social justice. I have a lecture to finish. If you'll allow me . . ." He stood.

We took one more walk. At the door he yawned and

excused himself. He was calm again. "I'm sorry Gil let you down. He can be a little erratic. He's always had trouble sustaining an interest in a project. Actually now that I think of it, his current job has been the one that's lasted the longest."

He opened the door. I glimpsed the elevator I'd come up on.

"He hasn't mentioned a job."

"He wouldn't. That's his character."

"What sort of work does he do?"

"He's chief of the security division for Sypher-Breaks and the Institute."

21

I was back in the same empty vestibule. My torn theater ticket was still atop the canister, a crushed cigarette butt keeping it company. When I pushed the button, the elevator doors immediately slid open. Everything I thought I knew about the father started to slide onto the son. Funny he never told me about his job. Funny I never asked. The doors started to close so I slid between them and faced front. I pushed three and the elevator started down. There was a fair chance I'd catch Frederick and Taylor still doing their homework. That was a chance I wanted to take. I had to, didn't I?

Funny I didn't know anything about Gil. You trust somebody like him because he's young and good-looking and open and easily influenced—and even emotional. Because he makes love so single-mindedly. Does it make you distrust passion? Was it passion? Whom was it passion for? He told you whom you reminded him of. I felt a little queasy. Was that why he gave me the .32?

I kept my finger on the open-door button of the elevator. The doors wanted to close but I wouldn't let them. I got out. I would take any chance now. That's all there was. With my help, they'd made me into a fugitive, and all fugitives can do is take chances. The third floor was well-lit and empty. No nurses carrying trays of hypodermics. No Ridley nervously gripping a clipboard. This was strictly a one-shift torture chamber. It looked safe now—like an Institute of Philosophical Healing. Nothing to be afraid of. I found the door to the library. I opened it and stepped inside, closing it behind me.

Taylor grinned at me under his impeccable mustache. "Hi," he said. "You sure are a slippery one, girlie." Then he stepped in front of the door as if I was about to slip under it.

"You were ordered to back off, Taylor. Aren't you worried about job security?"

He mugged, raising his eyebrows. "That's right. Job security. No room to fuck up when you have a delicate position like mine. A tightrope!" He shrugged. "Will there be a recession with Nixon out? Maybe Sypher-Breaks will fall on hard times. Data control is a slippery business. You can never be sure. That's why I like to plug up all the holes."

"Play it safe."

"Right."

"Then you should feed me to the cops. That would be safe, wouldn't it?"

"We thought of that," Frederick said, sitting at the far end of the long walnut table. "But that might bring up more questions than answers. Know what I mean? The law has to have it all there on the blotter."

"Let's figure it," I said. "Maybe there's some way we can all come out of this smiling."

"I don't believe in happiness," Frederick said. "I believe in security."

"It's a shame we don't have the same values," I said.

"Sit down."

I chose the chair closest to the door. A cigarette burned in the ashtray nearest Frederick. There were four more ashtrays spread in a line down the table like oases in a desert. The library must double as a conference room.

"You guys have to keep your job with Breakstone, right?" I asked, putting my bag on the table in front of me. The .32 was in it, resting.

"Not Breakstone," Taylor whined, shifting his weight from one leg to the other, "Sypher-Breaks Inc. Personal security's not our line."

"Shut up," Frederick said.

"Don't tell me what to do."

"Maybe you guys can straighten me out on a few things," I said.

"We don't wanna straighten you out. We like you the way you are," Taylor smirked.

Frederick heaved a disgusted sigh. Taylor leaned both hands on his end of the table, looking down at Frederick. "You don't like it. Tough. We don't agree. We have different ways of conducting our business affairs."

Frederick scowled and waved him away. "You don't conduct business, schmuck. You're just muscle. That's all you are and that's all I am. So come off it."

Taylor stood up to dust off his hands. He looked very pleased with himself. "We are under contract. Under contract. If that's not business, I don't know what would be so designated."

Their discussion allowed me time to free the catch on the bag. "What we need," I said, "is a story we can agree on. I'm not after you guys, so if we can figure out a story . . ."

"*You're* not after *us*?" Frederick said, pointing a finger at me and then thumping his immaculate shirt front. "You got a lot of nerve, kid. You woulda been just another dead ass zero on the debit sheet long ago—if Breakstone didn't hold us back. You want to know what's a threat to our job security? You, that's what."

"That's what," Taylor said and backed closer to the door.

"Breakstone says you guys were working on your own time, not for him."

Frederick scowled. "You gotta be kiddin'. You mean that old fart upstairs who don't know a crack in the sidewalk from the crack in his ass? We don't work for him. He's too busy buying art."

"Quiet a minute," Taylor said, "I hear something." He shushed us with a gesture and then turned his back to us, reaching for the door handle and the light switch. His stubby fingers reached them both at the same moment. Suddenly it seemed too quiet. I had an impulse to grab for the .32 but didn't follow it.

The lights went out and the door burst open, slamming Taylor against the wall. He gave a wrenching groan and screamed, "My hand!" The doorknob pinned it to the wall.

A huge backlit figure filled the doorway, blocking most of the yellow light trying to squeeze past it. One arm propped the door against Taylor's squirming body. Taylor kept groaning. His splayed fingers wriggled under the doorknob like worms around a rock.

"Gil?" I said. The figure took one step into the dark room. The door loosened. Taylor's knees sagged.

Frederick said, "The other Break—"

If he finished what he had to say I didn't hear it. A roar deafened the room. A spurt of fire lit the dark figure for an instant. I saw a golden head and flushed cheeks and a small crescent-shaped scar. I stood up, pushing my chair away. A brick fell on the back of my head. My knees refused to bend to help me get to the floor where I wanted to lie down. I took a step. It was like treading water. Taylor shoved me forward, always there to lend a helping hand. I told my arms to raise themselves. They wouldn't listen. I pitched forward, my head spilling away from my body. My eyes as they spun away caught Taylor lumbering through the doorway. He must be late for an appointment, I thought. My head hit Gil. There was a second roar. It sounded as if it was going off inside my left ear.

My head is becoming an explosive weapon I thought. My ear burned. I closed my eyes for a moment just to regain my equilibrium. The last thing I wanted to do was pass out. I had to talk to Gil. Gil? Gilbert B. Breakstone, Jr., you mean? That's the one. Tall, young, husky, gentle—not so tall, middle-aged, flaccid, insensitive, both at the same time. Unusual guy. Is he armed? Two of them, muscular. Does he carry bricks? I don't think so, not that I noticed. I thought maybe . . . No. That was Taylor. Taylor did it in the library with a brick. Where did he get the brick? From the bricklayer, where else? How much did he pay the bricklayer? He didn't have to pay the bricklayer—the idiot was dumb enough to give it to him free of charge. Then he stole it from the dummy. Right, he stole it, he stole it from a hundred bricklayers. Then they got together and built him a house out of all the bricks. Red bricks. Nice place, I'll take it. You don't have to take it—it's yours gratis. Step right in so we can brick up the doorway. It takes exactly one hundred bricks.

22

In the interim I died.

Very slowly I raised my head from wherever I was and looked at the carpet to regain the focus of my eyes. It took so long I was beginning to think double vision normal, but I slowly snapped to by concentrating on the fact that I had a headache and it was normal to feel a little fuzzy. Then I changed my focus, like changing a slide on a projector, and saw my bag. The bag was lying on a table. That meant that I was lying on a table. My hand slid along the table toward the bag. I pulled the gun out. It was heavy, so I left it on the table with my hand over it.

"That won't do you any good. It's too late." The voice sounded just like Breakstone's.

"You can never tell what'll do somebody good," I said.

I righted myself. Breakstone, sitting on the other side of the table, was looking at his hands. So did I. There was some blood on them. He reached into his off-white suit coat. He was awkward about it because of the danger of staining the suit.

He pulled out a linen handkerchief. I could see he was reluctant about staining that as well. He rubbed his fingers until they were presentable, fouling the linen. He pursed his lips.

While he was still engaged, I massaged my temples and the back of my neck. I didn't want to black out again. Breakstone put the linen on the table and flicked it away. Then he inspected his fingertips, his brow furrowed.

"If you dislike blood so much, it must be a little rough to have a son like Gil."

"Gil? What has Gil to do with blood?"

There was a snort from the far end of the table. Frederick, paler than before and slumped a little lower, was still seated in the same chair. His immaculate shirt front was now mostly red. He snorted again. "What has horseshit to do with Citation?"

Breakstone didn't even look his way. "He claims Gil shot at him. I'm making him sit here until I hear a better story." He calmly folded his hands in front of him.

"Listen, kid," Frederick said, "he's flipped. Call an ambulance. I'm on the absolute shit-side of death, I swear. Look at my shirt. If I lose any more blood I'll go straight into convulsions. Then you'll be sorry."

He really thought I'd be sorry. I liked that, in a way. But I couldn't choose to get the police in on this just yet, sorry or not. "You deserve a little hard luck, Frederick," I said.

He grimaced to show me his pain. It served to remind me of my own. I caught Breakstone's eyelids fluttering and tried to meet his gaze before it faltered.

"I checked him out. He's not dying. He bled a little, that's all. Just a scratch. You're not much of a shot, young lady."

"I didn't get a chance to shoot him."

"Nonsense," Breakstone said and pointed to the gun.

"Where are the others?" I asked. Whom I did or didn't shoot wouldn't make an interesting argument.

"What others?" Breakstone said blankly.

I couldn't expect much more from him. He acted almost as if he'd been shot.

I turned to Frederick. "Gil's been your employer all along, hasn't he?"

He looked at me impassively. "You knew that. You were working with that Erland character."

He glanced at Breakstone as if he wasn't sure how much to say in front of him. "I'm sure Erland knew that much. He was flaky, but he was no dummy. If we hadn't decided on that squeeze play that day I hailed your cab, I wouldn't be sitting here now bleeding like a stuck pig." He cocked his head, trying to look charming. "I hope you don't think it was anything of a personal nature we had against you. It was on account of your association we had to lean on you. Now how 'bout something in the medical area? I would do something myself but for fear of instituting shock."

"Soon," I said. "If you were just doing your job, why did Gil shoot you?"

"Do I know? He's a nut case." He nodded to Breakstone who was tuned in to another station. "With all due respect to the older generation."

I picked up the gun. "Listen, Freddy, we've had a lot of laughs together. But that's over. You can quit clowning around. I'm in trouble thanks to you guys, and I need a way out. If you can't help me find it"—I released the safety catch on the gun—"then I'll have to make sure you don't find a way out either."

He coughed and leaned forward, putting out a hand to calm me until he could quit coughing. Breakstone stood up.

Frederick said, "I'm at your complete disposal."

"Sit down," I said to Breakstone. I pointed the gun at the chair, and he tumbled into it. The exercise seemed to do him good. He looked more alert.

I waved it at Frederick. "Say something. Captivate me."

"We work. We investigate mainly. Well, we push people around mainly. But we contract as investigators."

"Gil."

"Right. The kid is hot to find his long-lost sister. Okay. We are already employed as security agents by S.B.I. so he finds us that way. The first thing we do for him is to muscle the Berndt girl."

"He asked you to muscle her?"

"He asked us to question her and to use our own discretion as to methodology."

"So your methodology is to drown her."

"Drown her? The Berndt girl? Nah. In fact we did muscle her just a little—or tried to—but she didn't go for it one bit. She was as tough as you. She told us to bug off."

"She didn't tell you anything?"

"Are you kidding? She sits there and says, 'Tell your master I'll tear off his right thumb if he bothers me again.'"

"Right thumb?" Breakstone asked. "She said his right thumb?" He was excited, so excited he forgot he wasn't speaking to Frederick.

"That's what I said she said," Frederick said curtly.

Breakstone opened his mouth and let it shut without speaking.

Frederick looked at the muzzle of the gun. "I'm going to black out," he said, "and it'll be your fault."

"I'll have to live with the guilt. Why did Gil plug you?"

"Why did Sirhan Sirhan plug Bobby? Was there any sense in that? I'm in favor of legislation to outlaw handguns. Incidents such as happened here tonight—"

"I need an answer, not a soapbox, Freddy. Do you want me to lose my temper?"

His tone changed. "He wasn't after me, I figure."

"How?"

"He wanted Taylor."

"How do you know?"

"He fired two shots, one at me, and Taylor, the little

worm, managed to duck out. When the kid saw it was me he got, he looked real chagrined and made out after my erstwhile partner. He wasn't after me. I figure he wasn't rational on the subject of Taylor. You led the kid here, didn't you? Rotten Taylor's probably rotting in the gutter right about this very second."

"At least Taylor stayed on his feet, Freddy."

"Quit calling me that." He turned to Breakstone. "Your son is out-to-lunch, Mr. B, out-to-lunch."

Breakstone's eyes were looking down at his manicured thumbs, as if they were talking to him. There's an anthropological theory in which primeval human development depends on the thumb. Man is a prehensile creature. He'd have a hard time holding a pencil without a thumb. When I read such things I try to read accurately and end up wondering where women fit into the theorizing. If I read Breakstone accurately, he had something to say but didn't know whether to say it. He gripped his hands tighter. His knuckles turned white. The tips of his fingers dug into his skin.

"Your best bet," he said to me, still looking at his hands, "may be my partner Sypher."

"How so?"

"He may be able to help you."

"Give me a reason to think so. He hasn't even been in town the past few days."

He said it slowly and said it three ways, as if to give me a choice. "He has only one thumb. He only has a right thumb. He has one thumb only, the right one."

23

My headache kept me moving. I found a closet for Frederick and Breakstone to hang out in for a while. Breakstone used his handkerchief to staunch the trickling flow of blood from Frederick's shoulder. He was still tending to him as I closed the door on them and a few brooms and a wash bucket. Frederick looked up and said, "That's a really mean thing to do to an invalid and an old man."

"I'll make it up to you some time," I said.

Breakstone said nothing. It seemed he didn't mind being put away in a closet. I propped the door so that it would be virtually impossible for them to break out without help.

I walked east toward the river thinking of the tableau the two of them made in the closet, another touching case of master and man. My head rang with each step and the sound it made was a low-pitched hollow slur, "Gil," "Gil," "Gil." Gil sent Frederick and Taylor to my apartment, Gil encouraged them to rip-off the files and terrorize Mrs. Berndt, to tear after Hoyt. I turned around. Somehow I expected to be followed. Nothing pursued me except the logic of events. I walked faster. I still carried the .32 Gil had planted on me. I was clear about one thing: I wanted to wrap the .32 around his thick neck. Gil's confused, guilt-ridden obsessiveness about a woman seven years dead put a warp in all these people's lives, even Frederick's and Taylor's, even mine. We all have obsessions, but we don't all pursue our worst obsessions to fatality. Only a few of us, like Gil, could because he was young enough and rich enough. His life was empty enough that he could afford to waste it.

Sypher lived in a penthouse overlooking the river. Breakstone obligingly told me where and told me what to say to get past the doorman. About to violate one of those invulnerable sanctuaries I routinely cursed as a cabdriver, I stood across the street to watch it glitter—the glass and mirrors, the gold, the lights, the buttons on the doorman's coat and his smile as a limousine pulled up the half-circle driveway. A series of reflecting surfaces registered the progress of a man in a tuxedo toward the gilt elevators. A woman in a silver fox wrap turned and looked at the night as if it belonged to her. The car door made a solid sound when the doorman gave it a push with his white-gloved hand. The woman strolled through the lobby. Each of her high-heeled steps reflected certainty and order. I bent my head painfully back to look for Sypher's penthouse. It was too high to see.

Arriving on foot at so late an hour didn't dispose the doorman to me. He watched me approach from the safety of his post and didn't budge to relieve me of the burden of opening the big glass door. These terms of equality helped give me the courage to utter Breakstone's magic words, passwords apparently uttered by all of Sypher's late-night messengers from reality. The doorman, pink-faced and Irish, eyed me under his cap, saying nothing, his narrow mouth tight. As I finished my little set piece he nodded. He bowed to the wisdom of his patrons. He marched to the elevator and ushered me into it, reaching in to press the top button.

The doors opened on an anteroom facing a single door. Less gilt, fewer mirrors, but in one corner a babbling brook babbling away, complete with rocks, shrubs and a small waterfall. When I went over to it a dozen fish winked at me. Apart from my normal appreciation of nature, I liked this brook because it showed that Sypher wasn't missing just a thumb.

I pushed the bell beside the door but heard only the brook. After a while somebody opened the door and took a cocky stance in front of me. Somebody was a small man, dressed for bed in powder-blue pajamas, a wine-colored robe and slippers, none of them bargain basement. His black eyebrows were tilted up, making something of a V shape. This effect seemed so overdefined to me I decided it was cultivated.

"Nice fish," I said.

Instead of inviting me in, he stepped out. "I never get over the fact that I haven't dumped that piece of wildlife," he said, looking down at it with interest. "Come on in." He walked ahead. I followed, but I left the door ajar, just in case of emergency. The room we walked into was well appointed. Presumably it had all the things modern penthouse living rooms are required to have, but I never noticed what was in it. He was in it, and that was all that seemed to matter.

"The problem is," he said, after he'd stopped at the bar, "I'm fixing you a drink—Scotch'll be all right, won't it?—the problem is, you don't give up. You keep going. I like that. It's a good quality in both men and women. Rare. But it's a problem." He fixed the drink, mulling over the problem. "You're not one of the fish, that's it." He pressed a button on his side of the bar. The wall of curtain behind the bar parted slowly. New York fell into the room, the pretty New York of skyscrapers and bright lights. He opened one of the sliding glass panels. A breeze swept through the room. "Fresh air," he said. "You're not one of the fish out there," he pointed out to the night, "swimming around and around, never quite awake, eating whatever crumbs come their way. You're not like the rest."

"Maybe not," I said.

"In other words, I've been keeping an eye on you."

"You aren't the only one. I've had lots of eyes on me."

"Not enough. Otherwise you'd never have ended up here. Or in the papers, for that matter. Now I have to figure out what to do with you. One more headache. But that's life. I shouldn't complain. Especially me. Because I've been very lucky in life. Right place at the right moment."

"What do you mean you have to decide what to do with me?"

"You're here, aren't you?"

I took the drink he held out to me with his good hand and sipped it. It was strong. "You weren't surprised to see me."

"You had to turn up sooner or later. The way things have been going." He walked over to the sliding glass and back to the bar. "Tell me what you know—or what you think you know—and we'll go from there." He paced back to the sliding glass.

"Evelyn was blackmailing you. But how those papers she had . . ." I stopped and started over. "The papers show that Sypher-Breaks is as disgustingly profit-oriented as any other corporation. That's normal. Maybe there's even some evidence of criminal intent on the part of your company, using chemical agents, for example, on blissfully unaware salesgirls and secretaries, just to see if you've got a hot product. Something that numbs the central nervous system but leaves the brain functions intact. A way to tap into the human brain just like any other machine. Another computer. Awful stuff, okay, and more awful because you stumbled onto the whole thing in a laboratory called South Vietnam, using guinea pigs called Viet Cong. But a lot of that has come out already. It's not common knowledge, but it's known. So what was she blackmailing you for?"

He sipped his drink, kept his eyes on it as if hypnotized by the ice cubes, and didn't react. "She wasn't."

"I think she was. I have the documents now. I could start blackmailing you. Since I know what you're doing."

"You don't know, and the fact is those papers could embarrass a company of our stature, despite your diabolical fantasies about corporate madness. That's why I had my two little scouts out looking—"

"Your two scouts? I thought Frederick and Taylor—"

"They work for me and report to me. Their little mission for young Gil is just moonlighting. Extra pocket money. And I make sure they report to me about anything they might dig up for our security chief."

I looked through the window. The moon was hanging out above the penthouse, awaiting orders.

Sypher cleared his throat. "In any case, if it is cash that interests you, there is a small possibility of an accommodation. But I don't believe that is your interest. My researchers tell me you emerged from the black depths of the sixties at their worst. You were an antiwar creep. You were involved with your community. You coddled interracial ragamuffin crybabies. You had your consciousness raised in at least one group of jobless females. Everything tells me you can't be had with cash. I'm not so crass as you might think."

"I don't think you're crass. Not at all. Breakstone—"

Suddenly he raised his thumbless hand to stop me speaking, as if mentioning Breakstone's name was a physical affront. "My partner, in crime as you'd say, inherited his fortune. I made it on my own, one of the last of the evil breed of individualists. So I am crass. I rose through the managerial ranks to my present eminence. I am a representative of that hard-nosed anything-for-a-profit class you read about in your sentimental magazines over espresso and carrot cake. That is why I can if necessary be cavalier about experimenting on working girls. For instance." He downed his drink. It wasn't the first he'd downed tonight. Maybe the fifth.

"Aren't companies like yours usually a little more cautious?"

"Usually. But we're pushing into a new field. We have to hit hard. We have to make a splash. Behind this research, however you may disparage it, there is a greater vision. We can refurbish the old idea of data control—"

I interrupted him, impatient with rubbish. "If she wasn't blackmailing you, then—" Sypher was looking straight at me with a peculiarly intense expression. I was facing him with my back to the rest of the room. I felt an arm grip my elbow firmly. I tried to pull away even before turning to see who it was. It wouldn't let go. "Take it easy, Emma," Gil said. "I won't hurt you."

His voice didn't make me believe him, nor did his face when I looked at it. Stripped of a natural layer of warmth, as if astringently wiped clean of make-up, his face was mottled, his skin stretched thin across his cheekbones, and chafed raw around his eyes. I was shaken by his look of vulnerability screwed too tight and now turned like a weapon against the world. I finally understood what he was about and wished I'd seen it last night, or even seen beyond myself while sitting in his car earlier. Like everyone else in his life, I'd kept him at a distance, and now he'd crossed over the line. There was no calling him back. At the time I'd had my reasons. Now I was shaken by my regrets.

Sypher banged his glass down on the bar. "For God's sake, what do you want, Gil?"

He let go of my arm. "I want to talk about Evelyn Berndt. Both Emma and I do."

Sweat poured down his face. Maybe he'd jogged the steps up to Sypher's penthouse. His blond hair was plastered to his forehead. He said nothing, just stared at

Sypher. His body was trembling. His hands were dirty, his shirt mostly unbuttoned, his chest hair matted.

Sypher's hand was still around his empty glass. "What have you been doing, Gil? Playing stickball in the gutter?"

I thought irrelevantly of all the times I've walked across the West Side late at night after work and seen kids playing ball under the streetlamps.

Gil said, "That's right. In the gutter. What happened to Evelyn Berndt, Sypher? Tell Emma what happened."

"She killed herself, Gil. Because her nasty little affair with the congressman was going down the drain."

"How do you happen to know that, Sypher?"

"A source close—Wincey told me. You know that yourself, Gil. Why play dumb?"

"What about the documents Josie gave her? When did she tell you about them?"

"Don't be an ass. I bought those documents from her years ago when it was a necessary expedient, because of your own father's incompetence. That was the beginning and end of my relationship to that sorry woman."

Gil stepped quickly to the bar and lunged over it to grab Sypher. He managed to get the edge of Sypher's robe lapel in his hand and rip it as Sypher backed away. Startled, Sypher stepped back near the open sliding door.

Gil dropped the torn shred of Sypher's lapel and moved around the bar. Sypher, still facing him, backed into the open doorway. Gil advanced another step.

I said, "Gil, what are you after? What do you think Sypher did? Please say it before you go any farther."

He made a half-turn toward me. His face was distorted. "I didn't shoot you, did I? Isn't that enough? I didn't hurt you." Breaking through the distortion was the appeal of a fifteen-year-old. Behind him Sypher backed onto the terrace. The breeze whipped his pajamas.

"Didn't you tell Frederick and Taylor to get me?" He hesitated, not moving. "Didn't you?" I said.

"I only said to neutralize you. Put you out of action. Really, that's all. I like you. I even gave you a gun. Why would I do anything to hurt you?"

Sypher yelled from the terrace. "Why would you! You're an asshole, that's why. You're obsessed with yourself and your sister, your goddamn doornail sister. You haven't got anything to think about, that's why. Why don't you jump off this building and put us all out of your misery? Give us a break."

Gil's enormously tensed body shrank a little under Sypher's harangue.

Sypher kept it up. "I gave you this little pickaninny job as security officer only because you're too unbalanced to do anything useful. I had to create the goddamn position for you. Your old man begged me."

Sypher was good, but he didn't know when to quit. Or maybe he didn't know how to quit. He was having too much fun puncturing the rich boy. It's hard to destroy someone verbally. Gil swung resiliently away from me to face him. Sypher backed away another step. He was doing just fine walking backwards. The inside light marked out a lurid green perimeter of grass on the terrace. Sypher stood in the middle of it, his thick black brows etching his face like a mask under a spotlight.

They were going to tear at each other and hurt each other, just as they'd arranged to hurt Evelyn and Hoyt and the Berndts and how many others. I wanted to know exactly what the stakes were. Why did they hate each other so much at this moment? What did Gil know, or think he knew, that he didn't earlier?

"It's terrific you guys hate each other," I said. "You've got me convinced. But I'm the one who's going to pay. The cops are after me. They're never going to come after either of you. By the accidents of birth and temperament, I don't have the money to charm them away."

"Emma," Gil said, "I can give you the money. This has nothing to do with money." His hands were fists.

"You're here twenty-five floors above the rest of the city because you can afford to be. You can afford to waste your life mooning over a girl seven years dead. You can hire other people to clear the road ahead of you."

"She's right, she's dead right," said Taylor. I swung around. He stood several feet behind me, his nose bloodied, one ear ragged and swollen, his clothes more rumpled than mine.

"Come in, come in," Sypher called from outside. "I always have an open-door policy this time of night. Now we can have a party." The distance made his voice cold and tinny.

Taylor stole a quick look at Gil. He held his hands at hip level like a gunslinger. He looked onto the terrace, bending his head and squinting. "What you doin' out there, boss? Big boy threatening you?"

Caught halfway between Sypher and Taylor, Gil looked back and forth and then edged behind the bar for cover. It wasn't much cover, but it was better than nothing. From his side, Taylor eased over to the bar and poured some Scotch into Sypher's empty glass. Sypher stepped into the doorway again as if he'd just been out to catch the air. He cupped his hands to light a cigarette. His hands were steady. Gil was immobile again. Maybe he couldn't figure his chances and move at the same time. We all have our own ways of concentrating. Gil's way had cost him seven years so far.

Sypher broke the silence. "There's not much to say," he said and waved his hand with the cigarette in it at me. "This woman's situation is unfortunate. That much is clear. But I can't imagine what she expects. I have nothing to do with her problems. I only recognized her because her hack picture was on *Eyewitness News* tonight." He looked at Taylor for corroboration. It was time to settle my hash, time for a united front.

"Right," Taylor said, "she's in hock cause Ridley fell on her. Mostly that. She can probably wriggle out of that hit-and-run incident, but Ridley's a hard nut to swallow."

"I'm not swallowing it. I'm not even tasting it," I said.

"You're gonna have to," Taylor said, a trace of sympathy in his voice. "You sure don't think our security chief here is going to tumble for it, do you?"

"What's he got to do with it?" I looked at Gil, who put his fingertips on the bar and leaned toward Taylor.

He said, "Let's quit faking it, we have something to settle you and I. I'm after you, Taylor, and I'm going to get you. Understand that?"

"After me? I thought you was after my partner. I mean I was hoping. What did I ever do to you, up to the minute, you should be after me?" He put his hand in his pocket as he spoke, and I wondered if he kept a helpmate there.

"You've been stringing me along, Taylor. You visited my sister's dorm room after she disappeared, didn't you? You never mentioned that. Isn't that odd you never mentioned it all this time? What were you doing there, Taylor?"

Taylor shrugged.

Gil continued, "I've got a pretty good idea. That's why I'm glad you're here. I think we can find out tonight some things that have been waiting a long time."

"You won't find out from me, kid." Taylor glanced swiftly at Sypher. That was a mistake. It was like a signal to Gil and he smiled grimly.

"Maybe. Maybe not. But I'll find out."

"Wait a minute," I said. "Back up and start over. Taylor, what's Gil got to do with what happened to Ridley?"

Taylor considered that, his eyes passing across all of us. "You knew he had you set up with the police after we got a little rough with Ridley, didn't you?"

"No, I didn't know that. Up to now I don't think I'd have believed it."

I'd been wrong about Gil straight through. He'd dumped Ridley on me. The good son and brother was as ruthless as Sypher in his own special way. Or he was so used to being betrayed that betraying others came naturally to him. I realized now how fully alone I stood in this room.

"You ought to learn when to keep your mouth shut, Taylor," Gil said.

"I am through protecting you, kid. I don't take kindly to being shot at." He turned to Sypher. "Why don't you set the punk straight, boss? I don't like being a sitting duck."

Sypher puffed nervously on his cigarette. "I'm not sure I understand your meaning."

"Sure, you do. Tell him to back off. Tell him to leave me alone."

Sypher waited a moment before answering. "It sounds to me as if you have some personal problem to settle with Gil. I'd rather not step into the middle of it. I'm only your employer."

Taylor did a take, his head jutting back. "You're only what? What is this?" He bit his mustache. He looked at me. "Are you getting this? Notice how I'm being edged out?"

Sypher said, "Taylor, I can't be responsible—"

"Responsible? What about seven years ago? Tell me about responsible."

"Shut up," Sypher said coldly. "I've had enough."

"You have? You two"—Taylor looked across the bar at Gil and then at Sypher—"make almost as good a team as Fred and I." He poured another Scotch and held the glass up in my direction. "They got us behind the eight ball, honey. I can see the big white cue ball coming right for us. Only it looks more like a cement-mixer with NYPD stenciled on the drum. Don't you want to add a little something, Sypher? Don't you want to review our common past, for instance?"

I cried, "Why don't you say what you have to say?"

Taylor wiped his mustache with the back of his hand. "I'd rather the man in the pajamas did the talking. I want to back him up seven years. He has so much to say."

Sypher said again, "Shut up, Taylor."

Gil's eyes moved back and forth between them three times. Then he chose. "What about seven years?"

"Nothing," Sypher said.

"Begin at the beginning," Taylor said slowly. He was the only one of us enjoying himself.

Sypher said, "I have nothing to say. In fact, I'm very tired. I'd like you all to leave."

No one budged. "Talk about seven years ago, Taylor," I said.

He filled his glass again. He nodded as he put down the bottle. "Good Scotch. But it would have to be, wouldn't it? Seven years ago I was a member of New York's finest. An ace on the TPF. But I needed more bucks. My money had evaporated on certain bad bets on which I needed recoupment. So I moonlighted. I got a good job. Personal security for a VIP. One very cold night in December I got a call from my employer. He wanted me to interview a certain spoiled nasty little rich girl who was pestering him. She had some papers, he said, and she was taking them very early in the morning to a demonstration downtown on Whitehall Street. He needed the papers because they belonged to his company."

"That's enough," Sypher said. "I warn you, Taylor."

"It's too late, boss. You had your choice. I cut you loose."

I stepped closer to the bar, nearer to Gil. His breathing was shallow, a blue vein pulsed in his temple.

Taylor sat down on one of the high stools near the bar. He looked almost relaxed. He liked finally sticking it in the faces of these two. But he told me the story, as if the other two were just eavesdroppers. "It was like three A.M., and it was snowing, but a job is a job so I went. I took the IRT uptown. He didn't want her hurt, this little

VIP said, but tell her I was a TPF so she'd dump the papers in my L-A-P. Sure thing. I met the girl just as she was leaving her dorm. She was wrapped up in a sheepskin coat but no cap. She should have wore a cap. I followed her along the walk. Then I stopped her before she could get to the IRT. It wasn't snowing any more, but it was goddamn fucking cold. She tried to pull away from me, but I wouldn't let her. When I told her what I was after, she cursed me under her breath." Taylor alternated his gaze between me and his glass, now empty again.

Gil didn't move except for the blue vein twitching.

"What happened was strictly accidental—on account of the ice. It's not my fault there was all that ice. The VIP, the lousy creep, held it over me all this time." He looked at Sypher. "I had to tell him, but it was his fault as much as mine. More his fault. On the way back to the dorm—she didn't have the papers on her, she said—she lectured me about the war and innocent people dying because of profit-nuts businessmen like her old man. She stopped and wouldn't go any farther. She said there was a principle involved. So I gave her a little shove 'cause I was getting tired of all the malarkey. I remember thinking it's funny with all that money that she lives in a dormitory. You wouldn't catch me living in no dorm room like that."

"What happened after you gave her the shove?" I said.

"Nothing happened. She fell on one knee near an iron railing where there was these big icicles hanging down. She grabbed one of them with her gloved hand and hit me in the head with it. That's pretty nervy, isn't it? Well, it really pissed me. She drew blood and everything. So I gave her a real shove. And she bounced back and slid on the fucking ice so she couldn't land proper. I thought she'd land on her knee and break it and then I'd be screwed but she didn't—she cracked her head. She cracked it open on the edge of the sidewalk by the curb. It was strictly accidental."

Along the way, as his eyes traveled back and forth between me and the empty glass, I began to realize that even Taylor had once been seven years younger. He kept a rabbity little smile on his face during his monologue, but it wore thin at certain moments and you could see something else poking through, flesh that wasn't quite as hard, quite so used to being muscle and nothing else. But beyond Taylor I kept seeing Josie Breakstone tramping through the snow on the way to the same demonstration I went to that morning. I remembered how cold it was walking to the subway, and what that demonstration had been like, our clamor and the cops' violence and the frightened and angry people on Wall Street who spit at us as we marched past shouting "Stop the War" and the hardhats throwing bricks at us. I didn't remember being at Whitehall Street because the cops, the TPF, never allowed us anywhere near it. But if Josie had been there she could have made a difference. With those documents in her hands she could have galvanized us with the horror of what was written in them in the neutral tongue of businessese, and with her nerve in taking what she knew of her father and his business out of the warmth of her family life into the cold dawn of Battery Park where, as we lined up to march, a few blocks away eighteen-year-old boys lined up to be sucked into the war machine. I didn't think Josie's death could be covered under the word accidental, and I turned from sympathy with Taylor to a sad kind of anger as his monologue shifted from revenge on Sypher to self-justification. Taylor's pathos just wasn't pathetic enough. Since he didn't have the guts to dramatize it, it fell a little flat.

Gil was rocking slowly on his feet, breathing deeply now. Taylor looked over my shoulder to where Sypher must have been standing. "Telling the story is like buying back an IOU, know what I mean?" Then his gaze crossed me and landed on Gil. The way his head moved and stopped was very emphatic as if it was balanced on a tripod. He could just have shifted his eyes but he didn't.

Gil rocked back on his heels staring at Taylor. I started to count in my head. At eight he sprang forward over the bar. His hands were ahead of his body and they were way ahead of Taylor's ability to react. They grabbed Taylor's throat and squeezed it. His thumbs overlapped around Taylor's windpipe and squeezed into his flesh as they would into soft clay. As Taylor grabbed Gil's wrists his stool lunged back and the two of them keeled onto the floor, Gil on top. The bar glass jumped two inches as they landed. It was still rattling when Taylor shoved his knee into Gil's testicles. The second time it wasn't rattling, and I heard Gil suck air as Taylor's knee shoved in again. He groaned, as I must have when the electricity shocked my body, and his body drew in on itself, peeling away from Taylor except for his tight grip on his throat. Taylor sounded like a sewer draining, his face redder than when I had first seen it in my rearview mirror. He clawed an index finger away from his throat and holding on to it like the branch of a tree, twisted it to rip it off. Gil yelled and jerked that hand away. He kept one hand on Taylor's throat, thumb pressed over his windpipe. Taylor kept wriggling to break Gil's grip. Gil lifted his head and watched Taylor struggling. Taylor's heels pounded on the wood floor. Gil raised his free arm over Taylor's face and a fist the size of the iron end of a sledge hammer started pounding Taylor's head into the floor.

I looked away. But the noise was still there. The sound of the head hitting the floor. Nothing in it reminded me of anything human. After a while the noise quit. I looked back. Taylor was motionless, his face pulped like a blood orange.

Gil rose slowly to his knees above Taylor's inert heap and more slowly to his feet. He was hobbled, and one of his hands, the bloody one, was cupped over his crotch. His heaving chest shone with the sweat of gladiatorial combat. He raised his head. His mouth was slack, his lips parted, showing a line of white teeth, his eyes, which should have been sodden bloodshot balls, had some of the harsh gleam of polished trophies. Between gasps for breath he stammered out, "That was no accident."

I shuddered. Maybe Taylor was an animal, nevertheless he resembled a human being. But Gil didn't. He frightened me more thoroughly than anything ever had. I backed away, afraid to turn my head. He could have devoured me in an instant. On his crotch there was a red print of his fingers. I knew exactly what those fingers felt like.

"I'll get us out of this. Don't be scared," he said.

"Stay where you are, Gil," I said, as if I were pleading with a child. I didn't want those hands on me again.

"It was Taylor," he insisted. "It needed doing. I'm only taking care of business, Emma."

My back butted against glass. I'd missed the opening to the terrace. Maybe he wouldn't hurt me—but would he know if he did? He'd seen his sister in me, and she was now, he knew at last, dead. Maybe he thought I should join her. He wanted to calm me. He stepped closer, and I thought I could smell insanity like a fever on his body. "It's all right," he said.

The short piercing crack of a gun made him shiver and look at me in amazement. His chin touched his chest and we both stared at the neat round red hole growing there. His knees bent under him. "Emma," he said, reassuringly, "it's all right." Swaying on his knees, he nodded, as if he'd just thought it all over, and toppled headlong toward me. After that he didn't move.

Up to the last moment he'd wanted something of me, and up to the last moment I was backing away. He gave me no better choice, but the trapped, begging look in the beast's eyes still tore at me. I'd steered myself away from Gil. It didn't make it easier that he deserved it.

24

I thought then that I was next. It seemed that I had to be. I'd taken too many steps away from where I belonged, thinking each time that I was only making the detour that would bring me back, deposit me on the Lower East Side in one piece. This uptown mayhem was entirely foreign. I'd never ventured into territory like this. What I expected to be smooth and well-lit, polished by luxury and blunted by comfort, was instead a dark alley strewn with shattered lives, crawling with menace, and no exit visible. I thought being a cabdriver had made me hard enough and alert enough that I could steer my way down their streets so long as I kept both hands on the wheel. But I was way off. I was lost.

Sypher held the gun. I thought it would be smoking. It wasn't, but the long muzzle was pointed at me. It was a bigger gun than the one in my canvas bag. He wasn't saying anything. He hadn't said anything to Gil either. He just squeezed the trigger. He wasn't the kind that wastes too much time thinking it over or talking about it. Once he decided, he squeezed out the decision like a bullet.

The only things moving in the room were the wings of

his nose. I thought maybe he'd shoot me when his nose quit trying to take off. It was lasting so long I couldn't think of any reason why it wouldn't last forever.

You kept coming after them because of Hoyt, because you loved him and you were damned if you were going to let them snuff out another life and walk away from it. And they tried everything to convince you you were being overemotional. They tried money and rough stuff and lies and fixed it so the cops wanted you too and you'd barely eaten or slept and your clothes felt as if they were rotting on your body and then when they still couldn't cut you to size they quit playing around. You aren't a kid anymore, they said, and they pointed a gun at you. This is the way it had to be—they always had the gun in their hands first because they weren't wasting time being overemotional.

But then Sypher fooled me. He must have made his career fooling people. He didn't squeeze the trigger. Motioning with the muzzle he said, "Drop your bag to the floor."

I let it slide off my shoulder. When it hit the floor, the strap dropped near Gil's outstretched fingers. It looked as if he were about to reach for it. Fighting nausea, I kicked it away.

"You did this," Sypher said. "Not me. And I'm going to make you pay."

I couldn't begin to count the number of distortions in his ledger.

He stood close enough to the bar to grab the neck of the Scotch bottle without losing sight of me. I watched his Adam's apple bounce as he gulped the stuff down. It was better than watching the gun. He slapped the bottle on the bar. "I'm not letting you off as easy as I let Gil off."

The way he said it you'd think Gil was in the corner sniveling because Sypher had pocketed his allowance. But he wasn't joking, he wasn't even being ironic. I felt the flesh behind my ears crawl.

"This room is too foul. I can't think," he said and looked around. "All right." He directed his pointer to the terrace. "Get out there."

My legs moved, but they had a hard time of it. All the way through the sliding glass doorway onto the perfect grass I listened, but you can't hear a finger squeeze a trigger, and it's questionable if you hear anything after it does.

The stars that had been out on break rushed to fill the empty black sky. Like the moon, they worked overtime for SBI. Trying not to turn my head too much, I looked to see what chances the terrace gave me. But this wasn't a raffle; there was no chance of escape I could see except by the sliding doors.

And Sypher was standing in front of those, an ordinary little man in powder-blue pajamas and a wine-colored silk robe holding a gun that looked too big for his hand. His lips parted and stretched over his teeth, which were small and neatly placed. That was a smile, and it was as sunny as the light in a morgue. "Gil wasn't bright. Well-meaning, but not bright. But you are. You're bright."

"If I was bright I'd be holding the gun." I wasn't feeling bright or funny. My eyes oscillated between the long-nosed weapon and the sharp angles of Sypher's face.

"Evelyn Berndt asked for it, just like you're asking for it," he said. He pulled the glass door closed behind him and motioned with the muzzle for me to back up. I stepped all the way to the three-and-a-half-foot brick wall, the farther away the better.

"Too far," he said and followed me out, crossing the grass but keeping six feet of wall between us. Holding the gun up, he leaned over for a moment. Way below on the far side of the FDR Drive was his moat, the East River, a narrow inversion of the starred black sky. The computer prince must have been looking for the barges filled to overflowing with thousands of miles of data print-outs, each bearing his name like a million death warrants.

We were perhaps twenty-five feet from the glass door. Twenty-five separate feet to stop me in my tracks before I got to it, and had he bothered to throw the lock when he closed it? It would have been more sporting of him to leave it open. I wanted, if possible, to keep him from playing with me as he must have played with Evelyn. But I couldn't see talking him out of it. "I'm not asking for it," I said tentatively, not knowing if he'd turn and pull the trigger just for the fun of it.

"You're not asking for it, you're begging for it. Evelyn didn't get a chance to beg. I'll tell you about Evelyn. It will be an object lesson. A little too late to be terribly instructive, but it will set the scene for your own departure. She was frightened when she called me, but like you she liked to pretend she wasn't. She wanted to dredge up our past association, it seems, because Wincey had cut her loose. But I'm not interested in other people's sewage. You can understand that, can't you?" He started to let his head rock slowly side to side. It was as if we were on one of those barges down there on the black river instead of way up here on this terrace swaying above the black earth.

"I don't suffer blackmailers gladly. But I did admire one thing about her. She took a chance that came her way, a little stack of papers left in her dorm room, and she made the most of them. She even dealt with the odious Taylor, got by him, and got to me. And she was bright too, she didn't want just money. So I set her up with Wincey. But when Wincey cut her loose, she tried to threaten me again. She even ordered me to her apartment. Are you learning from this? Or do I have to point out each little lesson to you?"

"I'm getting some of it."

"She had the same flaw in her character that you had, excuse me, have. She didn't know when to leave well enough alone."

His cold sneer was much more desolating than anything he could say about Evelyn. A woman with her ambition who thinks not unexpectedly that power can be had by tying oneself to a man could never know what "well enough" meant. She'd never reach that point because the man, whether Wincey or Sypher, held the strings and could, as Sypher kept repeating with relish, "cut her loose," any time. And, since she treated herself as a vessel without moorings, she foundered.

"When I got there she started sputtering that I'd set Wincey against her and like nonsense." He looked down at the turf and then at me again, considering. "You are fundamentally a much more unmanageable type. I don't, in fact, understand altogether what type you are, but I know that much. I know you must be eliminated. It's too bad really, because it's not your fault. If this country were better engineered, people like you could be caught early on while still malleable. But that's a problem for the future, not the unfortunate present."

So far I'd been happy to live in the knowledge that Sypher, more completely than Taylor and more consciously than Gil, was a rational monster. But even monsters suffer because their world is darkened, deformed and sometimes swamped by the existence of relatively normal human beings. He gave me a glimpse of a well-engineered country in which all the engineers wore Sypher's sharp-angled mask. I put my hand on top of the wall to steady myself.

Sypher caught my moment of weakness and smiled. "She was more unrelenting than you. She kept trying to provoke me. I admit I bore her some grudge because she'd been the one person I'd ever known who got the best of me. She paraded around in a silk robe taunting me." His voice took on a nervous intensity. Whatever had happened between him and Evelyn keyed him up to deal with me. He kept wanting to turn her into me, but his brain wouldn't let him, and he'd have to reconsider. His little movements became shorter, jerkier. His pajamas and robe seemed a little big, as if letting these words out of his body depleted him.

"At one point, she said she'd had enough of me and retired to her bath. She'd been running one nearly all the time I'd been there. I remember the sound of it through the thin walls. She called out to me to leave. She had a nice voice until she raised it and then it became a seagull's screech. 'Find your own way out,' she said, 'and I'll find my own way out of this mess.' I stood in the open doorway of her bathroom. If she'd said no more I'd have left, and none of the rest would have occurred. You'd be home tonight in your grubby little dive. 'It's your own mess you've been unable to escape,' I said to her, 'the smell of sausage, beer pretzels and sauerkraut. You have an immigrant's soul.' Her head was visible above the rim of the white tub. A wicked smile was on her lips, an annihilating smile. I dreaded setting foot in that bathroom. She leaned back in her bath; the water and the suds from the bubble bath sloshed along the side and she said, 'Whatever my unfortunate background is, at least unlike some people, I'm not all thumbs.' 'You think so,' I said, and I took this thumb"—and he produced it now before me as if I could never have caught sight of it before—"and I stepped over to her and her smile became even broader and I pushed on her head with my thumb. She sank into the suds and choked on the water instantly. She shouldn't have, but she did. I thought she was trying to make a fool of me by pretending to choke. I held her down a while longer. She was the kind of woman I can't abide," he said and paused. "You're another." He stood waiting for me to say something, to see if he'd put a proper scare into me.

One woman killed seven years ago because she defended herself with an icicle, another less than two months ago drowned because she had a wicked smile and knew how to hurt an invulnerable man. I was third in line tonight, without either accident or spontaneity to excuse my assailant. But all three of us touched those papers and thought about them and tried to use them in our own way. And all three of us were vulnerable because we didn't, as Hoyt would say, protect our ass."

"And what about Hoyt Erland?" I asked, keeping my voice low and firm.

"Who? The reporter? What does he . . .? Well, as I understand it, that was more-or-less unintentional." He said it hurriedly, as if preoccupied.

"I started all this because of Hoyt."

"It was an accident," he said, dismissing it. "And when the police come, and I show them what you did here tonight, I'll tell them that I shot at you and hit you, but that I certainly never meant to kill you. That it was an accident." His face had that pleased, well-fed look of a man lately risen from the dinner table.

"There are no accidents," I said. "Ever."

He raised his thick eyebrows. He was a little less than six feet away. The gun's muzzle drooped in his hand. He'd been holding it a long time and it was heavy and he was a small man.

I rushed directly at his chest to knock him over. His right side hit the wall hard, knocking some wind out of him, and he fell backward on his gun hand. I leaned over to get at it.

"Christ," he said and grabbed my ankle, giving it a pull. I pitched onto the grass. He rolled over and sat up pulling out the gun. "You're dead," he said, puffing. "It's all over."

I got up on one elbow. "Not while I'm breathing," I said, looking into the gun. "I think there's something wrong with my leg. I can't get up."

"Well"—he smiled thinly—"that doesn't matter at all." Everything mattered. The heat, telephone calls, potato pirogen, right turns, drugstores, wisecracks, posters, tuna, faces, subway tokens, pink autograph books, pea soup, the taste of salt on a man's back, the sound a body makes falling through the air, money piled on a coffee table, a picture in the newspaper, gray hair, a towaway truck, an ashtray, what somebody said to you at an angry moment two months ago.

All of it mattered, all of it was in my head as I looked at the gun pointed at me.

"Have you thought in which direction you should shoot? It wouldn't do to make it look planned."

He wrinkled his face and stood up a foot or two from me, nearer the parapet. He rubbed his side with his elbow. "I'm going to be black and blue," he said.

"Aren't you afraid I'll try to throw you over the wall?"

"No, I'm not. You're not strong enough."

"Was Evelyn strong?"

"Not strong enough."

I didn't want to go out lying on the grass. "Then let me get up."

"Go ahead," he said and started to back away. He lowered the gun slightly. I dragged myself up as if one leg was useless. And looking at it I took a step toward him, testing my weight on it, ignoring him. "That's enough," he said.

I leaned over to massage the damaged knee, bending it slightly. As soon as I was bent, I took off, head and shoulders against his knee. His gun exploded but I didn't feel anything except the two of us shove against the brick wall. His knees started to crack. He was trying to weigh me down with them. I could feel each of his bones press into me. I lifted his knees automatically to get them out from under while still pushing hard against the wall. His light body scraped up the bricks with me and landed on its back atop the wall. He flailed wildly at me and raised his far arm with the gun in it to shoot. But he was sideways and on his back and moving, and the second shot was still wide. Two chances seemed enough. I pushed him away, ducking at the same time, and he hooked his lone thumb on my belt while falling over. He dropped the gun as he slid over and scrambled to catch the top of the wall. His hooked thumb caught and his weight pressed me against the wall so I could barely move. He was screaming now and squirming, and one leg was fighting to come up over the wall. Slowly I turned my body to release his grip on me. His leg didn't make it. The fingers of his good hand started to give way. He felt like an anchor. I wanted more than anything now to be free of him, of all of this. I didn't look at his face. I don't remember if I could even see it. The whole weight of his body and mine centered on his thumb. Then the weight shifted. It was a long way down.

25

That night I stood for a long while in the fresh air above the city until I noticed the red lights flashing down below on the street. Then I turned away from the wall and started to walk across the grass. I nearly made it across before I passed out.

The obituaries never mentioned he lacked a thumb, but for a week or two afterward the columnists did. They all told the bizarre story about how the self-made tycoon lost his digit. In each case it was a good story and each story was different, but they all sounded authentic. I had my own story to tell and to tell, over and over and over again, about what had happened.

Eventually, with the help of the proper authorities, everything that could be straightened out was bent in half including me. Breakstone, Frederick and even Taylor survived that August night to join a babble of conflicting stories supplemented by everyone who had ever even looked up SBI in the yellow pages.

It started with my being booked, still later that night, on several serious charges. I spent almost two weeks in jail until those charges were reduced and my mother, justifiably wringing her hands, could afford to post bail.

Then those charges disappeared, in part for lack of evidence, in part because Frederick and Taylor, characteristically and at length, proclaimed themselves guilty of nothing until they totally convinced the police that they were guilty of everything.

In the eyes of the daily press I became "a liberated but not unattractive female hack," and "a new-left drop-out of the trouble-making, thumb-waving school," and "a colorful red," all of whom, it was suggested, might be getting away with murder. I stopped reading the papers as soon as I realized that what had happened was both too complicated and too full of unflattering references to people in power for the press to handle in three hundred words or less, except in terms of scandal. The story itself was one thing, but its implications were another. These were never even raised. What was sold on newsstands was a lurid tale of murder, accidental murder and revenge.

There were certain repercussions. For instance, the Institute quietly closed its doors; Wincey, who steadfastly denied any part in the events, was by a narrow margin not reelected; SBI stock temporarily nose-dived; and the Hack Commission revoked my license.

So since 1974 I've made an adjustment. You could say I had to, but you'd be wrong. There was a choice. I don't mean an adjustment to reality. I've made no appointments with my local shrink. The fight I went through during those few days burned away the part of myself I disliked the most. Not all by itself, but it set the process in motion, and maybe the motion is still in process and I am still figuring out how to cut through the deadly temper of the times without abandoning the edge I always kept as a cabdriver. If I have abandoned anything it's part of my irony, the part that no longer tasted so good.

In recompense, those few days proved I possessed a few skills I never knew I had, and I found once I got out of jail that I didn't want to let those skills rust. The time in jail had made me more restless and impatient with myself. I had more respect now for Hoyt's choice of investigative reporting—it was tougher than I thought—but I knew I'd never learn how to be polite to people who wore expensive business suits no matter which side of the eight-ball they were on. And I'd lived in this neighborhood—or state of mind—too long to make my life elsewhere.

I had to think of a way to make myself useful here, responsible somehow to forces circulating beyond the confines of my apartment. While awake, I kept thinking of Connie, of Mrs. Berndt, of torture and chemical additives. When I slept, I dreamed about Hoyt and about woman after woman in a slide show somebody was forcing me to watch. The women were all working I realized as they spun past me, but they were all doing someone else's job. They kept looking up at the time clock, one after the other.

I had a little savings; I borrowed a little more. My apartment, I decided, could become a trap if I stayed in it much longer. I found a storefront on East Fifth Street. I decided to hire myself out to community groups—welfare rights, environmental, women's groups—that might be moving in the same direction, if not at the same speed, as I. I could do research, investigation, trouble-making, phone-calling, protection, organization, and interference-running. I propped a hand-lettered sign spelling that out in the storefront window and taped some of my clippings next to the sign. These two elements were the extent of my certification and were as close as I could come to calling myself a private detective in this neighborhood and have hopes of making any money. Then I went on unemployment and made some of my best contacts while standing in line downtown.

The catch, if that's what it is, is that I still move all too slowly and what I want keeps changing slightly as I go on. Now I am more than six years older than in 1974, and I look it. In those few days I forced myself to live through a hundred things I'd never done before. Some of them I'd never do again. Some of them I do now without thinking. The sense I had that hot August I still possess: that the way things are is monstrous. But in those few days, with each second weighted by death and the possibility of death, I felt the explicit passion to struggle. Nearly every day since then, when not petting my cat, whose life hasn't changed at all, I've been left with the necessity to struggle to allow room for that passion.

About the Author

ERNEST LARSEN, born in Chicago in 1946, has put himself through the rigorous training American literary mythology requires of American writers. Despite getting his M.F.A. at Columbia University, he has spent most of the last fifteen years working at low-paying, low-status jobs ranging from housepainter and department-store Santa Claus to karate-lesson salesman and cabdriver. He is currently an editor of the film journal *Jump Cut*.